Mishaps of the Mythical Kind

The Mishaps Series, Volume 1

Audra Killian

Published by Audra Killian, 2024.

MISHAPS OF THE MYTHICAL KIND

First edition. August 30, 2024.

Copyright © 2024 Audra Killian.

ISBN: 979-8227830364

Written by Audra Killian.

Book cover design by Gombar Sanja
www.bookcoverforyou.com.

Chapter 1

"**H**ave you ever given someone ticks?"

The genuinely thoughtful...and odd question failed to shock me. My roommate, Leta, often expressed bizarre inquiries.

"Ticks? Like the insects?"

"They're part of the arachnid family actually," she explained with a ponderous expression. "As I was saying," she abruptly turned serious. "Elena, sex is healthy."

What connection there was between sex and ticks, I couldn't say.

"All kinds of good benefits. Neurochemicals and such things," she continued.

The pronouncement attracted the attention of our coworkers. Heads popped up and curious eyes peered over the network of partitions. With a groan, I sank below the gray wall of my cubicle to avoid further embarrassment.

"Really, Leta?" I whispered.

With a radiant smile, she nodded enthusiastically. Somehow, Leta embodied innocence and nymphomania simultaneously.

She had instantly befriended me when I started an internship at Madame Advertising Firm over a year ago. When I was offered a full-time position, she suggested I move into her apartment, at least until I settled into the city. I jumped at the offer.

The past two months had been...interesting. Leta was an over-the-top personality but had a heart as big as Texas. It was easy to overlook her quirks.

Like making outrageous statements in front of our coworkers.

"I'm not sure you've had sex since you got here," she said thoughtfully.

I caught one of my male colleagues staring at me with new interest.

Uncomfortable heat warmed my cheeks, and I covered my face as if that could protect me from the discomfort.

"Could we maybe talk about this at home?" I asked quietly.

From the cubicle across from mine, that same coworker smiled while giving me an eyebrow raise and a head nod. I shook my head, and he returned his attention to his monitor.

"Of course," she said reasonably. "Congratulations by the way."

I stared blankly at her, and her twinkly laughter filled the space. "You were assigned as Selene's assistant for the new account. Glenda is ecstatic about it, and she doesn't get worked up by many things."

"Oh! Thank you. I'm excited to be a part of it."

She glanced at her watch. "The clients should be here in about an hour. Good luck."

With a mischievous smile, she sashayed her way down the hall. I breathed a sigh of relief.

"Don't forget what I said about sex. It's good for your health," she called over her shoulder.

I slunk even further into my chair. New friend rule for me and Leta...no talking about sex at work.

Selene, two of the more senior members of our team, and our boss Glenda spent the morning in the main conference room with Michael Reinier. The representative from our new account was an attractive man with coffee-colored eyes and the body of a Greek marble. Despite the warmth of his male beauty, his attitude was cold and superior. He graced Glenda with a charming smile but gave Selene and the rest of the team a condescending glance. I was glad that I hadn't ranked important enough to be introduced.

Instead, I hovered periodically outside the room, in hopefully not too obvious a way, waiting to be of any assistance. Selene looked up at one point and gave me a reassuring smile before focusing back on the meeting.

I decided to return to my desk where I might actually be productive, but my feet stalled. The man walking down the hall towards me stole my breath away. Wearing a navy suit that contrasted beautifully with his pale skin and displayed his tall, muscled body, he was the epitome of perfection. His piercing blue eyes focused on mine, and I almost swooned.

Everything that happened next was Leta's fault really. All that talk of sex and neurochemicals muddled my brain. My feet fumbled, and I vaguely felt the pain as my ankle rolled in, thrown off balance by the heels that I rarely wore. The motion was enough to pitch me forward. I grimaced and waited for my body to hit the ground. Instead, I felt a solid arm wrap around my waist and pull me against a muscular chest.

A breath escaped my lips in a rush as my eyes stared at the buttons on a crisp, white shirt. My gaze traveled up to where the shirt parted and exposed pale skin. It continued up past a square jaw and full pale lips and stopped on a pair of amused, blue eyes.

"Are you well?" An Eastern European voice asked the soft question. His hand brushed against my forehead, and his eyes narrowed in concern. "You feel feverish."

My mind went completely blank as I stared at him. The pain of my unstable ankle rolling inward again refocused my attention.

"Yes...thank you...I, ah, I tripped."

He was right. The press of his body against mine had my internal temperature climbing. Thoughts of our bodies skin to skin, hot and sweaty...

My cheeks flushed, and I just barely managed to not fan myself like some fainting damsel. He was incredibly beautiful, and I forced myself to look away so I could form a coherent sentence.

"Thank you for saving me from crashing to the floor."

The amusement in his expression returned. "My pleasure, Miss..."

My mind threatened to go offline again. "Elena. I'm Elena."

"I'm Nolan."

I smiled. "It's nice to meet you, Nolan."

We stared at each other for what seemed like forever before I realized that our bodies were still pressed together. I took a careful step back

"Can I help you with anything, Nolan?" My voice was much huskier than it should have been.

"I have a meeting, one I'm late for. I was told the main conference room." His smile was absolutely dazzling. "Perhaps you can point me in the right direction."

All at once, the pleasant heat filling me disappeared. "You have a meeting?" Realization struck hard, and I said softly, "Oh, you're a client."

Before either of us could respond, Leta her head peeked out of the conference room.

"Mr. Tasev?" Her voice was naturally sultry and lyrical.

She stepped into the hall, closing the door behind her. As she approached, she eyed first me and then him with an impish smile.

"Mr. Tasev?" She asked again and drew Nolan's attention.

"Yes, I'm Nolan Tasev," he said as he turned to her with a smile.

"I'm Leta. We've conversed so much over the past few months, it's a pleasure to finally meet you. And I see that you've also met another member of our team...Elena."

"Indeed, I did."

I was surprised to realize that he was looking at me again. Clearing my throat, I ignored the smirk on Leta's face and decided it was time to go hide in my cubicle.

"It was a pleasure to meet you, Mr. Tasev. I look forward to working on your account."

"I also look forward to us working together." He took a slight step closer and leaned just a little closer than what was proper. "And you must call me Nolan," he said softly.

I couldn't do more than nod while Leta watched us with amusement. She made a little noise of interest and guided Nolan... Mr. Tasev, to the conference room. I hobbled back to my cubicle, praying that no one else witnessed the exchange.

I focused on a few tasks that Selene had given me that morning and tried to ignore the throbbing in my ankle. I'd somehow missed Mr. Tasev on his way out of the meeting, which was probably for the best. I would have undoubtedly made a fool of myself again.

I got through the rest of the morning with a limp. By noon, my heels were gone, and I hobbled around the office barefoot.

"How's the ankle?" Leta appeared at the partition of my cubicle just after lunch.

I looked up from my work. "Eh, I'll survive. Nothing some ice and ibuprofen won't fix."

She smiled, and I swear flowers went into full bloom throughout the city even though it was mid-September. "I'm glad you took my words to heart."

"What?" I asked with confusion.

Leta just laughed. "Our new client couldn't take his eyes off you, and you couldn't take your eyes off him. He's not bad if you like that pretty boy look. I go for the more rugged type myself, but I get it. Do you feel the neurochemicals?"

"No, I did not feel the neurochemicals." I didn't even know what those were.

"Liar. You are giving off a ton of heat right now, Elena."

I was feeling really hot...but it had nothing to do with a sexy client.

"Don't worry, your secret's safe with me," Leta said with a wink. "I'm proud of you."

I shook my head as she walked away. There was no secret. I was not getting involved with a client.

Chapter 2

I wrapped up my work for the week and was packing up my stuff when Selene peered around the corner.

"Are you ready?"

Chandelier earrings in red and orange hung from her ears and complimented her rich, ebony skin. The deep V of her clingy black blouse showcased an equally dramatic necklace. A delicately knit scarf covered her usual short hairdo, and the outfit was completed by brown slacks and metallic sandals.

Selene was slightly taller than me and uniquely attractive. Leta exuded sex whereas Selene gave off a more subtle sexuality. And something else. I couldn't quite put my finger on it. She was the kind of woman who could change your life in ways that you would never be aware of...maybe not always in a good way.

"Ready for what?"

"Drinks."

I stared at her for a moment before it clicked. With a little groan, "My ankle has been killing me all day. I'm just not up for drinks tonight."

Despite icing, resting, and elevating it for the past two days, it still throbbed. I'd sacrificed looking cute for comfort and wore a pair of flats with my dull sweater and slacks.

"You look great," she stated.

I narrowed my eyes at her. Selene had a knack for knowing what I was thinking. Sometimes it was scary how accurately she seemed to read my thoughts.

"Are we going?" Leta appeared around the corner. Dressed in a cute skirt that fell loosely around her full hips and a light pink blouse that looked great against her tanned skin, she looked as good as Selene.

"I really don't feel up to it," I tried to whine, but they looked even more determined.

"The alcohol will make you feel so much better, and it'll take away the pain," Leta stated.

"That would take a lot of alcohol," I muttered. She smiled encouragingly.

"Come on, you know you want to," Selene said. "Besides, Farah is already at the bar saving us a table."

I felt like I had just fallen nine stories onto concrete. It had been a rough day, and all I wanted was to crawl onto the sofa and not move until Saturday night...at the very earliest.

"One drink," I conceded.

They exchanged a knowing look and then nodded in agreement. I gathered my things and shut down my workstation as they excitedly talked about all the things we could do tonight. Conversely, I listed off the things that we were not going to do tonight.

No more than one drink, no dancing, no bar hopping...They ignored me while simultaneously guiding me out of the office and into a taxi.

The bar they picked was a nice place. Upon walking in, the intimate lighting and the color scheme instantly struck me. Warm, earthy red and cream tones on the walls contrasted with a shiny black bar accented with mahogany trim. Booth seats with low tables lined the back wall and high-top tables crowded the space in front of the small stage. Energy reverberated from the brassy trumpets and saxophones of the swing band playing on stage.

Farah sat at a high top to the right of the stage. Her long copper waves were unmistakable and framed a pale face with icy blue eyes. She wore jeans and a crop top sweater that hung off one shoulder.

She caught sight of us and waved. Selene waved back and led the way through the mob of dancers.

I tried my best to avoid bumping into people, but I got jostled a few times. Each time, I put more pressure on my ankle to keep from falling into someone else. My limp was more pronounced by the time we made it to the table.

"What did you do to yourself?" Farah asked in place of greeting. She studied me like a hawk.

However, before I could explain, Leta launched into the story of how I had tripped all over myself in front of our new client. Farah snorted with amusement while Selene waved down a server.

Thankfully, the waiter appeared a moment later and everyone was too concerned with their drink orders to care about my embarrassing encounter. When he left, they updated each other on people I didn't know. Every so often, I asked a question or answered one, but I really wasn't following the conversation. I massaged my ankle in a futile attempt to find some relief. It wasn't time for another Advil dose, but the pain was excruciating. I could feel little tears threatening to form at the corners of my eyes.

"Elena?"

I was not sure who spoke my name, but I looked up to see three very concerned faces staring at me.

"Are you okay?" Leta asked.

I almost said yes, but they knew I wasn't okay. "No, I just can't take the pain in my ankle anymore. I don't know what I did, but it is so unbearable right now. I'm sorry, but could we do this another night? Maybe when I can enjoy it?"

"Of course," Farah responded. "You should go home and rest it. It looks more swollen."

"We'll do this again when you're feeling better," Selene reassured.

Leta looked the most concerned. "Do you want me to go home with you?"

"No, no, no. You stay here and have fun. I'll get a cab." I smiled to reassure them and did my best not to fall off the stool as I eased myself to the floor.

"I'll walk you outside," Farah said.

Before I knew it, she was at my side. I said goodbye and walked towards the exit with Farah. She led the way, and the crowd cleared like the Red Sea in front of her. Unfortunately, the crowd stuffed right back in behind her.

I fought valiantly towards the door, but I stepped right, twisted left, and stumbled back, twisting my ankle all over again. I found myself falling backward.

When I fell this time, it was into the arms of a man with warm brown eyes.

It's not every day that a girl finds herself in the arms of a handsome stranger. I'd done it twice in the last few days. Apparently, it was my lucky week.

"Well, what have I caught here?"

His voice was exactly as it should be, rich and kind with an underlying hint of playfulness. His black hair was a little longer in the front but trimmed neatly on the sides and back. He looked to be early thirties. He smiled down at me, and I almost giggled it was so warm and inviting.

But then I remembered I was in some strange man's arms and no matter how nice they felt at the

moment, I should not be in them.

"I am so sorry," I began to apologize.

He continued to hold me while I stared into his soulful eyes.

We stared at each other until Farah approached. She cleared her throat and reality came crashing back.

He too seemed a little startled by my friend as his attention turned to her.

"Do you need help?" she asked him.

Farah stared fiercely at my rescuer. They maintained intense eye contact for a few moments while I hung there in the air. It was like watching two dogs on the verge of a fight.

"Excuse me," I projected over the music. That succeeded in getting their attention. "I think you can set me back onto my feet now."

He stared at me for a moment. "Of course." In one smooth move, I went from dipped to fully upright. Thankfully, he didn't let go of me completely as I struggled to regain my balance.

"What happened?" Farah asked as she took a step towards me while continuing to glare at my rescuer.

"I got lost in the crowd, and I twisted my ankle again."

"You hurt your ankle?" His voice filled my ear, and I turned towards it. He studied me with concern.

"Yes, but I'm fine. Thank you." I smiled and tried to step away but couldn't put weight on the injured side. I stifled a groan and gave him another reassuring smile, but he refused to release me until he was sure I was okay. It was oddly charming.

"She hurt it earlier this week," I heard Leta say from behind us. I looked over my shoulder and saw Selene and Leta approaching us.

"She's been limping around on it since," Selene added. Farah made a noise that sounded an awful lot like a growl, and Selene arched a reproving brow.

"Relax," Selene instructed, and Farah relaxed... a little.

"I told her she should see a doctor, but she wouldn't listen to me," Leta continued as if completely unaware of Farah's growl.

"He's a doctor," Selene said.

"How do you know?" Farah, the man holding me, and I all asked at once.

Leta rolled her eyes at us like we were the most clueless bunch of people she had ever met.

"Because that is what his ID says. Dr. Miguel Brown."

She reached around his left shoulder and held up a badge that did indeed read Miguel Brown, MD, St. Francis Clinic on 98th St. Farah and I studied the picture, then verified it with the face. Yep, it checked out.

"I would be happy to take a look at that ankle for you," he offered.

"Oh, no that's okay. Thank you, really, but..."

Four pairs of eyes stared at me. Farah's were untrusting, Leta's were wide with amusement, Selene's were thoughtful, and Dr. Brown's were concerned.

"Sit down, Elena, and let him look at it," Leta said with a mischievous expression.

"Maybe you should just bite the bullet and get it looked at," Selene added.

Farah growled softly again but shrugged her agreement.

I stood there silent with indecision.

"Okay, fine," I conceded. My three friends looked relieved, as did my new doctor.

Then without warning, he swept me off my feet and placed me gently on the chair that was still warm from his body heat. He'd obviously just vacated it.

"I'm going to take a look now, Ms...I'm sorry, but I don't think we had a chance to introduce ourselves," he laughed softly.

"I'm Elena McNeal." I held out my hand. He took it in his and gave it a firm handshake. I loved a good handshake.

"Miguel Brown."

"And these are my coworkers Leta, Farah, and Selene," I gestured to the three women encircling us.

With the introductions complete, he returned to gently inspecting my ankle. "How did you injure this?" he asked.

Before any of them could launch into a retelling of my embarrassing encounter, I threatened them with a look, and I simply explained that I twisted it at work. He gently moved my foot in different directions, paying close attention when I winced in pain.

"I suspect it's a sprain, though I can't rule out a fracture without an X-ray."

The objection was on the tip of my tongue when he smiled and rushed to add, "However, I think you will be okay not getting one. The swelling isn't too bad, and you have full movement. You might have some bruising. I'd recommend that you take it easy over the weekend, alternate Tylenol and ibuprofen, ice, and elevate."

I nodded. "Can do. Thank you."

"My pleasure." His smile was quite wonderful. "I would feel much better if I was able to check up on you, and make sure that you're completely recovered."

Surprised by his interest, I didn't immediately respond. Behind him, Leta gave me a threatening look and mouthed "Give him your number!"

I tried to hide my smile.

"That's not necessary, you've been so kind already."

"My reasons aren't entirely altruistic," he teased, and I laughed.

We exchanged numbers, and he insisted on assisting me outside where he flagged down a cab. I said my goodbyes to the ladies and made them promise they'd have a great time. As I rode home, I couldn't help but smile at the strange turn of events.

Chapter 3

I spent the weekend following doctor's orders, and Leta happily fussed over me. We watched a few movies together interrupted by calls from her boyfriend. She explained to me that he was unhappy about not seeing her over the weekend. I assured her that I would be fine on my own, but with a devilish smile, she told me it was better to make him beg for it. And she assured me, she'd make it up to him later in the week.

Wednesday afternoon Leta announced that she was going to have a friend over for the night. Her smile indicated that she was finally going to make it up to her boyfriend.

"Sounds good; I'll stick to my room tonight." With headphones and very loud music.

"Or you could stick to Dr. Miguel's bedroom," she suggested mischievously.

I shook my head. The doctor and I had talked on the phone a few times. We hadn't been able to meet up with his schedule. Leta expressed several times her disappointment that I had not yet slept with him.

I didn't see Leta at work the next day, but she sent me a text saying she was going to be at Corbett's for the weekend. I assumed they made up.

Miguel called around two o'clock asking me to dinner, and I met him at a small Italian place after getting off work. The place he picked was casual and inviting with lazy instrumental music playing low in the background. Strategically arranged tables maximized the space while creating an atmosphere of intimacy.

Of course, it could have been Miguel's appreciative and sultry stares that made the whole situation feel so intimate. His brown eyes were soft, and his lips formed a relaxed smile as he studied my face. I found myself overwhelmed by the attention.

We ordered a glass of wine each. He got red, and I got white. Miguel assured me the calamari appetizer was not to be missed, and we added that to the order. I decided on the alfredo, and he confessed that he ordered the spaghetti and meatballs every time. The waitress scribbled our choices onto a small notepad and assured us the appetizer would be right out. She returned quickly with the glasses of wine.

"So, why a doctor?" I asked as I gently swirled the wine in my glass.

He smiled. "I wanted to make a difference." With a soft laugh, "That sounds cliché, but I spent a great deal of time in the emergency room as a child, and I can tell you from experience that a good doctor makes all the difference. I can remember Dr. Hawkins. He was a retired medic who had seen far too many battlefields, but every time I came in with a new laceration or fracture, he made me feel brave and heroic. That's important to boys."

I smiled at his memory. "Is that what you do now, emergency medicine?"

He nodded and took a drink.

"And do you make little boys feel brave and heroic?"

"I hope so."

"You're in advertising?"

"Yep."

"Tell me about that."

"Advertising is about selling the product. But, sometimes, you aren't just selling a product, you're selling an idea, a hope, a dream, or a fantasy. Currently, I'm on an account for a perfume company. So, we're selling the perfume but also the desire that women have to be attractive and sexy and beautiful. You make them believe that they can be those things.

"If they wear the perfume," he teased.

"Yeah." I took another sip. "It's kind of like giving them a placebo. A great-smelling perfume doesn't make a woman more beautiful, but if she thinks it does and conveys that, suddenly her self-confidence increases her attractiveness. That is what we sell."

He gazed at me with those soft brown eyes. "I think you might be the least evil ad person I have ever met."

I laughed. "Well, we can't all go around being doctors and making children feel like heroes."

It was his turn to laugh.

The calamari came as he talked about his job. He vaguely described a few of the patients that concerned him, surprised him, and made him question things. My belief that people in healthcare were crazy was only confirmed by his stories. However, I was thankful that someone felt the calling to do it.

The calamari dipped in spicy marinara sauce was everything he said it would be. I was selfishly happy that he let me have the last piece.

The conversation was light as we both ate. I couldn't help but consider what his appearance said about him, something I had started doing since my internship in advertising. He dressed well. His blue-striped shirt and black slacks conveyed professionalism and male confidence. The conservativeness of the look reminded me of his age and spoke of a man who was concerned with his appearance but not overly so. He was attractive, but I didn't feel the rush of lust that the romance novels of my college years promised. I tried not to be disappointed by it.

After filling our stomachs, we talked about the towns we had grown up in. He had that same openness and friendliness that I associated with my neighbors back home. As he talked about growing up in the South, I wondered if this was where he had picked up his old-fashioned manners.

I smiled as he told me about playing football in a place where quarterbacks and wide receivers were something akin to gods. Miguel was not lacking in masculinity, and I wasn't surprised that he went to college on a football scholarship.

We sat at the restaurant talking for a couple of hours before I made an excuse to leave. As we departed, he reached for my arm.

"I had a wonderful time."

I smiled. "Me too, but next time I pay."

"Not a chance." He grinned.

I huffed dramatically, then said good night. I gave him a brief hug and hailed a taxi, not willing to brave the subway at this time alone. One pulled up immediately, and Miguel opened the door. I thanked him and was about to climb in when he gently turned me around, placed his hands on my hips, and brushed his lips softly over mine. It was a short and sweet kiss.

"I couldn't wait to see you," he whispered against my lips. "Two days was almost too much." I felt his lips parting into a smile. "How about Monday night? Dinner, you and me?"

"Sure," I said a little befuddled.

"I might let you pay," he said playfully before giving me another brief kiss.

I laughed. "I doubt that, but we'll see."

"Good night, Elena."

He handed me into the cab and closed the door. I waved as he watched the cab pull out into traffic.

"Where to?" the driver asked.

I gave him the address and fell back against the seat, trying not to fixate on why I felt so underwhelmed with what should have been a perfect date. I couldn't pick out anything that had gone badly. But, no matter how I tried to get excited by it, I was still left feeling lukewarm.

I wasn't expecting my roommate to be home, so the lights on in the front room surprised me. The apartment was quiet. I figured Leta was asleep, so I tiptoed through the living room toward my room. Two steps from my door, I heard an agonizing scream come from the direction of Leta's room. The sound of things crashing to the floor followed soon after.

I frantically looked around for a weapon as I heard another scream. Eying the umbrella by the door, I made a quick dash for it while pulling out my phone. I dialed nine-one-one and headed stealthily towards Leta's room. She whimpered on the other side of the door as something that sounded like glass hit the floor.

The phone rang.

And rang some more.

Finally, a voice came on, and I inhaled sharply, ready to report that something was terrorizing my roommate. The adrenaline pumped through my body, and my muscles tightened, readying for either fight or flight.

Nine-one-one put me on hold.

On hold.

Leta shrieked. Someone was killing my roommate, and nine-one-one had me on hold!

I stuffed the phone into my pocket and raised the umbrella over my head. It was up to me to save Leta. I gulped before laying my hand on the doorknob. My heartbeat pounded in my ears. On the count of three, I told myself.

One. Umbrella poised to attack in one hand and the other wrapped around the knob.

Two. Was I really going to charge in with only an umbrella?

Three.

Yep, I was. I took a deep breath, opened my eyes, and charged into the room with a squeak of a battle cry.

Broken shards of porcelain and glass, shreds of fabric, and torn pictures littered the floor of the trashed room. Downy feathers floated in the air. I scanned for an attacker, unable to find one. Leta was nowhere to be found either.

I heard a sniffle. "Leta?"

A head covered in down rose from the other side of the bed. "What are you doing with the umbrella?" She sniffled again and looked utterly confused.

I stared at her in silence. "I was going to save you from whoever was killing you."

Sniffle. "You're too late," she wailed and fell out of sight.

"Leta," I yelled as I traversed the chaos on the floor. I half expected to see her lying in a pool of blood. Yet as I rounded the bed, I found Leta in her underwear. She was curled in the fetal position beside the bed. Her body shook with sobs, but there was no sign of blood.

I squatted down to touch her and remembered the phone in my pocket. Still on hold. I hung up and placed it on what was left of the bedding.

"Leta, what happened? Are you okay?"

She rolled over, flinging her head back and her arms out. Her face was wet, and her eyes were red and puffy. She stared at the ceiling so long in silence that I looked up to see what was there. The ceiling was clear. I looked back to see Leta staring at me.

"What's with the umbrella? Is that smoke coming off it?" Her voice was steady as she eyed me like I was the crazy one.

I rolled my eyes and sat down on the floor, relinquishing my weapon, which was strangely hot in my hand. "I thought someone was in here...killing you. Remember?"

She looked thoughtful for about a second then snorted and dropped her head back to the floor with her eyes closed.

"What happened?" I waited for her to move, but she remained frighteningly still. I listened for breathing, but it grew fainter.

"Leta?"

No response. I leaned over to see if she was still breathing.

She shot up so fast I fell back on my bottom and lost my breath. I looked up in shock. Leta looked like a person I had never met. She was downright terrifying.

"Termites."

I watched in dismay as she tapped her finger thoughtfully against her chin.

"No, no, that won't work. Ticks...that will be so much better." She nodded and stood up, leaving me on the floor.

I sat there, deep in confusion while she started throwing things off the bed, looking for something buried under the shredded fabric and feathers. As she continued to launch items into the air, I was forced to dodge.

"Can you tell me what is going on?" I asked.

Leta looked down at me. "I am going to give Corbett ticks." It was stated matter-of-factly as she returned to her mission of furious sorting.

"Corbett, as in your boyfriend Corbett?"

"Yep," she said in a cheery voice.

Oh, that explained everything. "What?"

"That piece of crap is going to get what's coming to him if he thinks that he can just break my heart and move on unscathed." She shrieked with maniacal glee. "Yes, I found it!"

A silky pair of red boxers with "Sexy Beast" written all over the fabric hung from her hands.

I scrambled to my knees and approached the bed. Leta held the boxers to her chest and giggled maniacally. I waved my hands in front of her a few times before she looked down at me.

"What happened?" I asked slowly and almost regretted the question.

She crawled towards me like a lion on the hunt. "He dumped me. Said I was losing my sex appeal." Anger visibly filled every line of her body.

I should have dropped the subject, but I was too flabbergasted to think clearly.

"You? You ooze sex like a bodybuilder oozes sweat."

"I know." She sat back down on the bed concentrating fully on the boxers.

I'm surprised they didn't just burst into flames.

"I am so tired of him making me feel bad. No more." She twirled the boxers around her fingers and smiled. "But he's gonna feel horrible by the time I get done with him."

She jumped off the bed and flew out of the room. I needed a moment to regain my senses. Tripping over the clutter, I quickly followed her out. She sat at the tiny table in our kitchen with a laptop open in front of her. The fingers of one hand maneuvered and clicked the mousepad while the fingers of the other hand absently stroked the red boxers. Her narrowed eyes focused intently on the screen.

"Okay, I understand that you're angry and hurt, but you really don't want to do anything hurtful to your ex-boyfriend." I tried to reason from the doorway.

"Yes, I do," she responded calmly, not at all the way you would expect a crazy person to respond.

"Seriously, Leta?"

She ignored me.

I grunted in frustration. "Do you remember the last time that you guys fought? You were so mad at him, but then you talked things out and the two of you were able to make up. Do you remember that? Is it possible that you are overreacting just a bit?"

"We had great make-up sex. No talking." She looked up at me then. I saw the determination in her expression. "Trust me, you don't waste your time talking to an animal like that. Nope, no talking."

My lips pursed with my own determination. "So, what are you going to do? I mean, do you really plan on giving him ticks? Can humans even get ticks?"

A wickedly satisfied smile was my answer. "He can. All that fur of his will be just perfect."

I stared at her again in disbelief, realizing that she was completely committed to her plan of vengeance.

"Oh, wow," I said slowly, "you are crazy."

"Yep." With a sound of approval, she closed the laptop and rushed to her room.

I leaned against the doorway and pushed my hair back off my face. "Where will you even get ticks?" I called out.

"I have my ways. Wish me luck." She glided past me in a beige trench coat to grab her keys.

"You know this is unhealthy, right?"

She walked towards the door without pausing. "I know."

With a peppy smile, she set out to unleash ticks on her ex.

Chapter 4

I stood outside my office building, clutching my cup of coffee and so deep in thought that I didn't even see the night security guard approach.

"Ms. McNeal?"

"Hey, Stan. Just getting off your shift?" I turned to him with a smile.

Stan had a habit of walking with his hands in his pockets. He nodded and stood shoulder to shoulder with me while I stared up at the building. "Something bothering you?"

There were a lot of things on my mind. "Did I tell you that I tripped in front of my new client last week?"

"Ah, the ankle," he nodded knowingly.

I nodded back. We stood in silence for a moment.

"He was that good-looking?"

I laughed. "Maybe."

"Nothing to worry about. A guy likes having a pretty girl fall for him."

I nodded.

"Something else on your mind?"

I sighed. It was impossible to not vent everything to Stan. I couldn't count the number of times I'd cried out all my fears and frustrations to him since the first day here.

"I think my roommate might be crazy."

He nodded seriously. "I've known Leta for a few years now. She's a passionate girl, a bit headstrong at times."

I snorted but couldn't help smiling. "That's a bit of an understatement."

"Maybe, but there's a big heart under all that crazy."

"Yeah," I said, still not convinced that made up for the crazy.

"Did the date go well?" Stan asked.

"It did," I responded. I'd mentioned to Stan the night before that I was going on a date with Miguel.

The night guard looked thoughtful. "Was he a gentleman?"

Amused with his concern, "Yes, he was. I think you would like him, he's an ex-military guy like yourself."

Stan nodded. "Did he buy you dinner?"

"Yes, sir."

Stan made a noise of approval while looking like a father on prom night. "He walked you home?"

"No, I took a cab home."

He nodded approvingly. "Good girl."

I smiled at the show of parental endorsement despite the fact I was a grown woman.

"You looking forward to another date?"

"I guess."

He eyed me for a moment before chuckling. "Must have been quite some date," he teased. "You know, you're not obligated to go on another one."

He raised a brow questioningly.

"Yeah, of course. I'm just preoccupied with all the stuff at work."

He had a knowing look when he said, "I'm sure you are. Don't let that new client distract you too much. And keep an eye open. You never know when something is lurking around the corner."

Putting his hands into his pockets, he started down the street. "Have a good day, Ms. McNeal."

I procured a cup of steaming herbal tea from the staff lounge and settled into my cubicle to start another day. Immersed in work, I hummed softly to myself as Selene came around the corner.

"Well, how did it go? Did you sleep with him last night?"

I nearly spit hot tea all over the papers in front of me. Thankfully, I caught myself in time and merely dribbled down the side of my mouth and onto my pretty pink blouse.

"What is with your and Leta's obsession with my sex life? I did not sleep with anyone last night," I said much louder than intended as I looked up at Selene with shock.

"What a shame that is," said a familiar voice.

Mr. Tasev stopped next to Selene with a smile on his face.

I managed not to slap myself in the forehead, and instead, sat there gaping at him with my mouth open. Would the embarrassment ever end? Was some divine force above using me for a good laugh?

Much to my surprise, Selene struggled hard not to laugh, unable to say something professional-like that might get us out of this awkward situation. With no distraction, I had to reel my jaw in and ignore the blood rushing to my face.

"Mr. Tasev, what a pleasure it is to see you. How are you?" I sat up straighter, because somewhere in the back of my mind that seemed like just the thing to do and pasted a friendly smile on my face.

He returned the smile though it wasn't quite what I'd call friendly. I got the impression something more inspired it. "I thought that you were going to call me Nolan." His lips pursed in a seductive pout.

Tingling shot up and down my spine and reverberated to every other part of my body, and I do mean EVERY part. I exhaled to dispense the sudden flush of lust, desperately wanting to fan the growing heat of my face.

"Of course." One small phrase at a time. That was the plan.

I'd expected Selene to recover, but she turned away to keep from laughing in our client's face. Nolan leaned over the partition of my cubicle and brought his hands together in front of him. And what beautiful hands they were. Just so big and capable of doing things to a woman that...

I put the brakes on that thought very quickly. I had been in the company of a very attractive man last night and though he had given me a perfectly acceptable kiss, my thoughts had not once turned this lust-driven towards him.

Sternly, I told myself to concentrate...on something other than Nolan's fascinating body parts. He watched me with amusement as if he knew exactly what inner battle I fought.

"I am saddened."

I waited for him to finish that statement and leaned in a little when I realized that he was waiting for a prompt. "What saddens you?" I asked with slight confusion.

He gave me a devilish smile followed by a look of mock sadness. "It saddens me that you slept alone last night," he paused, pursing his lips in a way that was both thoughtful and exceedingly attractive. "Such a disappointment. A beautiful woman should never be lonely in bed."

More heat rushed to my face.

"Oh, well, thank you for your concern, Nolan. That is very...sweet."

A snort came from Selene's corner. I shot her a dirty look.

"I assure you, it is not sweet," he said those words so softly that I wasn't sure if I'd heard him correctly. He had another unconvincing look of concern on his face again.

Leta saved me from any further embarrassment as she came down the hall and spotted Nolan. She called out his name in a pleasantly surprised tone. Reaching the three of us, she quickly assessed the situation, taking in my blush, Selene's barely restrained snort, and Nolan's slightly amused smile.

With a terrific show of charisma, she pretended not to notice a thing and swept Nolan down the hall with her before he could object. She was a passing magnet, and he could not resist her pull. I listened to her chat cheerfully with him as they walked towards her office. When their voices were no longer audible, Selene burst into a mixture of laughter and snorts. I gave her another dirty look, but it failed to quiet her.

"Wow," she said as she grabbed her side. "You have…" She couldn't finish the statement she was laughing so hard.

"The worst luck imaginable," I finished for her. She nodded, unable to respond in any other way. "Why? Why do I keep humiliating myself in front of that guy?" I was very careful not to raise my voice again.

She took another minute to pull herself together while I put my head on the desk and tried to disappear. I hadn't quite figured out that trick yet.

Selene laughed again as I groaned from underneath the sanctuary of my covered head.

"It wasn't that bad," she tried to comfort.

I looked up from my desk with a look that conveyed my disbelief and continued to stare at her with narrowed eyes until she admitted that it really had been that bad.

"Come on, it's got to feel good to have a guy like that flirting with you."

I narrowed my eyes at her new attempt to comfort me, but she returned the look and refused to back down.

"Admit it. I don't see him flirting with anyone else here. He wasn't flirting with me or Leta."

"That doesn't make me feel better. He doesn't mess with you and Leta because you two don't respond to him the way I do."

Selene looked confused.

"Every woman here just about melts when he walks into the room, everyone, but you and Leta. You guys looked at him like he was just any other man."

"Besides being a client, he is just any other man." She still looked confused. Looking around the hall before leaning over the partition, she asked in a hushed voice, "You don't think there's anything strange about him, do you?"

She seemed to want a particular answer from me, though I wasn't sure what.

"Anything strange?" I suddenly felt suspicious. "What do you mean by that? Like..." I looked around, "sex offender strange?"

Selene instantly stood up straight and adamantly responded, "No, no, that is not what I mean. I just was wondering if you thought that there was something different about him." She gave me that look again like I knew the answer that she wanted.

Unfortunately, I didn't. "No, I just think that he's an attractive man. That's all. Nothing strange though." She looked a little disappointed but nodded. "I still find it strange that none of you are attracted to him or his partner."

Selene looked relieved. "Yeah, I can understand that. We just tend to like guys who are a little...different. You know?"

I had no idea, but Selene seemed uncomfortable, so I said sure, and she smiled. Her head turned in the direction of Leta's office.

"Your playboy is on his way back," she said with amusement.

I groaned and threw my head back onto the desk. "I really don't need another embarrassing moment right now, but there's nowhere to hide."

"Don't worry about it. I'll take care of it."

I looked up to see her smile in a way that was warm and comforting.

Nolan and Leta appeared around the corner. He looked confused as Leta led him down the hall and past my cubicle. He stopped and though his eyes met mine, there was no recognition that he even saw me. I realized that Nolan and Leta both looked a little blurry, and I couldn't quite hear what Leta was saying to him as she coaxed him down the hall. His apparent confusion deepened.

I looked at Selene, who stood watching Leta and Nolan. She was still clear. I stood up and took a step forward. The space between Nolan and me seemed off. It was like I was in a bubble, and he was outside the bubble. I looked up and could almost see the domed top of it with its clear, slippery surface extending down and around me and Selene.

Nolan gave up his search and allowed Leta to lead him down the hall. I shook my head with closed eyes, certain that I was seeing things. I opened them to find the bubble gone, but just in time to see Leta wink over her shoulder at us.

"What just happened?" I asked Selene.

She shrugged her shoulders and slipped stealthily down the hall before I could ask another question. I turned to look at the disappearing back of Nolan and shook my head again. Whatever I thought had just happened was far too strange to have really happened. At least, I tried to assure myself. There was no way that Selene had just encased me in a bubble.

Right? Those sorts of things just didn't happen.

"Oh," Selene popped her head in. "Miguel's calling, and I'm pretty sure that it's important." Then she disappeared, and what do you know, the phone rang.

Guess who was calling.

It was Miguel, calling to reschedule our date.

Chapter 5

It had been days since I had seen my roommate, other than a few times at work. I missed her. On Saturday morning, the sound of her heels tapping against the floor drew my attention, and I watched as she sauntered into the apartment with hips swaying victoriously. I put down the tablet I had been reading and shifted in the chair.

"Wow, you look great." I seriously admired the short red dress and strappy stilettos that laced up her shapely calves.

She stood just inside the living area with her hands on her full hips, looking immensely pleased, but my comment seemed to surprise her a bit.

"What? Oh, this? I just got it on my way to Corbett's house the other night," she purred. "I wish you could have seen the look on his face. His jaw just dropped to the floor."

I bet it did. It was the kind of outfit that looked more like high-end designer lingerie. It had a corset top that made even Leta's small breasts look pumped and ready for action. The silky red fabric tailored perfectly to her pear shape and was cut so short, I was afraid of what Leta might reveal if she bent over. But it was a fantasy dress for sure, the kind that I would dream of wearing, but would never have the confidence for. Leta, though, had more than enough confidence to pull it off. She wore it like a second skin.

"So, I guess you guys made up, and you didn't give him ticks... did you?" I really hoped that she had exaggerated that part.

She laughed. "Of course not."

I breathed a sigh of relief. My roommate was not a complete psycho.

"I didn't get the chance when he saw me in this."

"What happened?"

"He dropped to his knees and begged for my forgiveness, which of course I made him earn." Oh, dear.

"The last time you guys made up it took a couple of days." And, I had been unable to escape.

"We didn't have sex," she quickly corrected.

"That's enough information. I don't want to know anymore." I held my hands tentatively over my ears, prepared to block out the details. But she just laughed, and I relaxed.

Leta threw her purse and jacket over the back of the sofa before reclining on the cushions. "He'll have to show me that he cares before he gets any."

"Good for you," I encouraged. "He should treat you better because you deserve better."

Leta smiled and then broke into hearty giggles.

"What?" I asked defensively.

"I'm sorry," she managed to say. "It's just," more uncontrollable laughter, "just that everyone says that as some sort of cheery antidote, and it is so stupid. Deserves better? Who really gets what they deserve in this life? Good things happen to bad people and bad things happen to good people." She wiped the tears from her eyes as the laughter subsided.

I couldn't help but feel hurt. Maybe I was sensitive about being naïve in comparison to Leta, but I was just trying to support her. But apparently, it was all just stupid. I knew life wasn't always fair, but I still wanted to believe that there was some justice in the universe. Then again, I was just an idealistic small-town girl.

I stood up and tried to make my voice as pleasant as possible, unable to stay in the same room. "Well, I'm glad that you worked things out, excuse me."

My voice wasn't very convincing. I saw it in Leta's face as she sat up. "Oh, don't get upset. I know that you were just trying to be nice, but the world just doesn't work that way."

I went to grab my coat, thinking that a walk would be just the thing. She stood and was in front of the door before I had finished putting the coat on.

"Wait," she said more firmly than I had ever heard. "There is no reason to get this upset. I appreciate what you were trying to do, but I'm just being realistic."

I'm not sure if it was the implication that I was unrealistic or the overly patient tone she used, but I was suddenly too furious now to leave quietly.

"Excuse my silly little ideals. Where I'm from, we don't live in the real world there and couldn't possibly understand things the way you city folks do."

"That is not what I was saying," she quickly interjected.

"Maybe not directly; it's hard to tell with you city folks."

I felt the blood rushing to my face as my voice rose with every word I was saying. Usually, it took so much more for me to lose my temper, but maybe the stress and excitement of the past few weeks had made my fuse shorter. Either way, this uncharacteristic show of anger felt oddly good. The heat building inside me was comforting, and the expression of so much emotion was like releasing years' worth of pent-up frustrations.

"But we small-town folk like to just say what we mean."

"Would you stop calling me 'city folk', I grew up in a forest in Greece. I am the furthest thing from city that you can get." Leta also uncharacteristically raised her voice. The tension in the room was so thick you could have cut it with a knife.

I narrowed my eyes. "Well, maybe condescending pessimist is just part of your personality then." I immediately felt guilty.

She gasped and took a step back. A few moments of silence passed with both of us glaring at each other. Leta took a breath, and as she exhaled, I saw a brief expression of pain. Instantly, I felt myself begin to cool off. Heartburn shot up my chest, and my gut felt twisted inside out, no doubt a result of the anger and now guilt. I began to utter my apology, but she interrupted.

Her voice was colder than I had ever heard, and her eyes were razor-sharp. "And naïve foolishness must be a part of yours."

I don't think I had ever seen vengeance before, but there it was, written all over Leta's face. Funnily, I had always thought that it was about drastic acts of retribution, but this was really what it was all about. Someone had hurt her and now she was going to hurt them back. Simple. Eye for an eye. A wound was given for one received, and still, neither of us would be even. Neither of us would feel better, and none of the hurt would go away. It seemed to make so much sense, yet it didn't make any.

That heat rose in my chest again, and I could have said so many things back to her that were just as mean. But we could be here for hours exchanging insults, and what would I get? A worse stomachache no doubt.

"Right," I said softly. I stepped around her and headed out the door.

My walk to cool off only took me to the park two streets down. Sitting on a park bench was great for reflecting. Not that I did much of it while I watched people pass by me. Instead, I wondered about the color of the grass, the feeling of the cold wind, the stamina of the cyclists in their neon riding outfits, the stories of the homeless pair huddled against a tree...

My thoughts didn't wander too much in the direction of my roommate or our fight or my strange display of anger. All of that was much too deep to focus on right now. Solving the mysteries of the universe seemed like an easier pursuit. I stayed on the park bench even as the temperature dropped, but it was the little drops of rain on my face that finally made me leave. I had forgotten to grab an umbrella.

I didn't realize how cold I was until I stood up and left the bench. Still unwilling to face my roommate, I left the park and headed to a nearby coffee shop. The afternoon was cold and wet, and the shop was full. People chatted at the few tables set up near the windows while others crowded together in the small space waiting for their drinks.

I ordered my usual, and the cashier asked, "You okay?"

Surprised, I looked around first to see if she was talking to me.

She smiled, and her lip piercing glinted in the low light. "Yeah, you. Are you okay?"

"Umm, yeah. Thanks. And y-you?" I stuttered.

"I'm good." She grabbed a cup and wrote my order on it before handing it to the barista. "You've come in here before, but today you seem different. So, I was just wondering if you were okay."

I stepped aside so she could help the next person, but something about the knowing look in her eyes disturbed me.

The rush of coffee-goers seemed to end a few people after I had gotten my white chocolate mocha. I browsed the few items that were on sale, eclectic mugs and such, waiting for the cashier to be free. When the opportunity presented itself, I rushed forward. "Excuse me."

She turned around with a polite smile. Her orange hair had looked redder from afar, but it was definitely orange and trimmed close to her head. "Hey. What can I get for you?"

"This is sort of a strange question, but what did you mean when you said that I was different today?"

"Oh, you just didn't seem all aglow today. You know?"

"Nope," I said shaking my head.

She smiled kindly as she leaned against the counter. "You usually come in happy and throwing off this warm, fuzzy vibe. But today, the vibe was weird." She inhaled and looked thoughtfully up. Thick black lined her brown eyes. "It was kinda like," she continued to look around as if the answer was written somewhere on the walls. I followed her gaze as if I too might find the answer there. Maybe the answer was that obvious.

A gasp and slap on the counter drew my attention back to her. She was staring at me with a smile. "It was like your inner fire had burned out." She shook her head. "Yeahhhh, that's it."

Okay...all that New Age stuff was beyond my comprehension.

"Well, thanks." I smiled at her and decided that maybe it was time to face my roommate, with my burned-out inner fire and all.

I was at the door when I heard her call out, "You really should do something about your inner fire, though. It's like your life force, you know."

She looked concerned and excited at the same time while all the other faces in the room just looked concerned. I tried not to let my embarrassment show as I nodded my head at her.

"Thanks, I'll keep that in mind."

I looked at her one last time, and her entire presence changed. No longer did she look like the girl with outrageous hair and a lip piercing, but instead she looked older and almost maternal as she smiled. The light around her looked vaguely orange, yellow, and red, and there was a bluish-white glow to her face.

"I know that doesn't mean much now, but one day it will." Even her voice sounded older and wiser.

I blinked and the special effects were gone. Shaking the whole thing off, I left the coffee shop and headed home, writing the hallucinations off as emotional stress.

Standing outside the apartment door, I took a deep breath and told myself to remain calm. I didn't need another show of irrational temper. That was not me. Instead of getting angry and defensive, I was going to sit Leta down and talk about all this nonsense calmly. I would start with an apology and explain my feelings while also letting her explain her own.

Feeling more capable of handling my roommate, I put my hand on the door handle, but it turned on its own.

I looked up as the door opened and found Leta standing there. Her eye makeup was smudged, and her massacre had run down her cheeks. Her hair looked dry and thin, not at all like it usually did. She had changed out of her dress and was now wearing ratty old sweats that were way too big. And when our eyes met, she looked like she would cry.

Actually, she did cry as she wrapped her arms around me in a crushing hug.

"Leta," I struggled to say against her chest. "Leta, I can't breathe." I yanked on her sweats a few times before she took the hint and pulled back.

"I am so glad that you are here," she cried and smothered me again.

"Leta," I barely managed. More vigorous pulling was required this time. When she finally let go, I took a deep breath and steadied myself against the doorframe. "Are you okay?" I asked even though I was sure she was not okay.

"They're trying to kill me," she shrieked.

I winced, and more tears poured down her face.

"Okay, calm down. Who's trying to kill you?" Maybe it was the ticks revolting.

"Come on." She grabbed me and whirled me towards the stairs. I tried to stop her, but my options quickly became apparent: go with her willingly or be dragged. I chose to go willingly, figuring I could reason with her on the way.

"Leta, it would help me if you told me exactly what is going on," I said calmly as we descended the stairs. "Maybe we should call the police."

"The police won't care about a tree," she cried. We descended so quickly, that I started to feel dizzy.

"Wait," I said firmly with a strong yank on her hand, which had mine in a death grip. She responded this time and stopped on the step just below me. "You said that someone was trying to kill you. What does that have to do with a tree?"

"They're trying to kill the tree which will also kill me," she said shortly, as if that answer was clear as day.

I took a moment to process that information and shook my head sadly. I'm sure I wore an expression similar to my mother's worried scowl because I was deeply concerned that my friend really was crazy.

"Leta, it's been a tough week. Let's go back to the apartment. I'll make you some tea, and we can talk."

"We don't have time for that! They are going to kill my tree and wipe out my soul."

She made no sense at all, and I didn't doubt that my face showed confusion. "I don't understand what a tree has to do with your soul. Come on, let's go up to the apartment."

She stood staring up at me before getting a very determined look on her face.

"I'll just have to show you."

Without warning, she started down the stairs again taking me with her. I tried to tell her to slow down or stop, but nothing I did dissuaded her. My friend was obviously on her way to a mental breakdown, and I had no choice but to follow.

Chapter 6

"Leta, will you please slow down!" I reverted to yelling, not that it was helping any more than my logical reasoning had. Leta continued to firmly hold my hand as she dragged me through the rain.

"My ankle is just now starting to recover. Do you want me to reinjure it?"

No response.

I huffed and pushed the wet hair out of my face. The pouring rain was enough of a visual hindrance. With the stinging little globules piercing my eyes and the growing soreness of my stiff ankle, hair in the face was just one more thing leading to the inevitable disaster we were furiously rushing towards.

"Leta!" Nothing got through to her. I was going to collapse at some point, and she was just going to continue dragging my body to this tree of hers. My clothes were saturated, my ankle hurt, my body was exhausted, and still no hope in sight.

We continued down the nearly empty street, completely overlooked by the people we passed. I had thought about calling out for help about two streets back, but I was in the city, where people kept their heads down and minded their own business. I remembered reading that a person could be attacked in front of a building full of people and no one would call the police because they assumed that somebody else would.

I was doomed.

Despite being in decent condition, I was starting to feel the four blocks that we had sprinted so far.

Wait, could it be? Was Leta looking both ways up and down the street? Were we about to cross a major intersection?

My pleas for help were heard. Cars were coming in both directions. We would have to stop and wait for the light, which we just missed. The plan began formulating in my head. First, I had to get out of Leta's death grip, and then I could get her some help. The on/off nonsense of her relationship was just too much. She would be okay though. She just needed some rest and quiet time.

Maybe some counseling, but she would be fine. I just had to get help.

Escape... then help for Leta. That was the plan.

She turned towards the street, and I waited to feel her slow down. I watched her step into the street before me. I watched the cars coming quickly towards us and realized that Leta had no intention of stopping for traffic. She expected the traffic to stop for her.

I was so about to die.

I screamed and covered my face with my free arm as the headlights of the oncoming car blinded my eyes. Any second now, it was going to hit me, and I was going to be filled with unimaginable pain.

Any second now I was going to die.

Any second now.

Terrified, I dared to peek open one eye. Nothing. I saw nothing but the pouring rain. I opened both eyes, and my gaze fell to the spot just over my left shoulder, where I saw the white Honda pass within inches of my body. I think I squeaked; couldn't quite manage a shriek at the moment.

Panicked, I turned my head forward to see Leta. She leaped gracefully to the curb ahead of me, reminding me of a stag. I managed not to fall on my face while stumbling over it. We continued to beat tracks over the sidewalk.

When my feet hit the soft though slick surface of the grass, my ankle breathed a sigh of relief. The park was unfamiliar to me, though I knew it was one of the older and larger ones in the city. All but the evergreens were bare, and the trees were eerie figures against the gray sky. I stared up at them thinking that this was the weirdest thing that had ever happened to me. If you had told me a few days ago that I would be dragged by my sweet but crazy roommate across the city in the rain and through a creepy park, I would have laughed at the silliness of it all.

Freaked out by the trees, I continued to stare up at them while my feet slipped out from underneath me. It wasn't until I pain exploded in my head that I realized I had fallen on the ground. It took a few more seconds before the shock cleared enough that I remembered to close my mouth before the polluted city rain drowned me.

Honestly, I was surprised Leta stopped. I'm not sure if it was my violent coughing or maybe just that she didn't have the strength to drag my dead body.

Her face came into view over me. She blocked the rain enough that I could fully open my stinging eyes. Water dripped down her chin and the waves of her drenched hair. She looked concerned. "Are you okay?"

What! I sputtered up more rainwater and rose up on my elbows. "Now you're asking?" I yelled.

"Well, yeah, you just fell." She took a step back with another classic Leta look; the one that seemed confused because I somehow missed the obvious.

"You just dragged me across the city at a dead run with my injured ankle, pulled me into a busy street where I almost got hit and now you are asking me if I'm okay!"

"Do you want to rest for a minute?" It was the concerned seriousness of her face that completely flabbergasted me.

I gave up trying to reason with her and fell back on the grass with my eyes, and mouth, closed. I even groaned aloud at that point.

"If you're okay, we need to get going. They could be cutting down my tree as we speak." The matter-of-fact tone had replaced her concerned one.

I hoisted myself up on my elbows again. Shielding my eyes from the rain, I glared at her with one eyebrow raised. "I am not moving again until you explain to me what the hell is going on."

She looked shocked, then panicked, and then just plain irritated.

"That or you drag my lifeless body there." We stared at each other, neither willing to give in. "Fine." I laid back down, about eighty percent sure that she really wasn't going to drag me there.

"But we don't have time for this!" she cried.

"Your choice." I couldn't see her, but I imagined her biting her nails as she pondered her options. Peevishly, I smiled at the thought of her having chewed-up nails- one less perfect thing about her.

I'll give it to her. She was stubborn as a bull. It was at least three minutes before she caved, and she was pouty about it.

I cracked one eye. "I said okay," she snapped.

Sitting up with my legs crossed, I guarded my eyes against the rain again and waited.

She looked so uncomfortable standing there in the rain, but that wasn't the reason for her discomfort. Leta didn't want to explain this to me. After watching her fidget in place, I reminded her that we did have a limited amount of time; I was getting cold sitting on the muddy ground. She glared but kneeled in front of me and sighed. She said something so softly that I couldn't hear her.

"What did you say?" I asked as I leaned towards her.

She looked slightly miffed again. "I'm a dryad," she said in a louder voice.

"A dry-head?" Was that like a pothead?

She looked furious. "A DRY-AD!" I heard her loud and clear this time. She stood with her face red and tight, hands clenched at her sides.

"What's that?"

Her eyes widened, to a scary size. "You don't know what a dryad is?" It was more of a shriek than a question. "Do you know what a nymph is?"

"A slutty character from Greek mythology?" I was very confused.

"I am not slutty." If Leta had been a volcano, she would have blown her top. It was going to be Pompeii all over again.

Okay... "I didn't say that you are."

"Don't you get it?" She cried with obvious frustration.

"I am so far from getting it right now." I'm sure I had one of those dumbfounded looks on my face. Trees, fairy tale creatures, and dry-heads... what did all these things have to do with each other?

"I am a dryad." She said it slowly and beseechingly as if that would help me to understand any of this better.

I leaned closer to her. "What is a dryad?"

She groaned and stomped her foot. Mud spattered up on my face.

"Hey," I started to complain when I saw the thorny little plants growing out of the ground and up Leta's legs. My eyes widened in disbelief. I pointed at the plants and made a few incomprehensible sounds before real words came out. "Leta, look... look down. What is that?"

Her angry eyes shifted down, and her mouth made a small "o".

"No, it's okay. Everything is okay." Those words were not said for my benefit.

She was talking to the thorn bushes actively growing up her legs. Growing inches every second that I sat there staring at them. Plants didn't grow that fast. Normal plants didn't do that.

"Leta, are you talking to the plant?"

She spared me a glance before looking back at her legs.

I stood and stared at her in silence for several minutes while she continued to talk soothingly to the plants. My disbelief grew as the thorny things turned into beautiful iliac flowers that bloomed right in front of me before closing again and returning to the ground. And, just in case all that strangeness was not enough, I looked up to see Leta's smooth perfectly tanned skin changing into a grayish-brown bark.

"Oh, my..." was all I could say as I stood. She suddenly took notice of my disbelieving stare and looked down at her hands, which also resembled tree bark.

"This wasn't exactly the way I wanted you to find out, but here it is." She held her hands out and shrugged her shoulders.

"What am I finding out?" I was still a few pages behind.

She sighed again. "I'm a dryad. It's a type of nymph that lives in and is associated with a tree."

"But you live in an apartment with me, Leta," I pointed out slowly. "I know; I can hear you snoring in the middle of the night."

She scrunched her nose at that last bit. "I don't physically live in the tree though every once in a while, I do have to be inside my tree because that is where my soul lives."

I don't think I sat voluntarily. It was more like just landing on my bottom when my legs gave out. The muddy water splashed up around me, but I didn't notice. My life had suddenly become something out of a fantasy novel. My roommate was not human; at least, I didn't think so.

"So, you're not human?" It was one last shot at normalcy, but she shot me down with a shake of her head.

Okay, deep breaths. My life had just taken a hard turn into the unbelievable.

What was I going to do? Sit here in the cold mud trying to convince myself that everything was okay when my roommate was still sporting her bark skin? I'm not sure how long I sat there turning thoughts over and over in my head. It wasn't until Leta spoke that I remembered I was in the park.

"Elena, please."

That was it. Those desperately pleaded words were all it took to get me off my bottom. I pushed past the craziness my life had suddenly become and figured there was always the possibility that this was all a dream. I wasn't going to bet on it, but a girl could hope.

"Alright, where is this tree of yours?" I asked as I pushed the hair off my face again.

Leta stared at me in silence for a while.

"That's it? I thought for sure that we would need to do this a couple more times before it really sunk in. You're just going to accept it?"

"What else would I do? Tell myself that it's okay- my roommate just needs to exfoliate more. Eventually, it would click that no pumice stone is going to fix that." I pointed to her skin. "Besides, I'm still hoping I'll wake up soon."

"You want to touch it?"

I reeled my hand in. "That's a little more than I can handle right now."

She smiled and pulled her sleeves over her hands.

"So, let's go save your soul."

She smiled brilliantly, and even with the fading bark skin, she was beautiful.

"It's not far."

Leta grabbed my hand and began towing me through the park once more. However, this time she was a little more conscious of my requests to slow down or plead to go around park benches. I didn't have the stag leaping abilities that she did.

"Wait!"

Without warning she stopped in front of me, and my momentum forced me to collide with her. She stood unaffected; I struggled to regain my balance after bouncing off her.

"There it is," she said in a wistful voice.

I regained my balance and stood next to her looking for the tree. "Where?"

Before I could locate it, Leta made a noise beside me that was half scream half shriek. I immediately turned to her. "What? What's wrong?"

Her eyes filled with tears as she held her hands over her mouth. Whimpering was the only reply she made. I firmly grabbed her by the shoulders and shook gently. "Leta, what is wrong?"

She whimpered more loudly this time and raised her hand to point. Following the line of her finger, I saw a man standing by a small tree. It was no more than six to seven feet high with a trunk of gray-brown bark. From the three major branches, many smaller ones sprouted, all leafless.

"Is that your tree?" I asked with a bit of disbelief. I had expected something bigger.

She nodded with fearful eyes.

"Well, let's go save it." That was the reason she had dragged me all this way through the rain. I started towards the tree with Leta right behind me.

The man beside the tree was large, both in girth and height. He was obviously the kind of guy who had done a lot of hard jobs in his life. With gloves on both hands, he picked a shovel off the ground just as we were nearing the tree.

"Excuse me," I called out.

He did not appear to hear me as he continued to position the shovel at the base of the tree and drive it into the ground with his foot. Leta gasped beside me and dug her fingers into my arm. I held in a shriek of pain and gave her a look to release my arm. She took the hint and sheepishly let go.

I rushed forward before the man could drive the shovel into the ground again. "Excuse me, sir." I leaned over and waved in his face.

He seemed a bit startled and stood up. "What do you want, lady?" His voice was full of irritation, and his aggressive stare was more than a little intimidating.

I paused briefly as the self-preservation part of my brain kicked on. This man outweighed me by a good one hundred pounds and stood over me about seven inches with a shovel in his hand, looking very angry. And I glanced around to find that my backup was a good three feet behind me.

I motioned for Leta to stand beside me, which she did...reluctantly. I waited to see if she was going to say anything. It was her tree after all. She stood there giving him the kind of smile you would imagine a hare giving a wolf...the kind that says please, oh please don't hurt me. Where was the seductive man charmer that I worked with?

"You gonna waste my time some more?" the gruff voice asked. He shifted his weight to the other leg and wrung his big hands around the shovel's handle, further reminding us that he was a lot bigger than Leta and I put together.

"Um..." What was I supposed to do?

He shifted again uncomfortably and looked even more annoyed. "We don't want you to hurt this tree," was what I blurted. It was the best I could manage.

He snorted and went back to digging up the tree. Leta gasped again and possibly bruised my arm as she gripped it for the second time.

"Hey," I started to object as I took a step closer to him.

He turned and gave me a look that stopped me in my tracks and caused the words in my head to flit away like little butterflies.

"What?" I had never heard such varying degrees of irritation.

"We really don't want you to hurt this tree." All I got this time was a look of disbelief.

He stayed frozen like that just staring at us. Then he shook his head, stood to his full height, and dropped the shovel. This man knew he was intimating. He took one step towards us, and we shuffled back two steps. After a brief smile, his face became hard and determined.

"Look, I got a job to do, and that job includes getting rid of this dead tree."

"It's not dead!" Leta objected over my shoulder. I looked back at her with surprise. It was about time.

"It's dead." He replied firmly.

"It is not!" I could feel the strength of her conviction pushing against me as she opposed him more fervently this time.

"It's unwanted, that's what it is." That was the tone that ended all objections, and Leta shrank back in the presence of it. "The city wants it gone, so I'm here to get rid of it. Now, leave me alone." He bent to pick up the shovel.

I heard Leta make a faint whimpering noise behind me and took a step forward. "Please, this tree is very important to my friend," I said beseechingly.

He turned towards me looking like he was about to erupt. Instead, he looked at me, then behind me, and finally, his eyes shifted right and left. He started laughing.

"Yeah, I can tell it's real important to your friend. Is that why she took off?" He chuckled again.

My brows creased in confusion. Leta would never abandon me. Never.

I looked over my shoulder, to the left and the right. No sign whatsoever of Leta. I was so going to wring her neck when I caught up to her.

Still chuckling, the man resumed his digging. The rain had made the ground soft, and with ease, he was able to uncover the more superficial roots. He continued to unearth the tree and whistled happily as he did it. I stood watching him, trying to figure out where on earth Leta had gone, and trying to find a reasonable explanation for why she would just abandon me like that. Nothing made sense.

Just as he struck the actual roots, the worst high-pitched scream I have ever heard, filled the air. I covered my ears and groaned as it bent me over with pain.

The sound stopped suddenly. I looked up and found that the man had stopped shoveling and was staring down at me strangely. "You okay?" He had a look that clearly said he was convinced I was crazy.

"Didn't you just hear that?" I nearly yelled. The pain had lessened enough that I was able to stand up and look around. The small clearing was empty. It was him, the tree, and me.

"Nope," was all he said as he stared.

"I swear I heard a high-pitched scream." I stared at him in disbelief. "How could you not have heard it?"

"Do you hear that sort of thing often?"

I started to answer then realized what he was implying. "I am not crazy," I informed him instead.

"Whatever. It's just you, the tree, and me. And neither one of us was screaming," he shrugged his shoulders and turned back to the tree. He drove the shovel just below the tree and thrust it upward, ripping the tree from the ground.

The screaming started again, and even covering my ears was not enough to drown it out. I watched as he continued to dig, unaffected by the noise that was no doubt going to make me deaf. That was when it hit me. It had to be the tree screaming. After seeing my roommate's skin turn to bark, a screaming tree didn't seem all that far-fetched. Besides, he was macerating that tree's roots.

I had to do something. The tree was suffering, and I was going to go deaf before he finished killing it. Besides, it was Leta's tree. Even though she had disappeared, this tree meant the world to her. I had seen it in her eyes, and I told her I would help her save it.

I did the only thing I could think of; I positioned myself between the guy and the tree, wrapped my arms around the thin truck, and shouted, "Save the tree!"

My actions forced him to avert the shovel mid-thrust. I held my breath as I waited for it to slam into my foot. At some point, I had closed my eyes. When I heard a grunt, I opened them and managed a ragged exhale upon seeing that the shovel had avoided my body entirely.

"What are you doing?" I heard him ask with renewed anger.

Stealing a glance in his direction. "This is a matter of life or death. I must save this tree."

He groaned and rubbed his forehead. "Lady, I have to get rid of this tree. If it's not gone, my job could be a stake." He sounded so tired.

I didn't want to cause a man to lose his job, especially one who was working so hard to get it done. But I had to save this tree. Supposedly, this was Leta's soul we were talking about.

"I don't want you to lose your job, but I can't let you kill this tree."

He stared at me before groaning again. "I'll make you a deal. I have two other trees I got to dig up and dispose of. You have until then to get this tree out of the park. If I come back and it's still here, it's going in the trash with the other two. You got it?"

"How am I going to get it out of here?" I said more to myself than to him.

"I don't know and don't care. But it better be gone when I get back." He picked up the shovel and started to walk off.

"How long do I have?" I asked a bit frantic.

"I'd say you have about an hour." He said over his shoulder.

I had one hour. I watched him walk away before I snapped back to reality; one hour to find some way of digging the rest of the tree up and carting it out of the park. I looked around and found nothing useful.

Releasing the tree, I stepped back and told myself to think quickly. Gloves, shovel, and a wheelbarrow would all be very useful right about now. What I really needed was a Home Depot. Even a Wal-Mart would suffice.

The light rain turned to a downpour, and I shook my head. I had to find a store and quickly. Of course, I wasn't familiar with the area, and it would take too much time to go back to the area that I did know. I could call someone, but I wasn't sure where Selene and Farah lived. It was very likely that they wouldn't get here in time. And thanks to the rain, the park was empty.

Just standing there was a waste of time. So, I followed the cemented path at the far end of the clearing until it took me to the street. After crossing the street and walking a few blocks away from the park, I found a person who pointed me in the direction of a hardware store. A few more blocks down from the park, I found the store. It was a hardware store, yet it specialized in plumbing. If the kitchen sink stopped working, I now knew where to go. The gentlemen at the store were nice enough to direct me to another hardware store, another two blocks away.

Time was running out. Already twenty minutes passed. I had to find something quickly. I stopped to look at the street sign and realized that my ankle was throbbing, almost as badly as when I first injured it. A heavy feeling of doubt settled in my stomach. I wouldn't make it to the other store and back. Feeling a bit defeated, I turned around, hoping that I would see something, but feared that I was just going to have to drag Leta's tree back to the apartment, praying the whole way that I wasn't killing it.

I was within sight of the park when a sharp pain in my ankle caused me to stop. Approximately twenty minutes remained. There had been no miracle store on the way back, and I dreaded dragging a six-foot tree all the way to the apartment. I wondered as I rubbed my aching appendage, where the hell my roommate had gone. Leta had made this seem like a life-or-death situation yet had suddenly disappeared.

How was that possible? However, despite her disappearance, I was still convinced of the gravity of the situation. Maybe it was not life or death, but it was important, and I was going to do everything I could to save that tree.

With my resolve strengthened, I resumed my trek to the park, passing some small stores and little mom-and-pop places as I went. I paused briefly as an elderly woman stepped out of a store and opened her umbrella right in front of me. I barely managed to skirt her. She looked up as I dodged to the side, apologizing with a warm smile. I told her it was all right and watched as a little boy, her grandson no doubt, emerged from behind her carrying a toy shovel and pail...what was I going to do with a plastic shovel?

At this point, any little thing could help.

Desperate and out of options and time, I went into the secondhand toy store, hoping that I would find something. The man behind the counter was an older Asian man, about my height with graying black hair and wide glasses. He smiled and politely greeted me. Poor man, he had no idea what kind of mess had just walked into his store.

I proceeded to quickly tell him about my crazy friend and the tree that was important to her and how I had to dig it up and transport it back to my apartment all in the next fifteen minutes. I was impressed with his calm, especially in the face of my near hysteria.

He smiled and nodded his head the entire time. When I finally finished, he asked, "You want a shovel?" His voice was soft and accented.

"Yes," I almost cried with relief. He seemed happy with my answer and moved around the counter, disappearing amongst the shelves of toys. I fidgeted at the counter as I waited. He returned shortly carrying a yellow pale and blue shovel like the little boy's.

It wasn't perfect, but it was more than the plumbing store had offered. What luck that the used toy store happened to have two shovel and pail sets.

"Here, you need this." He set it down on the counter.

"Thank you so," I began to say as he disappeared again. "This is great, thank you," I called.

"Good, good," was all I heard in reply.

I waited a minute for him to return. "Sir," I called again. The shelves were too tall for me to see him. "Sir?" I really had to go. The clock was ticking.

I decided that I would just find him and pay for the toys, when he reappeared, pulling something behind him.

"You will need this too." He said with a big smile.

I watched as he pulled an old Red Flyer Wagon. It was one of the bigger ones. I remember being able to fit me and my cousin into the one at my grandmother's house when we were ten. Surely, I could figure out a way to fit that tree into it.

I hugged the store owner. He remained very still at first, then lightly patted my back and spoke. "Very good. Very good."

I pulled away and handed him two twenties, which he objected was too much. I loaded my shovel and pail into the wagon and headed out of the store. He followed me, trying to give me back one of the bills.

"It's okay," I assured him.

He was a stubborn man and took a few steps after me. "Too much," he said.

A glance at the time told me that I had only about ten minutes left and that the hour limit had only been a rough estimate. I picked up the pace, but not before calling out over my shoulder, "Sir, you may have just saved a life. Thank you."

Somehow that was enough to pacify him, and he waved as I turned back towards the park.

I sprinted as best I could, considering my ankle and the wagon I was pulling. With a huge sigh of relief, I arrived at the clearing to find that the tree was still there, tilting slightly to the side. Without hesitation, I went to work.

Rainwater filled the hole, so I found myself kneeling in a puddle while using the pail to shovel out the mud. Digging as fast as I could, I managed to clear out a good chunk of mud around the roots. However, they went deep and far. Unlike the park guy, I was going to do my best not to damage them.

I started clearing the harder dirt beneath the roots away when something gray shot out from the tree and knocked me on my back. At first, I thought it might be the tree falling, but I looked up to see Leta staring at me in disbelief.

"You came back." It was a simply stated fact.

"Of course, we have to save your soul tree, remember?" I smiled to reassure her and then remembered that she had been MIA for the past hour. "And where have you been?"

"In there, of course," she nodded to the tree.

"You were in the tree?" That whole concept was still a little too far out there for me.

"Yes."

I knew we didn't have time for the cross-examination, but I just couldn't help it. "You just disappeared into the tree, leaving me all alone to save it?" My voice was a little shrewder than it needed to be.

Leta had the courtesy to at least look a little apologetic. "I couldn't help it. He started going for the roots, and I felt faint, and just thought about how I wished I were in a safe warm place and then I ended up in the tree." That whole sentence was managed in one breath. "That's my warm, safe place, and we dryads aren't the warrior types. Danger comes, and we hide in a tree. You want big and scary, get Farah."

I stared at her as her skin began to change back to its smooth olive brilliance, trying to figure out if I wanted to be mad at her. I considered being mad and then decided that we couldn't help what our instinctual responses were. She was a flight-er, so what? The important thing was that she had come back out of the tree and was here to help me dig it up.

"You forgive me?" She asked shyly.

I sighed deeply out of exhaustion. "Of course. Now, get off me so we can dig up the roots. It is going to take a lot of work, and we don't have much time."

She rolled off me and I sat up, rolling back onto my knees. I grabbed the pail while she stood there staring at me with a look of confusion.

"There is a small shovel over there that you can use." I filled the pail with the dirt I had removed from the roots. The pail was nearly full when I realized that she was still standing there, looking at me quizzically. "Aren't you going to help?"

She nodded, and in that matter-of-fact tone of hers, said, "I was just wondering what you were doing."

I blinked a few times as I stared up at her. "What?" An equally intelligent response to her statement.

"Why are you pulling the dirt out when all we need is the tree?"

It had been a long day. I was willing to concede that there was something that I was missing...again. "How else would we get just the tree out?"

She shook her head, no doubt, at the fact that I was clueless to so many things. "We pull it out." Leta wrapped her hands around the tree and settled into her tree-pulling position.

"What about the roots?"

She rolled her eyes and tsked at me.

"Just stand on the other side and get ready to pull," she instructed. I did as she asked and waited. Satisfied with my position, she leaned closer to the tree and whispered something I was unable to hear.

Without warning, the tree drew up its roots and began falling backward. We steadied it as best we could as the long roots wrapped around the base of the tree. It was close to being the strangest thing I had seen all day. I briefly remembered that scene in Lord of the Rings when the Ents go to war and some of the trees uproot themselves. I shook my head; my life had become a fantasy novel.

When the last root withdrew from the soil, Leta and I supported the tree's entire weight. "Now what?" She asked.

Apparently, I was in charge of things again. "Um, the wagon."

She looked over her shoulder and giggled. "You want to move it in that?"

My response reflected how cranky I was becoming. "It was the best I could find after you just abandoned me. You want better, go find it yourself!"

Leta's sad face immediately made me feel like a jerk. "I'm sorry, Leta," in a much gentler voice. "It wasn't easy to find anything useful, and that was the closest I could get."

Her bottom lip started to quiver, and her eyes watered.

"Oh, please don't cry, Leta." I couldn't handle crying at the moment. I would no doubt break into tears myself, and we didn't have time for that. We were on a tree-saving mission.

She sniffled a bit and drew up to her full height. "You are a great friend, Elena McNeal, and when this is all over, I am going to give you a great big hug."

I gave her a small smile. "Thanks. Now, let's just get your tree out of here and back to the apartment."

She nodded in agreement, and together we lifted the tree into the wagon. I jumped back when one of the roots brushed against my leg and wrapped itself over the edge. A few more followed suit, and soon the tree was loosely secured, but top-heavy.

"You hold the trunk still, and I'll pull the wagon." She nodded, and I pulled it towards the path that led to the street.

The sky still drizzled as we stood at the street corner waiting for the light to turn. Leta stood on one side of the tree glowing with happiness and relief. She was so excited I noticed that she could barely stand still. She might have even been humming a little song. Of course, she managed to look amazing while doing it. I, on the other hand, stood to the right of the tree...cold, wet, aching, and no doubt looking like the wet abused sewer rat that I felt like.

A few people stopped to wait for the light too. Leta didn't notice their looks, but I did. Couldn't blame them really, though. How often did they see two women soaked and muddy steal a park tree and cart it around the city in a little Red Flyer Wagon? I'm guessing that even in a city like this, we were a strange sight indeed.

The carting went a lot easier than I anticipated. It was almost dark when we arrived at our apartment complex. I smiled when I saw that there was no one around to see us haul the tree up to our apartment.

I worried about the tree as we hauled it up the stairs. The branches and bark seemed dry and brittle, meaning that I had to be very careful not to break them. I asked Leta if the tree was okay after the long walk back to the apartment, and she assured me it was fine. I figured she was the tree expert.

We were barely up the first set of stairs when our luck ran out. Our middle-aged landlord popped his head out of the room just next to the stairs. He looked up, saw the tree, and did a double take.

"What do you girls think you're doing?" he yelled up to us. Leta had the roots of the tree. That was the heavier part after all, and she was stronger than me. She gave me a smile and a wink while carefully setting down her end. Then she turned towards Mr. Franks and unleashed the charm.

She stood at the base of the stairs talking with the landlord. I couldn't hear what she was saying but slowly his grouchy expression melted away and was replaced by a wistful smile. He even skirted his way past the tree on the stairs and took over my load. I skittered out of the way as they carried the tree. Hurrying after them, I unlocked the door.

Per Leta's instruction, Mr. Franks carefully propped the tree in the corner of the living room by the window. He adjusted it repeatedly to please Leta's meticulous requests and left the apartment with a silly smile on his face. Ah...my man-charming-dryad-roommate to the rescue.

Leta fussed with the tree while I hurried into a warm shower. I stood under the spray for almost half an hour. Afterward, I dressed in my warmest PJs and buried myself beneath the covers, surrendering to sleep.

Chapter 7

U pon waking the next morning, I found myself buried under the warmth of a down comforter. A smile spread across my face as I emerged and felt the sunlight peeking through my curtains. The muscles in my arms ached as I stretched overheard and yawned loudly. Pausing in confusion, I turned onto my side, and soreness rippled through the rest of my body.

As I sat up, something popped in either my hip or spine.

Then it hit me.

Yesterday, I helped Leta rescue her tree. The tree that supposedly held her soul. After she had sprouted bark-like skin and emerged from inside the tree.

I rubbed my aching head, and a groan escaped my lips. Deciding that I wasn't ready to face anything, I fell back into the pillows and pulled the covers over my face.

I embraced the denial. My roommate was human, not a bark-covered monster. And, I hadn't helped her smuggle a tree into our apartment building after transporting it several blocks by toy wagon. There currently was not a sickly-looking tree residing in my living room.

Just summarizing the events of the past twenty-four hours made me feel silly. I mean, come on...Leta couldn't possibly be a nymph whose soul resided in a tree. I chalked it up to being nothing more than a crazy dream.

Having settled that, I threw the covers off once more. As I sat up, my stomach growled as if I had forgotten to fill it in days. I rubbed it reassuringly. Pancakes sounded like an excellent way to start this beautiful Sunday morning.

After relieving my equally angry bladder and brushing my teeth, I grabbed my robe and headed to the kitchen. Still in a sleep daze,

I almost missed the tree standing in the corner of our living. I did a double take and stood staring at it.

Oh, crap! Yesterday had not been just a dream...which meant that my roommate was not human. I wobbled a little bit and luckily found the coffee table to plop down on.

Yesterday, this had all been so easy to accept. Friend in trouble...must help...end of story.

However, today was a new day, and I struggled to wrap my head around this new reality. Leta was a nymph, a dryad to be precise, whose soul lived inside a tree. That was fairy tale stuff.

I rubbed my temples as the ache in my head steadily increased. I didn't want to accept any of it, but the signs were all around me.

Sign number one: a sickly tree in my living room.

Sign number two: the aching of my body to support the existence of the aforementioned tree.

Sign number three: there were so many weird things that had happened in my life since moving in with Leta. I should have picked up on her extraordinariness a long time ago. And what about the weird way that Selene always knew when things were going to happen right before they happened?

I didn't want to believe that my roommate was a dryad, but I was too pragmatic to deny the evidence. I feared what this change in perception would mean. Change brought challenges, and I was immature enough to resist the challenge. I wanted life to go back to being perfectly normal.

I wanted it known that not even my imagination could have come up with the strange events of the past twenty-four hours. Before the whole situation, I didn't even know what a dryad was.

A moan came from Leta's room. I ignored it; the world still seemed like it was spinning.

Another moan, this one sounding more strained. I contemplated whether I should get up and check...or maybe it would all go away if I just stayed here.

She groaned this time, and it did sound pained. I took a deep breath and seriously contemplated sneaking out of the apartment. There was a lovely little café located down the street.

Eventually, a sense of obligation drew me to her room. Leta was my friend after all, and I was fairly sure she wouldn't abandon me if I morphed into something out of Greek mythology.

I tiptoed to the corner and saw that the door was slightly open. After a brief moment of hesitation, I took a deep breath and committed myself to dealing with whatever was on the other side.

"Leta." I stepped further into the room. No answer. "Leta, are you okay?" It felt like I had been asking that question a lot lately.

She groaned in response. Approaching the bed, I noticed that she looked a little pale. Pale gray in fact. Peering closer, I realized that her skin was more like the smooth bark of the tree in the living room than normal skin. Despite that strange change, I put my hand to her forehead.

"You're burning up."

She opened her eyes and strangely enough, they seemed browner than usual, maybe even a bit darker. "What?" She stared up at me with wide-eyed confusion.

"I think you have a fever. Let me go get the thermometer." I stroked the damp hair away from her face gently and turned to go.

Her hand firmly gripped my forearm. She continued to stare at me with her big eyes. A little flicker of fear raced down my spine as those big brown eyes looked intently at me from within a gray bark face. I said her name gently as I tried to pry her fingers off my arm.

She shook her head at that point. When she looked back at me, she looked less crazed.

"Oh, no, I'm fine," she said in a hoarse voice. Upon hearing it, she shook her head again and tried to sit up. And didn't get very far. She sat up about halfway before groaning loudly and falling back against the bed.

"I'm just a little sore," she said when I gave her my best mom look.

"No, I'm sore. You're sick," I said firmly as I shifted her legs back under the covers. She weakly tried to push me away but gave up the effort once I started tucking the blankets around her.

"Now, you are going to stay here and rest while I get the thermometer. You also need to drink lots of fluids. Do you want tea or water?"

She peeked one eye open. "I can get it," though she made no attempt to move. "I'm okay. I just need to get up and move around." She followed that statement with a big yawn.

I ignored her as she continued to object. She closed her eyes again, and the objections seemed to make less and less sense.

After spraining my ankle, I learned that my roommate lacked all medical supplies and basic medications. At the time, I had given it very little thought and just proceeded to buy what I needed as I needed it. Now, it made more sense why she did not possess some of the basics. On that note, I reminded myself to check for a fire extinguisher later, especially since our new roommate was extremely flammable.

Thanks to my ever-prepared mother, I had a small first-aid kit packed away in my closet. It contained all the basics: gauze, Band-Aids, tape, burn ointment, saline, eye patches, Tylenol, and ibuprofen. Buried beneath the gauze was a small blue thermometer. I kissed it and thanked my mom for having the foresight that I seemed to lack.

Returning to Leta's room, I found her lying with an arm flung across her eyes. She was still talking. Her phrases lacked a word here and there, but she didn't seem to notice. In fact, she didn't even seem to realize that I had come and gone. She just kept on talking.

"So, you can see I mean that... by... when I say that dryads do not get sick." She stated it in that serious Leta tone.

"Uh-huh," I responded as I unsheathed the thermometer. "Here, open your mouth."

She did as told but jerked back when I leaned towards her with the thermometer.

"What are you doing?" She asked indignantly, looking highly offended.

"Taking your temp," I responded blandly. "Now, open up."

"Elena, I already explained to you that dryads do not get fevers," she explained haughtily. "My grandmother always said-"

I thrust the thermometer under her tongue. She stared at me in stunned surprise. It didn't last long though. "I do not need my temp," she mumbled with the probe in her mouth.

"Hold still and stop talking," I ordered.

Of course, she stubbornly continued to try to tell me about how her grandmother always said... I eventually just put one hand under her chin and forced her mouth shut. She made a disgruntled noise, trying to object with her mouth closed.

"Almost done." The thermometer beeped and read one hundred and five degrees. "Yep, you have a fever." I felt my brow creased in worry. "A really high one."

Leta pulled the probe out of her mouth. "I run at least three degrees warmer than you all the time." I was beginning to see that my little nymph friend was not the nicest sick person.

"Oh." That was a bit of a relief. "You still have a temp though."

"Elena, Elena, Elena," she said dramatically, throwing her arm across her forehead again. Leta would give Scarlett O'Hara a run for her money in the dramatic department.

I shook my head. I had never met a person who could be so practical and down-to-earth one minute and a full-out drama queen the next.

"Answer this for me. Do you have any of the following: chills, achy body, congestion, sore throat..." She raised an eyebrow at me.

"I am not sick," she objected hotly.

I patted her arm gently and said in a stern voice that sounded a lot like my mother's, "Now, you just stop trying to play it tough and let me take care of you."

She looked at me defiantly and swore under her breath that she was fine.

"Oh, I'm dying! I'm dying!"

Leta was fine for about an hour, and then she was dying.

At least, that's what she kept telling me. Apparently, my dryad roommate had never even had a runny nose, and this sudden onset of symptoms was beyond her coping.

Leta developed something that looked like chicken pox. I'm not entirely sure where a nymph gets something like chicken pox, especially since she hadn't been in contact with anyone recently infected. However, I noticed that her tree had similar-looking bumps and wondered if the tree got the bumps from her, or if she got them from the tree. After Googling tree diseases, I decided that Leta had some form of apple scab.

As if gray bark all over her body was not a strange enough sight, little dark brown and olive-green lesions developed all over her. And of course, Leta, being the mature and intelligent adult that she was, handled it with the grace of a dying goat.

Every five minutes she cried out in pain, or cried out because she was too hot or too cold, or because her skin itched, or the room was too bright, or because the air was poisoned. Leta found fault with everything imaginable, and I tried my hardest to keep her calm and fix what I could. However, there are some things that I just couldn't fix. I honestly didn't know how to assure her that the air was not poisoned in such a way that it would only kill dryads.

The development of dryad pox, as I dubbed it, made everything more difficult. It wasn't enough that every time she sneezed or blew her nose, little bits of bark went flying everywhere. Nope, and it wasn't enough that dryads don't respond to any pain medicine but pure opium, which Leta explained when I tried to coax her to take ibuprofen. Nor was it enough that the distress of being sick for the first time in her life had made Leta a complete emotional mess. The alternating outbreaks of sobbing and angry screams scared the neighbors. A few came by to make sure that I wasn't killing her.

I'm not sure they all believed my assurances.

Unfortunately for Leta, the bumps were under a thin layer of bark and no matter how hard she tried to scratch them, she just couldn't get under the bark to reach them. I might have gone a little crazy too.

Around noon, I made a quick run to the nearest pharmacy to pick up Aspirin (the Tylenol and ibuprofen weren't touching her fever), calamine lotion, Benadryl, and another couple of boxes of Kleenex. When I returned, I found Leta with her head out the living room window, wearing nothing but her pink underwear and matching bra. It was a crisp fall day, but Leta looked more relieved than cold by the fresh air. She turned to acknowledge me when I walked through the door.

"Do you feel better?" I asked.

She nodded and crawled onto the couch. "Soon, I will be dead."

She threw her head against the couch cushions and closed her eyes.

"Okay."

I went to the kitchen to unload my pharmacy bag. That was about the eighth time today she had told me she would be dead soon.

I figured there was no point in arguing with her. She stayed calmer that way.

"Elena," her weak voice called.

"Yes, Leta." I poked my head into the living room.

She pushed herself onto her elbows. "Can I get a cup of tea?"

"Sure, it's the least I can do for a dying woman."

I went back into the kitchen and put the kettle on. I also poured her a tall glass of ice water.

"Oh, I shall remember your kindness as I am floating down the River Styx. I will tell Hades all about you."

I rolled my eyes and shook my head as she continued to lament.

The kettle whistled while I dug ice cubes out of the freezer. I took the boiling water off the stove and poured it over a chamomile tea bag, figuring that a little relaxation and sleep was just what Leta needed.

A little sleep and relaxation were just what I needed, but I wasn't getting any until Leta was comfortable.

As the tea brewed, I opened a can of chicken noodle soup and threw it on the stove to heat. Grabbing the steaming tea and ice water, I joined Leta in the living room. She looked asleep but was mumbling softly to herself. I wondered if all dryads were this crazy. But then again, as Leta had explained earlier, it was rare for a dryad to be sick.

I'd learned from her ramblings that a dryad's health was connected to that of her tree. Whether it was Leta who had gotten the tree sick or vice versa, the chicken and the egg conundrum, it was obvious that they were both sick from the same thing.

"Tea," I said as I thrust the mug towards her.

She opened her eyes, took one look at the steaming liquid, and knitted her brows.

"Do you think I could just have some ice water instead?" She asked as I presented her with the ice water in my other hand. This was also becoming a pattern with Leta; she thought she wanted one thing, but instead wanted something else.

"Elena, you are so good," she said with a weak smile while taking the water. In one long gulp, she drank it all. Then she poured the ice on herself. "That is wonderful," she sighed and closed her eyes.

"I'll just leave this here in case you want some later." I had barely set the tea on the coffee table when she sprang up, flinging ice cubes everywhere.

"Oh, my tea," she declared happily while holding the mug to her chest. She sighed contently and closed her eyes.

I fell into the chair across from her and took a well-deserved nap.

I woke an hour later to the sound of heavy grunting. Stretching my arms over my head as I opened my sleepy eyes, I realized that Leta was no longer on the couch. My eyes followed the grunting noise, and I found her.

She had the most pained look on her face as she rubbed her back across the corner of the doorway.

"Leta, what are you doing?" I said as I jumped out of the chair. "Don't scratch them, otherwise you'll get a bunch of scars."

I tried to pull her away from the doorway, yet despite being ill, she was still stronger than me.

"I don't care," she cried. Her voice was harsh and stricken with pain. "I have mutating bark skin with disgusting pustules burying themselves beneath it."

I felt my face scrunch up involuntarily. When put that way, I'd consider the scars too. "They're not pustules." I tried to reassure her.

She paused and looked at me with distrusting eyes. "Really?"

I nodded my head.

"You didn't even look at them," she accused. So, I looked at them and frowned. The bumps on her back were swollen and opaque. Did that make them pustules?

"I knew it." She cried angrily. "That's it!" Pushing off the wall, she walked past me into the kitchen.

I watched her warily as she searched for the unknown. Suddenly, her eyes widened, and she smiled.

"Leta..."

I didn't immediately react as I watched her draw a knife out of the drawer. Then, I watched as she pointed the tip at one of the bumps on her arm.

"Leta, what are you doing!" I nearly screamed as I grabbed the knife from her. It only worked because she was too surprised to hold on to it.

"I'm gonna cut them out," she said vehemently.

"No, you are not." I put myself between her and the rest of the knives, still holding one in my hand. I never quite imagined myself in this position. "You can't cut them out."

Her eyes never left the knife as she began to scratch her arm. "How do you know? We haven't tried yet."

Looking at Leta at that moment made me glad that I was the one holding the knife because she looked like a complete psychopath. She stared at me with her wide brown eyes and reminded me of Gollum...just a crazier, more sinister version.

"Leta, you cannot cut out the tree pox. There are hundreds of those little bumps all over your body, and I didn't buy any extra gauze to keep you from bleeding to death."

She looked at me and then at the knife, obviously still considering it as an option.

"I have a lotion that will help."

She stared at me silently for a moment.

"We can always come back to the knife." It was one of the few times that I really hated Leta's matter-of-fact voice.

"Sure, okay." What else was I going to say?

It turned out the calamine lotion helped but not enough. Leta continued to look longingly at the kitchen. After about three coats, I decided to try something else. I led her to the bathroom, hosed her down, and sat her in the tub. She watched in confusion as I filled it with warm water and oats. Yet, all skepticism disappeared from her face as she relaxed into the mixture. Finally, I found something that worked.

Leta soaked until the water was cool. I carefully helped her to dry off but was only halfway finished when she started to complain of painful itching again.

"I can't just leave you in the bath all day," I told her.

But...I could coat her in oatmeal. Using the tub as my mixing bowl, I made an oatmeal paste that I applied to her body. The oatmeal was the magic potion for Leta. After covering her in the paste-like mixture, I wrapped her in a sheet and guided her to the couch, where she immediately fell asleep. The rest of my afternoon was spent hydrating my roommate, reapplying the oatmeal when she started towards the kitchen with that crazed glint in her eye, and trying to soothe her when her temperature spiked and she became slightly more delusional.

"Should I come see her?" Miguel's concerned voice asked. "It might be something serious."

He had called to reschedule our date. I explained that my roommate was sick and that I was playing nurse. He asked what her symptoms were, and not wanting to mention the brownish-green pustules and bark skin, I told him that she had flu-like symptoms. That was when he had asked if I wanted him to come over.

I was so stressed that just hearing his concern made me relax a bit. "Yeah, that would be great."

Then it clicked that the good doctor was not coming over to make me better. He was coming to examine my patient, who looked more like a Jim Henson creation than my roommate. Leta was now sprouting random little branches all over her body.

"I can be there in an hour just after-"

"No," I blurted quickly. "I mean you really don't need to come over. She just has the flu. She's just being a big baby about it."

Leta's head popped up, and she stuck her tongue out at me before finding the whole movement too exhausting. Her head fell back on the pillow, and she snored softly.

I stuck my tongue out at her though she was asleep and wouldn't see it.

There were a few seconds of silence between us. "And how are you doing? You sound tired. Should I bring you something?"

Ah, if only you could, I thought. I could use some one-on-one attention from the doctor. I realized that I wouldn't mind being taken care of just a little.

"Elena, do you want me to come over?" Such a soothing, comforting voice. I had no doubts that he was a good doctor.

"No, I'm okay. Really," I added to make it convincing. "We're presenting to those VIP clients I was telling you about tomorrow. I'm a bit nervous and have a lot of stuff to go over before then."

I could tell from the way he sighed that he was not pleased or convinced by my affirmations that I was indeed just fine. "Will you promise to call me if you need anything?"

I smiled. I wish he could know just how much better his concern made me feel. "Yes, I will call if I need anything; I promise."

"Good," I could hear the smile in his voice. "Let's get dinner tomorrow after your meeting. You can tell me all about it."

"Sounds good."

"Good night, Elena."

"Was that Dr. Wolf Boy," Leta asked from the couch as I hung up.

"Dr. Wolf Boy?" I repeated with confusion. "What does that mean?"

I had a strange heaviness in my stomach that warned of something unwanted to come. With the events of the last twenty-four hours, I failed to convince myself that the feeling was unimportant. Wolf Boy? What on earth could that mean?

"Leta," I said in an edged voice. She was back to softly snoring. I thought about not waking her up, but I would have no peace of mind if she didn't answer me. I shook her softly until she opened her eyes. "What did you mean when you said 'wolf boy'?"

She stared dazedly at me for a moment. "Oh, Elena, the world is full of wolf boys...and wolf girls...and genies in saffron yellow bottles." She dozed as she said the words and was asleep once more. I let go of her, trying to convince myself that it was gibberish caused by her fever-induced delirium.

"Tree-chopping...tree cropping...and weed making..." She muttered-singed in her sleep.

Oddly, that little bit of craziness made me feel better, and the wolf-boy comment was obviously complete nonsense.

Chapter 8

Despite my total lack of sleep due to Leta's worsening symptoms overnight, I smiled as I looked at the final product of the ad that we would be presenting to the clients. It was a beautiful mock-up that if accepted by Mr. Reiner and Mr. Tasev would only become more beautiful after the final revision process.

I sighed wistfully as I stood alone in the meeting room with a double shot white chocolate mocha in hand. No way I was getting through this day without a...lot of help. It had been difficult to leave Leta in the morning, though she had been sleeping peacefully since three AM. I had gotten a total of four hours of collective sleep. Waking up around five, I decided to just shower and head into work early given that it was going to be a very busy day. During her lucid moments, Leta had given me numerous advice tidbits on how to handle demanding clients, and the clients were undoubtedly high maintenance. However, what stuck with me was her reference to Miguel as a wolf-boy.

I refused to think about that. Too many other things demanded my concentration today. I groaned aloud and rubbed my temples. Lack of sleep and food always lead to a migraine for me. Of course, I pre-medicated myself before leaving for work but the unwelcome pain was too familiar. By noon, I'd be like a vampire, unable to bear the light of day.

I felt a firm but gentle touch at the small of my back and jumped, flinging a few drops of espresso on the table.

"I did not mean to startle you," a deep voice said behind me, and I quickly turned around.

I must have had a crazed look on my face because Mr. Reiner held his hands up in the universal gesture of "no harm meant."

"Mr. Reiner," I said a bit breathlessly.

Of course, I knew that he would be here today, but I had not expected the rush of emotion that I would experience upon seeing him. It should have been bubbling excitement. Instead, I felt anger, frustration, and irritation. It was completely unlike me to have such severe mood swings, but I realized that they had been happening more and more lately. It must be stress, I told myself. Taking a deep breath, I suppressed the strange myriad of emotions.

"Are you okay?" He asked with that arrogant, condescending expression of his.

"I'm fine, thank you, and yourself?" I winced internally at my clipped tone.

"I'm a bit confused, to be honest. It is not often that women look at me like that." His arrogant voice grated my nerves.

"And how is it that I am looking at you?" I asked in a more pleasant tone, though I heard how strained it sounded.

Pulling a napkin from the breakfast setup at the right, I mopped up the spilled coffee. I desperately needed to avert my attention from Mr. Reiner; otherwise, I was liable to shoot him a look that would offend more than confuse him.

He took a step closer, and I could hear the smile in his voice. "I don't usually have women jump away from me in fear of being attacked. Nor do I usually find a woman who stares at me with contempt that I know haven't earned...yet."

I silenced a groan and tried hard not to roll my eyes. What did he think he was? The seductive leading man in a romance novel? Because those were the only men who could get away with a statement that ridiculous. I took a deep breath and turned to him with a smile.

My smile faltered as I saw the self-satisfied look on his face.

"Mr. Renier," I began in a polite tone, "I did not mean to confuse you or offend you. I was just startled by the...by you."

"By 'the what'?" He pressed as he stepped closer. "And, I insist that you call me Micah."

I felt the heat of my blood increase and wondered if I blushed. However, instead of focusing on the building irritation, I turned my attention to fuss with the breakfast setup. I arranged the wine-colored cloth napkins even though Sarah had arrived before me this morning and had already arranged them in meticulous order.

On a side table was the usual setup of bagels, juice, and coffee, but in addition to that, we had ordered the most delicious pastries and croissants from a fantastic bakery down the street. A bottle of French champagne chilled off to the side in anticipation.

"What were you going to say?" I heard his voice very close to my ear and again was visibly startled.

He chuckled softly as I turned around.

"I have startled you again." I noticed with growing dislike that he was amused by my discomfort and that no apology followed his statement.

A fire inside me burned even higher, consuming every ounce of energy I had, and I felt unable to control it.

The coolness of my voice surprised me as I responded, "It's okay; some people have differing views on what is adequate personal space boundaries and what is not."

Oh, I couldn't believe those words left my mouth. I had never been so direct with anyone in my life. Of course, I had never felt this fired up before either, but that was no excuse. One complaint from him, and I could be off the team completely. And here I had listened to Leta for hours on how to handle situations like this, and not a single bit of her advice was put to use.

Luckily...well, I think it was lucky...he seemed even more amused as if he had been trying to get this reaction from me the whole time.

"I understand now." He said in a placating tone. "You thought that some gesture I made was inappropriate. You are right when you say that some people are fearful of physical intimacy whereas others are not. I understand it borders on phobic for some."

Nothing in his voice or expression conveyed understanding.

"Mr. Renier..."

"Micah," he said as if he was instructing a child.

"Mr. Renier," I said more firmly this time; I was not going to be pushed around. I waited to make sure that he was not going to interrupt, which he made no indication of doing. "There are acceptable forms of physical contact, depending on the relationship that two people have."

He took a slow step towards me. I wish I could say that my firm demeanor had made him unsure and weary; no, he approached like he was a predator closing in on his prey as if he thought that I was some timid bunny. Little did he know that the increase in my pulse was due to anger and not some silly sense of being endangered. I had nothing to fear from this man.

"Where I come from, it is acceptable to comfort someone when they appear to be distressed, and you appear to be distressed."

Maybe the lack of sleep and the stress of the past weekend showed. "That was very considerate of you, but it still was not appropriate to touch me that way."

Micah smiled even more smugly. "And how was it that I touched you?"

I saw the endless amusement in his eyes. What was it with these clients? Where Mr. Tasev's flirtations seemed like nothing more than harmless flirtations, Mr. Reiner's advances were much more predatory.

Heat rose so quickly in my chest, unlike anything that I had ever felt before that I did not respond, fearing that I might breathe fire. Scales could be sprouting over my body for all I knew.

It wouldn't be the strangest thing to happen in the last few days.

Micah seemed satisfied to answer his own question though. "Are you saying that it was wrong of me to touch the small of your back?" He moved closer even as he asked the question.

"Yes, that is exactly what I am saying," I managed calmly.

"For future reference, what is the appropriate way to comfort a lovely woman who is upset?"

I ignored the compliment. "A handshake, or no touch at all."

He raised an eyebrow. "A handshake?"

"Yes, it's professional and satisfies your...urge to touch." That did not sound as nice had it had in my head.

Micah stared at me intensely for a moment before he said softly, "I will remember that for the future." As if he expected I would need his consoling in the future.

No way in hell.

We stared at each other in silence. I was unsure of how to respond to this man who made me hotter than any I had ever felt, and not in a good way. He gave me that look that dared me to say something that would further amuse him.

Thankfully, Glenda chose that moment to come storming into the room.

"Where the hell is Leta? Sonia just told me that she called in." She studied a stack of papers in her hand as she strode into the room with a few powerful strides. Looking up to get my answer, she noted Micah and the scowl disappeared from her face completely.

"Micah, darling," she said in that husky voice of hers. She dropped the papers on the table and approached him with open arms. They embraced lightly while kissing each other's cheeks. Micah spared me a self-satisfied glance before giving his full attention to Glenda.

"What are you doing here so early? The meeting is not for at least another hour."

I could hear the slight tension in her voice though her smile was all confidence.

"I was excited to see your work; however, I understand that you have preparations to see to. I have several calls to make so if you will excuse me."

"Of course, Leta's office is available to you," Glenda offered.

"Thank you, but this room is a bit too warm, and I feel slightly overheated. I think that a walk in the fresh air will be nice."

"Yes, it is a cool morning. We will see you again shortly."

Micah excused himself and left the room. Glena watched him go and turned on me the minute the door to the conference room closed. "Why the hell isn't Leta here?"

"She was not feeling well," I responded lamely.

"And?" Glenda asked with a raised eyebrow.

"Well, she has the flu," I watched as Glenda's face didn't change at all. What the heck, I figured, the truth couldn't hurt at this moment. "And I think that she has the chicken pox."

That got a reaction. Glenda inhaled sharply and took a big step back from me as if I were the contagious one.

"You're not experiencing any symptoms, are you?" She asked while examining me for any signs of infection.

"No, I had the vaccine as a kid." That did not appear to ease her worry.

"Damn," she said finally. She turned and paced. "Well, the creative team will just have to be on top of their game today."

She gave me a meaningful look. As if I didn't already know how important today's meeting was.

"Where's Selene?" I was about to respond when she rushed from the room calling out Selene's name rather impatiently.

Oh, it was going to be such a good day...

They hated our team's idea. And the two other teams that Glenda had secretly directed to work on ideas. After three different presentations, Micah rose from his chair and buttoned the front of his navy suit.

"I think that we have seen enough, and unfortunately, nothing that we saw was impressive." His dark fierce eyes softened as he turned to Glenda. She rose to her feet beside him calmly issuing apologies. He shushed her with a gesture of his hand.

Glenda fell quiet as Micah kissed both her cheeks, speaking so softly the words could not be heard from where I was sitting; yet, Glenda seemed to relax a bit. Nolan followed suit offering Glenda a smile that was warmer than Micah's. Both men turned to leave the room.

But then Nolan turned back to the room. "Your team," he pointed to Selene. "One more opportunity. You have until this Friday to present me with a new ad that gives me everything I expect from a company with your reputation."

"You will have your ad on Friday, gentlemen," Glenda assured him. She sent Selene a silencing look. Selene acknowledged it with a slight head nod.

Glenda escorted the men from the room with Josh's team following behind. The door closed behind them, and Selene placed both hands on the table pinning her team with a determined stare.

"We have less than five days to sell this thing. Get ready to work people. At the end of this week, we better have an ad that would persuade the Devil himself to buy fire."

So started the day that wouldn't end.

Chapter 9

The conference room felt more and more like a prison cell as the day wore on. With Glenda's full endorsement, Selene declared that we were not leaving until we came up with the idea that would stabilize the rickety relationship with our clients. Unfortunately, none of us were sure which direction to go in. The first order of business had been to figure out exactly what the clients did not want.

Selene announced that sandwiches were ordered from a nearby place, probably because we could not be trusted to leave and come back. When it arrived around noon, I was looking longingly at the door. My headache reached record pain levels, and the second round of espresso shots barely kept my eyes open. My brain was nowhere near functioning.

As we all consumed the much-needed food, Selene turned the focus of the group toward the analysis of our project. It wasn't hard to pick apart the other two ads and list the faults of each; however, when it came to our project the room fell silent.

Selene, our unremitting leader, commented first. "It's gimmicky."

Her dark eyes studied the mock-up with such intensity I was surprised it did not melt under her stare.

"All perfume ads are that way," Sarah said before taking a bite of her ham and cheese.

"No," Selene said as she shifted her gaze to Sarah and then to the rest of the room. "We are not going to be defensive of this. We are going to view it as if it was our fiercest competitor's bid." Subtle fierceness infused her voice. "We are going to tear it apart, all the way to the smallest detail."

And so we did.

At seven thirty, Selene declared she was satisfied with our work. It didn't feel like much had been accomplished after spending the entire afternoon listing all the faults of our mock-up.

I believed in and loved the original mock-up, but after hours of examining every detail in as critical a manner as possible, I felt insecure about my ability to put together a good ad. I could only guess from the despondent faces of my coworkers that they felt as shaky about their talents as I did.

In addition to feeling like the biggest failure ever, my head felt like Mount St. Helen's. Any second now, toxic gases and ash were going to spew from my ears. Shortly after that, the top of my skull was going to blow right off my head, and then I would be even more useless than I already felt. Of course, that wouldn't deter Selene. She'd probably tell me to just put my head back on and analyze our ad on yet an even deeper level.

I dragged my aching body into the elevator beside Sarah. She also looked exhausted, her usual optimism missing.

Leaning against the back of the elevator, I closed my eyes and tried not to moan from the tiny bit of relief that complete darkness brought.

"You don't look so good," Sarah said bluntly.

I peeked an eye open to look at her. She decided to elaborate. "I think that meeting made all of us a little sick, but you look very unwell. Do you think you're getting what Leta has?"

I sure hope not, I thought to myself. "I just have a headache... it's been worsening since this morning."

Sarah, bless her heart, looked concerned and righteously confused. "Why didn't you just say something to Selene? I'm sure she would have...done something."

Despite the pain, I smiled. "Yeah. She would have given me an aspirin and said 'Look harder, Elena. Find the flaws, every little one.'"

Sarah responded with a sad smile, expressing her silent agreement with my assumption.

Despite the truth that assumption might have held, it was petty. That was not like me. It was just the pain and exhaustion making me so cranky. I closed my eyes as the elevator doors started to close.

"Hey, that was a rough day, wasn't it?" I opened my eyes to find that Selene had joined us in the elevator.

"No kidding," Sarah responded bravely.

Selene smiled at her before turning to me. Her brows tensed with concern. "How are you doing, Elena?"

"She's had a bad headache all day," Sarah answered for me.

"Really? Are you sure you're not getting sick?" Selene asked.

"I thought the same thing. Whatever Leta has must be horrible because she has never missed a day of work in the past three years that I've worked with her. Something like that must be contagious."

Great, people were going to start looking at me like I was the harbinger of the plague.

"I just didn't get a lot of sleep last night. A good night's sleep is all I need to feel better." I gave a weak smile of assurance.

It lacked conviction though.

Selene's dark eyes seemed to darken as she stared at me. "What does she have?"

"The flu... and possibly chicken pox."

Her eyes widened briefly before returning to their usual sharpness. It had happened so quickly that it was by pure luck that I witnessed the shift. However, it made me instantly uncomfortable. And suspicious. I could almost see Selene doing the math in her head and realizing that something did not add up. But why wouldn't it add up...unless Selene knew the truth.

But could she know?

Well, duh, she had known Leta a lot longer than I had. It was entirely possible that she knew. I instantly felt a weight lift off my shoulders. How incredible would it be to have someone else who knew! Someone else who could share in this insane realization that nymphs were running around.

I felt myself on the verge of asking Selene if she knew, what she knew, and how she knew it. But Sarah spoke, suddenly reminding me of her presence.

"Ugh, I remember having the chicken pox when I was younger. It was horrible!" She made a face to go with her memory of the experience.

Selene looked slightly confused as she asked, "Can adults even get chicken pox? I thought that only children got it."

"Miguel says that anyone can get it. Most kids are vaccinated against it these days, but I don't think Leta got the vaccination," I responded.

I watched the confusion and suspicion fade from Selene's face. She even smiled sympathetically. "That sucks."

The foundation of my theory that Selene might just know the truth about Leta felt shaky. Besides, could I take the risk of covertly extracting information from Selene, especially since I wasn't that skilled as an extractor. Of course, I could always just ask Leta who else was aware of her special relationship with a tree.

"Speaking of Miguel, how is the good doctor?" Selene asked as the elevator doors opened in front of us.

"Oh, who's Miguel?" Sarah asked with interest as she and Selene exited the elevators ahead of me.

I didn't answer either because I was standing there in the elevator with my hands rubbing my throbbing temples. The plan was to have dinner with Miguel tonight, and I was going to ask him in the least crazy way I could if he was a wolf boy as my fever-crazed roommate had implied.

They both stopped to look back at me as I stood there with wide eyes. Their smiles disappeared; I'm sure it had something to do with me looking like a crazy person.

"I'm supposed to have dinner with him tonight," I said to no one in particular.

My hands fell away from my head and down my cheeks where they decided to rest. I exited the elevator barely aware that the doors had started to close on me as I did so. Selene and Sarah rushed forward to hold them open as I walked past.

"I can't have dinner tonight. I can't do this. I'm not ready," I mumbled in shock.

Both of my colleagues looked at me before exchanging a worried glance.

"You don't have to do anything that you don't want," Sarah tried to comfort.

"You don't look well. Maybe you should just reschedule. I'm sure that he will understand," Selene said.

I quietly stood there with a million things passing through my head, yet I was unable to hold onto a single thought.

"Tell him that you're not feeling well," Selene said.

Before I could turn to her in confusion, my cell phone rang. It was Miguel.

"He'll understand," Selene assured.

Without really thinking about anything, I opened my cell phone and said hello.

"Hi." I was vaguely aware of the concern in his voice. "Hadn't heard from you yet. How was your day?"

"Ugh..." was my brilliant response.

"That good, huh?"

It was so hard to concentrate. I closed my eyes, trying to gather any thoughts in my head other than those screaming in pain.

"It wasn't good." I started to walk towards the exit. Selene and Sarah silently flanked me, passing looks of concern between them. I tried not to notice.

"I'm sorry to hear that. Should I grab takeout somewhere and meet you at your apartment?"

"My apartment?" I squeaked.

There was a soft chuckle on the other end. "Or my apartment. I just thought that you need to look in on your roommate, and I could help you take care of her if needed."

That sounded wonderful...except for the sick dryad waiting at home. Who knew, maybe Leta had grown leaves since the last time I saw her.

"I'm so sorry, Miguel," I began.

"Oh, that is never a good start to something," he joked.

"I have been fighting a killer headache all day and just really need to get some sleep."

"Do you want me to get you anything?"

"No, I'm sorry. I just want to crawl into bed and sleep. Thank you for being so sweet." I tried to convey my gratitude.

After a slight pause, "Of course. I just wish that there was something I could do for you. I was looking forward to seeing you, in any state of health."

"Thanks, I'll call you tomorrow."

"Okay. Call if you need anything."

"I will. Bye."

I hung up the phone as we exited the building. For the first time, I was not disappointed by Stan's absence. I couldn't handle any more talking. My head felt like it was going to explode. This was also one of the few times that I was willing to pay for a taxi. No way I was surviving the subway tonight.

The apartment was dead silent as I trudged through the front door. Relief was the first emotion that went through me. Quiet. Ah, wondrous quiet. I put my keys on the kitchen table softly, afraid that even the metallic clink would be torture. With eyes half-closed, I wandered into the living room. Leta was lying on the couch wrapped in a white sheet. Her eyes were closed, and she seemed to be sleeping peacefully, which was a relief. Yet, there was little change in her appearance. Her skin still looked like bark and a few odd twigs seemed to be growing out of her body.

Reassured enough, I continued the trek to my room. Throwing my purse and jacket on top of the dresser just inside my room, I paused only for a second to stare lovingly at the full-size bed that awaited me. I stumbled past a pair of shoes and a few discarded shirts on the floor and threw myself onto the bed. I don't even remember hitting the pillow.

Despite my genuine aspirations to sleep soundly through the night, I did not. The few hours of deep sleep had succeeded at curing my headache. Yet sometime around four a.m., I woke with a strangled scream.

With the images of my nightmare still lingering, I wasn't thinking clearly when a shadowed shape crept into my unlit room. A full-fledged scream made its way up my throat this time, but a rough hand clamped over my mouth before I could vocalize it.

"It's me. Are you okay?" The rough voice sounded oddly like Leta's. As my brain cleared, I realized that the contorted figure creeping towards me was my roommate.

She must have felt my body relax because her hand slid away from my mouth. "Are you okay? You were making the saddest noise I have ever heard. Was it a bad dream?"

I watched as she tried to sit on the edge of the bed. A few of her branches made it difficult, but in the end, she managed.

"Let me get a light," I said as I reached for the light on my nightstand. A soft warm glow filled the room. I turned back to Leta and shrieked involuntarily.

"Grotesque, right?"

She didn't seem to be all that bothered by the change in her appearance. Instead, it was said with the acceptance one has for an unwanted blemish. "Anyway, tell me what your dream was. I thought for sure you were going to wake up screaming."

She pulled one leg up on the bed, pulled it close to her chest, and waited for me to explain.

"I just had a bad dream, that's all," I said as I reached for my phone. "It's only four o'clock." I sighed. That wasn't enough time to go back to sleep, yet it left me short for the second night in a row.

Leta gave me an apologetic look. "Well, since you can't go back to sleep, you might as well tell me about the dream."

So much for taking a hint. I wasn't ready to relieve that dream yet; however, Leta continued to stare at me expectantly. With a heavy sigh, I conceded and told her about the dream.

I was lost in the woods. It was dark and cold, and I didn't know where I was going. I just knew that I had to keep running because there was something after me. The trees were coming to life as I ran past them. It got darker like night was coming fast and hard. I saw a light in the distance and ran towards it. There were sounds behind me, but I just kept going towards the light. My dress got caught on a branch, and the wind blew through me, saying in a ghostly voice, 'Don't go.'

"Oh, you never should go towards the light, very bad," Leta informed me.

I shook my head at that comment, "Right. So, I get to the light, coming from the window of this tiny cottage. You know the cute little ones you see in those home and garden magazines. Anyway, a shadow grabs me."

Leta leaned closer to me. "A shadow?"

"Yeah, it was black and smoky and didn't have a solid shape."

"Hmm..." Leta looked concerned.

"It told me to turn back, that whoever was inside would understand. I pulled away from it and went around to the door. I could feel the heat inside the house, and I was freezing. The inside was warm and lit. Then it was like I was outside my body watching myself in a Little Red Riding Hood costume, one of those skimpy ones that I would never wear. Miguel was there, but he didn't look quite right."

"Did you say, 'Why Miguel, what big hands you have?'" She asked suggestively.

I glared.

"Okay, I'll shut up and let you tell the story. But you have to admit that would have been so funny if dream-you had said it." She folded her hands in her lap. "I promise I won't interrupt again."

I eyed her for a few seconds longer before continuing.

"No, I told him he didn't look so good and asked if he was okay. He said, 'I feel fine. You don't look so good though.' We chatted a bit after that."

"You chatted?" Leta asked with skepticism.

"Yes, we chatted. Whose dream is this, yours or mine?"

She raised her hands in surrender. "Yours, of course. It's just that you were crying and almost screamed when you woke up. Unless his small talk is really that terrifying..."

"No, you just didn't let me finish. Anyway, we were talking, and his hair started to grow, all over his body. I asked him what was happening, and he said 'Nothing, everything is fine' and started to stalk towards me. His eyes turned red, and he got bigger. I wanted to get out of there, but he trapped me in a corner. Fangs grew out of his mouth, dripping with blood. I couldn't go, couldn't leave. I was crying and begging him not to eat me. He just kept coming, saying that everything was fine. This was just who he was. He reached out for me with his clawed hands and that's when I woke up screaming."

"That's it?"

"What do you mean that's it?" I threw the blankets off my legs with a huff of irritation. "You have a dream where the guy you like turns into a scary monster intent on eating you. You would wake up screaming too." I glared at her. The day was already off to a bad start.

"Well, I'm not sure." She looked thoughtful. "Big, strong, hairy guy wanted to eat me...might not be such a bad thing."

I was slow to catch her meaning. "That is not what I was talking about! Is sex all you think about?"

Leta's eyes widened as she held out her arms and looked down at her disfigured body. "Hello... nymph!" Her look added the silent duh.

"How could I forget!" I just about yelled as I looked her up and down.

"Whoa, Miss Crankypants, there are a lot of unsaid things in that comment. Want to let it out?" She sat there looking like the calm, poised Leta she always was except with things growing out of her gray-brown skin.

I rubbed my face and could feel the indentions of wrinkled sheets in my cheeks. My body protested as I got out of bed. Great.

"Leta, the last few days have just been a bit rough. I found out my roomie is a mythical sex machine-"

"Hmm, mythical sex machine...I kind of like that..."

"I had to care for you while you had whatever this is, haven't had a good night's sleep in two nights, had the worst headache of my life yesterday, possibly lost the first major account of my career, and now am paranoid that my sort-of-boyfriend is a werewolf. And that last one is also thanks to you."

It was childish to tack that on but apparently, pain and lack of sleep brought out the worst version of me.

"How is that last bit my fault?" Leta asked out of pure surprise.

"Really? You've been calling him my wolf-boy the past two days. Don't you remember?"

She shook her head. "I'm sorry. Those days are a blur to me. I do remember you being there and taking care of me." She reached for my hand, tugging it gently until I looked down at her. "And I appreciate it." She held a hand to her chest. "Truly I do."

The genuine look of gratitude in her eyes eased my crankiness just a bit.

"That's what friends do. They take care of you when you need it." She smiled.

"But you did call him wolf-boy, thus inspiring the dream." I was still cranky.

Leta shook her head in defeat. "I'm sorry that you had a bad dream because of what I said. I should not have said it."

"Why, because he's not really a werewolf?"

Leta's eyes and mouth became perfect circles before she shook her head. "I was delirious...out of my mind. In a hundred years, I have never been sick."

"Hundred years! How old are you?"

"A hundred and seven," she responded with a shrug as she got off the bed.

I groaned as I fell back on the bed and covered my head with the blankets. Maybe I should just stay in bed. Claim that I got whatever Leta had.

"That's not an answer to my question, by the way," I muttered from under my blanket. If Leta heard me, she decided not to answer. I waited a few moments, listening to the silence before throwing the blankets off.

Leta was gone.

Maybe she hadn't heard me.

Chapter 10

Espresso was my poison of choice as I sat in the conference room. Selene had pulled in a dry-erase board to organize the ideas as they were thrown around the room.

We each had samples of the perfume in front of us with a list of its component scents: rose, cinnamon, honeysuckle, apple, champagne, and vanilla. However, on the board we had nothing.

A whole board of nothing.

Even in my post-migraine, sleep-deprived state I could see that all the ideas on the board were crap.

"Well, Elena, do you have any better ideas?"

I sat slouched in my chair cradling the cup of espresso to my chest, but Selene's voice seemed to penetrate my semi-comatose state. The room around me was silent, and I noted the tired faces staring at me with obvious annoyance.

"You think everything up here is crap, so give us something that isn't." Selene was tired and agitated, crossing her arms and staring at me with her dark eyes.

Apparently, that last statement of mine had been said out loud. Great.

"Umm..." I sat up in my chair and put my precious caffeine on the table. I looked back at the board. What was it that made all these ideas bad? Even the coffee couldn't clear my head. "Well..."

The room continued to stare at me with hostility. I would have rather faced dream Miguel as he turned into a monster than stay here and face the group without any good ideas. Yep, I would go back to those creepy woods and run...

"Woods," I whispered to myself.

"Woods?" Selene leaned forward to hear me better. "What about woods?"

"Running in the woods...with trees," I said absently as I tried to clear the dream image from my head.

"Yes, Elena, woods have trees," I heard Brad say in a patronizing tone, but I ignored it.

The images came together in my head. I couldn't see the whole picture, but it was almost there. I jumped out of my seat and grabbed the marker from Selene, ignoring her objection. Hurriedly, I wiped the board clean. Objections followed my impulsive action, but I barely heard them as I was possessed by manic vision. My hand flew to different areas of the board as I started to quickly sketch different pictures.

"Are we playing Pictionary now?" Someone said in a snide voice. I'm sure it was Brad.

"Wait," Sarah said behind me, but I just kept drawing.

Finally, I stepped back and Selene came to stand next to me and stared at the board.

"I don't know how they go together. I just know they do," I said to her.

The room seemed quietly confused by the pictures. Skyscraper buildings, trees huddled together, flowers, a woman's face, a man's face, and the perfume bottle. What did they have to do with each other?

"Elena, can you draw a few more buildings putting them in the same kind of arrangement as the trees?" Sarah asked, apparently in deep thought.

"Yeah, sure," I quickly drew the buildings and stepped back again.

"I see it," Selene said suddenly. "Wow, I can see it," she said with some disbelief. She laughed as she stepped closer to the board. "Christina, read me the list of scent components we made."

The other woman nodded and started to shift through some papers. "Apple, vanilla, champagne, rose, cinnamon, and honeysuckle." She looked up to Selene.

"Champagne...sophisticated and modern. Wealth, celebration, good times," Selene began walking as she brainstormed out loud. "Apple- homey, sweet or tart, traditional, everyday fruit, common."

"The everyday woman," Brad said from his seat, getting Selene's attention. "The everyday woman works, has a family. The sophisticated woman might work a corporate job."

Selene pointed to him. "Yes."

She grabbed the marker from me and went to the board. She drew a line down the middle of the woman's face. On one side she wrote, everyday woman, modern and sophisticated.

"What is the other half of this woman?" She asked the room.

People around the table began staring at the board with interest. Different voices started calling out adjectives as Selene wrote them on the board.

"Free."

"Wild."

"Sexy and beautiful."

"Unattached."

"Carefree, happy."

Leta.

I smiled and couldn't help but think that my roommate fit all those words.

"Nymph," I said softly, certain that no one heard.

Selene looked at me. "What did you say?"

Again, the room looked at me.

"Nymph, nymph-like." My manic rush was gone, and I felt uncomfortable with all the attention. "You know, a creature of fantasy and unbelievable beauty."

"And sex," Sarah added.

"Yes, sex, with a capital S." I gave her a nod. How could I forget the sex?

"Okay, okay," Selene said as she wrote nymph on the board and circled it.

"The buildings could represent the real world, where a woman has to deal with work and kids and responsibilities," Christina said.

Selene nodded to her. "And the forest is the fantasy where our nymph lives."

It was fascinating to watch Christina and Selene play off each other. It was why they were such a dynamic team.

"The perfume takes our woman from this," she pointed to the everyday woman, "to this." She tapped the nymph half with the marker.

"What about the man's face?" Sarah asked.

"He's following her, watching the transformation, taken into the fantasy with her." Brad was leaning back in his chair tapping a pencil against his knuckles and smiling.

The energy in the room intensified. People were alert and excited. I watched it with a bit of surprise. Looking back at the board, I saw the story come together.

"She's walking with the reflective glass building beside her. She's wearing business clothes, something probably conservative and restrictive. Dark, drab colors maybe." I described the images as they played through my head like a movie. "She pulls out the perfume and applies some as the man walks by. He's intrigued by the smell, so he looks back, and we see a reflection of the woods in the glass of the building. The woman is still walking, her clothes morphing into something softer and more flowing. The buildings turn to forest as she enters it. The man follows her, and she looks back at him in her nymph phase and smiles. Cut to the perfume bottle."

I blinked and looked away from the board. My group sat silently imagining the scene.

"Damn," Brad said excitedly as he pumped his fist in the air.

"I want some of that perfume," Sarah said.

Christina twirled her chair towards Selene. "I think we have it." She smiled.

"We do have it," Selene said as she capped the marker. "We have it."

The room cheered.

I exhaled with a huge sigh of relief.

"Good job." Selene smiled, and I realized her praise was for me.

I wasn't sure where any of it had come from, but...wow! I fell back into my seat as Selene quieted the room.

"We have the idea, now we need to do the work. Christina, let's get a complete outline of this. Brad, we need demographics. Sarah," And on she went, issuing orders and organizing the rest of the work that needed to be done before the end of the week.

There was a lot to do, but Selene let the group go early. Though she gave us a warning that this was the last early night we could expect for the rest of the week, everyone left in good spirits.

Chapter 11

I talked to Miguel a handful of times that week. He insisted on taking me out to dinner or coming over with takeout, but I declined each time. I didn't have the energy to be pleasant company, and my anxiety dominated my consciousness.

It was Wednesday night, two nights before the presentation, and he called to check up on me.

"How is your roommate?"

The mention of my roommate brought to mind images of a grotesque half-tree, half-woman creature, bark and all.

"Leta's fine."

"And how are you doing? I know that you've been taking care of her."

"I'm okay. I had a lingering headache all week, but that's probably because I'm not sleeping very well on top of being stressed."

"Why aren't you sleeping well?"

"Oh, you know, bad dreams."

That stupid dream! The one where Miguel turned into a werewolf. The dream I had because my delusional roommate had called him 'wolf boy.'

I rubbed the bridge of my nose, where my headache had currently taken up residence. Miguel was not a werewolf.

That was my new mantra, not that my subconscious had taken note of it.

Of course, the knowledge that my roommate was a figure from Greek mythology didn't make that little affirmation very convincing. I'd thought Leta might be crazy, but I hadn't suspected for a minute that she was a mythical creature.

"Hello? Elena?"

"What?"

"Just wondering where you went for a moment. Are you okay?"

This was it. I could tell him about the dream, make a big joke out of it. *Isn't that funny...*I would say. *You aren't a werewolf because they don't exist. Right?*

And you're too nice a guy to be one if they do exist.

Which they don't.

I'm pretty sure they don't.

"Oh, there you go again," Miguel said with some amusement.

Werewolves do not exist, I firmly told myself.

Despite the affirmations, I wasn't convinced. But I desperately wanted him to not be a werewolf.

If he was...I wasn't sure what I'd do, and I refused to think about it tonight. Some other night, some other day, I would deal with that nagging doubt. Tonight, I would push the image of moonlight striking his skin and transforming him into a monster intent on devouring me from my mind. For the most part, I did well.

"Why don't you come over to my place tomorrow night? I'll make you dinner. You can relax before the big meeting."

I didn't want to say yes. I knew I'd be a complete mess tomorrow night.

However, instead of telling him no, I said maybe. After assuring him that I would call after work tomorrow, I hung up and went to bed to try to catch up on sleep.

My dreams were apparently on repeat too. I spent so many of my nights running through dark forests, waking up at times with gasping breaths. The scary trees stayed the same; shadowy shapes that loomed menacingly over me, but the things chasing me were different each time.

One night it was Miguel. I ran into his strong arms, seeking safety from the things in the darkness; yet as he drew me closer, I heard a low growl in my ear. I pulled back to ask if he had heard it, only he wasn't there anymore. A monster covered in grizzly black fur towered over me, saliva dripping from the protruding canines. Red eyes stared at me. I screamed and ran. He pursued me on all fours, swiping at my ankles with gigantic, clawed hands.

He caught me, sending me face-first into the ground. Heavy panting grew louder and closer, followed by a low growl. Just as I turned over to face him, I woke with my heart beating rapidly in my chest.

The others were similar. A warped tree-like creature chased me in a different dream. I tried to escape the forest, but a misshapen figure with branch-like projections always blocked my way. It moaned while the many branch-like limbs swung violently at my body. It wasn't a stretch of my imagination to figure out where that image had come from. Every time I left my room, I was confronted by the strange tree-woman hybrid that was my roommate.

Another dream started with the same forest, but nothing chased me in this dream. Instead, I was trapped in a small clearing circled tightly by trees. They grew like bamboo, so tight I couldn't escape. The darkness began to fade in the distance; fought by a growing light. But it was not the light of a dawning sun.

Hungry, violent flames consumed the trees and the sky, spreading on the ground like spilled water. I had nowhere to go, trapped in that small circle. The flames kept coming, drawing ever closer. The flames licked at my heels. I caught on fire like a dried log drenched in gasoline.

I didn't feel a burning pain, just the suffocating grip of the fire. It covered my legs in flames that rose further up my torso and to my shoulders. I could feel faint heat, but the inescapable feeling of helplessness was panic inducing. The fire threatened to consume me, and still, I couldn't do anything. The oxygen was stolen from my lungs each time I tried to call for help.

So, it was no wonder that each morning when I looked in the mirror, the dark circles under my eyes had darkened. I swore that my whole body sagged from the weight of my exhaustion, that any person walking past could see it. Leta tried to reassure me that I didn't look like some melting flesh monster, just a woman who hadn't slept well. My mind felt dull and clouded. And my mood was like a ship sinking in a sea of despair.

I tried not to snap at Leta, though she sweetly just ignored me when I did, sometimes even getting a look of such guilty concern that I had to look away. Though her skin was not yet back to normal, the branches were gone, and she felt much better. She anticipated that in another day her appearance would be back to normal. She had already returned to work in a way, taking calls from the creative team and the clients. With her seductive voice, she assured them that we were going to wow them.

Stan greeted me on Thursday morning as I arrived. "How you doing, Ms. McNeal?"

I was slow to respond.

The wrinkles on his face deepened with concern. "Elena?" He said in a firmer voice.

I stared for a second before shaking myself and managing a pitiful smile. "Oh, hey, Stan. How was your shift?"

The concern deepened. "Same ole', same ole'. By the looks of you, I'd say that you're not getting much sleep. Why is that?"

"Bad dreams. I go to sleep just fine, but I can't stay asleep because of the dreams. So, I wake earlier and earlier each day."

"What kind of dreams?"

"Oh, you know the usual nightmares- werewolves, killer tree roommates, death by fire..." I tried to sound nonchalant. But the alarm in Stan's eyes confirmed that I had failed.

"Why are you having nightmares?"

"Well..." how should I answer that. "There's a huge presentation with our biggest client tomorrow, and we already messed it up once, so we cannot afford to mess up this time."

Oh, and my roommate is infected with some branch-sprouting disease, and the guy I'm kind of seeing may be a werewolf.

"Elena, you can't go on like this. You look like the walking dead."

Leave it to Stan to tell it like it is. I knew Leta was lying to me.

"I know. Thanks for the concern, Stan."

"If you need to talk, I'm still here to listen." He tapped my nose. "Remember that."

"Thanks. I have to go, Stan."

He nodded, and I felt his worried gaze on me all the way to the elevator.

No one else commented on my death-warmed-over appearance, possibly because a few of them felt the same. There was so much to do. Even though the idea for the ad had been conceived, it had to be molded and reshaped before all the edges were smooth. Everyone labored away at their desks doing what they were best at. I was assisting Selene with the visual layout presentation.

I liked to think that it was the lack of sleep that made it so hard, but I went through so many designs, and nothing was right. I had just trashed the latest sketch before pounding my forehead on the desk.

"Rough day?"

I looked up and through the veil of my hair saw Farah, the freelance photographer who often contracted with the firm.

"More like a rough week." I pushed aside the hair and tried to arrange it presentably.

"Yeah, I heard a lot is riding on this presentation." She was lean perfection with her fiery red hair spilling over her off-the-shoulder blouse.

"What are you doing here?" I asked.

"I had some pics for one of the campaigns to drop off. Thought I would swing by and see how things were going." She paused to study me with keen eyes. "You look like hell."

Honesty was one of Farah's virtues, but I was too tired to be offended.

"Yeah, like I said, rough week." Without thinking, I muttered, "You should see Leta."

However, as I met gazes with Farah the intensity of her stare scared me.

"How is Leta doing?" She asked carefully. Another brief flare of hope that somebody else knew Leta's secret, but I couldn't risk giving anything away.

"She is doing much better. The bran- pox...chickenpox is mostly gone. You know those horrible little bumps? Yeah, they're almost gone."

"I've never had chickenpox." She continued to stare at me intensely. "Maybe I should go by and see her since she is feeling better."

"No," I almost shouted, then tried to cover it with a joking tone. "Are you crazy? You might get sick, especially since you've never had it. She's still contagious, which is why she hasn't come back to work yet."

With a brief flash of amusement in her eyes, she smiled at me as if satisfied by what I had said.

"Of course." She was about to leave, but added, "You know, with everything you've done for Leta...you're a good friend, Elena. I'm not sure if you know how much that means."

"Of course," was all I could think to say.

"I'll give her a call to check in. Hopefully, those bumps...will be gone soon. Then maybe we can all hang out again."

I smiled. "That would be nice. See you later."

Chapter 12

We trudged out of the office later than anyone else that night. I saw a mixture of relief and wariness among my co-workers. We all worried about the possibility of losing the contract tomorrow, yet what we had was great. It was better than any other ad I had seen since working with Madame Advertising. My small contribution was undoubtedly the best that I had ever done, and I was sure that tomorrow we would impress the clients.

Maybe it was too early to celebrate, but I wanted to...no needed to. I wanted to rid myself of the burden and stress of the project that had been with me all week. There was nothing else we could do. It was what it was. Good or bad. The clients would either love or hate it.

I felt lighter and happier as I left the office. Even though I was exhausted from work and still sleep-deprived, I felt an unexpected surge of energy. I didn't want to go home and coddle my sick roommate. I didn't want to join the others who were going out for a drink. Instead, I decided to take Miguel up on his offer.

I called him up as I stepped out of the elevator. He laughed at my enthusiasm, saying I sounded wired. I assured him that most likely I would come down from the high soon; but right now, I just wanted to forget about work and clients and roommates. He said he was cooking and gave me the address to his apartment.

Maybe an intimate dinner at his apartment was just what I needed. Maybe I would feel something more than just lukewarm. Maybe I'd even be bold and adventurous and let the night go much further than just our steamy kisses. I could regale Leta with the story later and prove to my nymph friend that I wasn't as uptight as she thought I was.

I took a cab because I just wanted to be there. Miguel greeted me at the door and before I could even say hello, he pulled me into a deep kiss. He left me breathless when he pulled away and took my hand, pulling me into the apartment.

"That was quite a hello," I joked, but I felt overwhelmed by his intensity.

He smiled as he closed the door behind us. "Want to see what 'I've been thinking of you' is like?"

He moved towards me, my body instinctually retreating from the assertiveness of his approach. I came up against the door, and his arms came up to box me in. I'd considered where this date might end up, but he was moving way too fast for me. He eyed me as a predator eyes prey. A small part of my brain alarmed.

"Maybe after dinner," I laughed as I put a hand on his chest.

"Why wait?" His body moved even closer, and my breath caught in my throat.

Again, warning bells.

I laughed nervously. "I'm a famished woman. I need sustenance." I ducked under his arm and put a few feet between us.

"Nice place," I commented as I took in the ultra-masculine surroundings.

His arms wrapped around my waist, and he pulled me into his body.

"Seriously, you should feed me first. I'm useless when I'm hungry." I smiled though my heart raced, and not for the good reasons.

He kissed me again, quick and hard this time, playfully biting my lip. A groan that sounded a bit like a growl followed as his attention became more passionate. I tried to reconcile this aggressive Miguel with the kind, concerned man I had talked to all week.

He growled. I immediately thought of my nightmares.

"I just want to eat you up," he whispered in my ear. The fine hairs on the back of my neck stood up as he ran his teeth over my skin.

I smothered a scream as I began to push at him. "Wait, please just wait!" I said a bit frantically as I pulled away.

He growled as I stepped away. "You didn't just growl, did you?"

The question surprised him. He paused briefly before shaking his head.

"I'm sorry." He pushed a hand through his hair. "Are you okay?"

There was the concerned voice that had offered comfort on the phone.

I stared at him, wondering at the drastic swings in his personality. "I'm really confused right now."

"This going too fast?"

My surprise at the idiocy of that question must have read in my eyes.

"Yeah, I guess so." He sighed and raked his hands through his hair again. "I don't know what came over me. It just felt like an animal instinct taking over."

I nodded, trying not to think of him as Wolf-Boy.

"It's just…" He looked so upset that I felt obligated to say something reassuring. I couldn't think of a way to nicely say that I was freaked out by the possibility that he was a werewolf.

Instead, I said, "It's just been a while. You know?"

"Yeah, of course," he said with a sigh. He held my hand but kept the distance between us.

The image started somewhere in the back of my mind. If I had been more cognoscente, I might have cut it off before it coalesced into the image of my nightmares. Suddenly, I wasn't seeing Miguel. Instead, I was seeing my nightmare version of him, the one where he turned from an attractive man into a ferocious monster. Dark thick hair covered his entire body, and his teeth elongated into sharp fangs dripping with blood.

I shook my head as if I could banish the image. But that hadn't worked at any point this week. I kept having that twisted Red Riding

Hood dream. I started to laugh, that uncomfortable, awkward-for-everyone-else sort of laugh. The on-the-verge-of-hysteria laugh.

I looked up at Miguel. He studied me with concern again.

"I'm sorry," I gasped, unable to stop the frantic laughter. "I'm sorry. I think I'm just a bit delusional with all the lack of sleep this week. That stupid dream just won't go away."

From the deepening concern in his eyes, I failed to alleviate his worries. Okay, the crazy laughter was not helping. I took a few deep breaths and squashed the hysterics.

"When Leta first got sick, she implied that you were some sort of werewolf." His worry deepened. More explanation was needed. "Crazy, I know."

I waited for him to nod or to say, yeah, that is crazy, but he just continued to stare at me.

"She was delirious, but it stuck with me. I started to have these nightmares where I was Little Red Riding Hood, and you turned into the Big Bad Wolf."

His silence troubled me.

"I think it was the stress from work. My imagination just got carried away with that silly comment, and I couldn't shake the dreams." I tried for a light laugh. "But if you just assure me right now that you are not in fact a werewolf, I can squash those silly dreams." I tried for a light tone, added an encouraging smile, and waited.

And waited.

All he had to was laugh and tell me how silly I was. Of course, he wasn't a werewolf. But he just looked at me with a bit of shock.

Maybe I had sounded too crazy. He was worried about my sanity now. Great, I had to say something to reassure him that I wasn't insane.

Before I could say anything, he said slowly in a quiet voice, "You didn't know."

You didn't know...those three words just about destroyed me. I didn't know what?

We stared at each other in silence.

"I just assumed that you knew..." he looked like he was in shock.

"You assumed I knew what?" My voice reached a new level of hysteria.

"It's just that...considering who you were with...I just thought that you had to have known."

Oh, my god! Oh, no, no, no! This was worse than the nightmares.

"What do you mean 'considering who you were with'?" My voice was surprisingly calm. *Like the calm before the storm*, I thought.

He looked shocked and alarmed at the same time. "You know, you were with Leta, and I thought you knew that she was..."

"What do you think Leta is?" I asked carefully.

"She's a nymph," he responded just as carefully.

I looked away, trying to maintain my calm. "I don't know or care how you know that. Right now, Miguel, I just need you to tell me that you are not a werewolf or any other mythical creature." He silently stared at me with an apology in his eyes. "Please." My voice broke.

"I thought you knew," was all he said.

That was all I could take. The calm broke. The hyperventilating started.

"I have to go." I pulled away, working my hand out of his grip. "I have to go."

"Wait. I'm sorry. I'm not handling this very well. Why don't you just sit down, and we will talk about this? I can explain."

"I really don't think I need any more explanation," I turned and grabbed the door handle.

"Elena, please. Don't leave." He touched my hand. As I whirled towards him, he pulled his hand away with a hiss, as if he'd been burned.

"No, I can't take any more of this. First, my roommate and her stupid tree and now you!" I flung the accusation at him with all the frustration and anger that had accumulated over the past week.

"I'm done! Just done," I said more to myself than to him. I flung open the door.

"Elena," he called as I raced for the stairs.

"Don't," I called over my shoulder. "Just don't."

My last glimpse of him showed all the pain and regret that I heard in his voice. I felt a moment of compassion for him, but the strength of my suffering was greater. I refused to look back again.

I also refused to cry on the subway even though the tears threatened to fall the entire ride.

My body hurt as I climbed the stairs to my apartment. My phone beeped for the tenth time since I had left Miguel's. That was the tenth message he had left.

How many ways was he going to say he didn't know? How many times was he going to avoid telling me what he was?

I felt like the biggest fool ever as I ascended that last set of stairs.

Mechanically, I put the key in the lock and opened the door. Throwing my keys on the kitchen table, I began to trudge to my room.

"Elena, is that you?" Leta's cheerful voice carried from the other room. "I can't wait to show you! It's so exciting."

I heard her voice behind me and turned slowly to look at her as she emerged from the other room.

"Look, all the twigs and bark are gone." She smiled brilliantly and did a little twirl. The bark and twigs were gone. She was back to her dazzling self.

"I just took a shower this afternoon and when I looked in the mirror," she continued to ramble on, looking down at her body with obvious joy. My shell-shock state had escaped her completely. Good, maybe I could slip into my room without her noticing.

"That's nice. Congratulations, Leta," I said over my shoulder. It lacked any emotion whatsoever, but I couldn't gather enough energy to care. I wanted to shut down. Right now, the shock of the truth had made me numb, and I just wanted to stay in that state as long as I could. Because when the numbness wore off, it was not going to be pretty.

"Thanks… oh, Elena, are you okay?" Her jubilant tone changed to concern.

"I'm tired and going to bed." A few more feet and I could hide behind the door.

"Do you want to talk about anything? Did something happen at work or with Miguel?" The gentleness of her voice was too much.

Without warning, I turned on her. "I just want to sleep, Leta! I haven't done it in almost a week so do you mind if I just crawl into bed!"

The hurt showed on her face, but I didn't care. "Of course, I'm sorry. I know it has been a rough week. You go to bed and get lots of sleep. Hopefully, without the nightmares." She tried a smile that was wasted on me.

"My life is a nightmare," I muttered. I know she heard. Her hearing was good and worry darkened her eyes.

I closed and locked the door behind me. Stripping down, I put on the first pair of pajamas I found, not caring if they were clean. Then I fell into bed, and when my head hit the pillow, the numbness began to wear off. Tears poured down my cheeks, and I sobbed into the pillow. A shadow lurked outside the door, but Leta left me alone. Luckily, I fell asleep crying before the full impact of the night could hit me.

For the first time in a week, I did not dream of werewolves, dark shadows, or tree monsters.

Chapter 13

Despite the debt of sleep that had accumulated over the past week and the absence of nightmares, I found myself awake at four in the morning, staring at the ceiling.

The numbness was back, for which I was exceedingly glad. I could almost feel the wave of emotion just barely contained behind it. It was huge, and I knew it would tear through me, sweeping me out into a sea of feelings that would drown me. And today, I needed to be in one piece. I needed to just keep it together for one more day. One more day, and then I could fall apart. Of course, it would be good to find a new place before I fell apart.

As I lay there, fully awake in the darkness, I realized that I had to find a new place to stay. I wasn't sure that I could handle any more craziness, and living with Leta was bound to bring more of it into my life. Guilt buzzed around my mind like an annoying little bee, and no matter how I mentally tried to swat it, I just couldn't get rid of it.

Maybe it was a little unfair of me to walk out on Leta when she had been so generous and welcoming. Maybe it was a bit cowardly. But I wanted normal! Was that so bad? I didn't want a best friend who grew branches or a boyfriend who sprouted fur on a full moon.

I turned to the cell phone on the shelf next to my bed. There had been ten messages when I had finally just turned it off. I didn't want to talk to Miguel yet...didn't want to hear his stupid excuses.

"'I just assumed you knew,'" I muttered his words to the dark. *Why, yes...I* thought...*I always assume that there is something freakishly wrong with wonderful, attractive men.*

On second thought, I should have thought that something was wrong.

Feeling sorry for myself, I crawled out of bed and showered. Without immediately realizing it, I tiptoed through the apartment, not wanting to wake my roommate. That was another confrontation that I was not ready to have. I knew that Leta would be going to work for the presentation. How could she not? She was her beautiful, bark-less-branch-less self again. However, I didn't wait for her.

How could she not tell me? The anger flared for only a moment before a snide inner voice replied. *But she did tell you, even if it was a delirium-induced confession.*

The subway ride was a bit of a blur. Robbery and murder could have happened right in front of me, and I wouldn't have noticed. I was too busy holding on to the numb. Thankfully, I managed to get on and off at the right places and found myself staring up at the right building as dawn began to light the streets.

Trudging through the glass doors, I stopped short at the sight of a smiling Stan. I didn't want to face him either.

"Aren't you the early bird," he said jovially.

I tried a smile, but the effort fell short. I didn't need to see it; I could feel that it was bad.

"After this presentation today, you need to go straight home and sleep, young lady," he pretended to look severe.

"I have to look for a new apartment after work today," I muttered.

His eyes got big as he stepped around the welcome counter. "What? You're not moving in with that new boyfriend of yours already, are you? You should give it a little more time before-"

"I'm never seeing him again."

He stopped and stared silently at me. I decided it was a good time to escape the conversation. Yet, Stan recovered quickly and stepped in front of me. "What happened?"

"Nothing."

He raised a brow. "You broke up with your boyfriend and decided to move out of your friend's apartment all in one day. I wouldn't say that that's nothing."

I tried arching a brow back at him. We proceeded to stare at each other.

I lost. "I don't want to talk about it, Stan. I want to go upstairs and prepare for that damn presentation."

His eyes softened at my raised voice. "I think you might need to talk this through. You're considering some big changes. And what does Leta think of this?"

I couldn't meet his eyes. "I haven't told her yet."

He pursed his lips this time.

"She's been sick, okay? I didn't want to stress her out. Besides, we just have different...lifestyles."

Stan straightened up, and I dared a look at his face. He looked concerned rather than disapproving. "I thought you and Leta were friends?"

"We were."

"And?"

"And...she wasn't who I thought she was."

"And who was it you thought she was?" I didn't answer so he continued. "Now, I've known Leta a little longer than you, and I know her to be a kind, caring, generous, and supportive person. Is that who you thought she was?" I nodded. "So, you are telling me that she is not those things?"

"That's not what I meant, Stan," I objected weakly.

"Well?"

"She didn't tell me..."

"Tell you what?"

How was I going to answer this? She didn't tell me she was a nymph...no, that was not going to work.

"There are just some important things that she didn't tell me." He wasn't convinced. "She's crazy, you know?" I tried defensively. "Her life is crazy. I don't want crazy. I want normal and quiet."

Stan started to smile. "Life is crazy, kiddo. And, if you think you can avoid the craziness, you are crazy." He rubbed his chin, and the smile deepened. "I will admit that Leta can be a bit high-strung at times, but that doesn't beat out all the good things about her. People can't help being...what they are."

Something about the way that he said it made me suspicious. Was the whole city secretly mythical creatures? Or did he know her secret too?

I wasn't in the mood to continue this conversation. "I have to go upstairs, Stan." I stepped around him and headed towards the elevator.

"Think about what I said Ms. McNeal," he called after me.

I don't know why, but I expected it to wear off slowly like the numbing shot I had once gotten for stitches in my foot. But it didn't.

No, one moment I was blissfully numb and the next, the pain was crashing into me like a head-on collision. Maybe it was the mock-up with its images of a nymph-like woman luring a gorgeous man into the realm of fantasy. Maybe it was the nymph herself.

Leta arrived at the office later than she usually did. I felt a tinge of guilt that she had probably been late waiting for me. She entered the conference room where the team gathered. I strategically placed myself between Sarah and Brad. I couldn't handle sitting next to her or anyone else who might see past the brave face. Fortunately for me, Sarah was just as exhausted as me, and we sat in silence, wordlessly acknowledging our inability to interact.

I tried to avoid those eyes as they stared intently at me...tried and failed. I figured that Leta would be mad at my abruptness last night, that she would be shooting daggers at me with her eyes, and who knew, maybe she actually could shoot missiles out of her eyes. Stranger things had happened in the past week. Finally giving in to the intense stare, I saw only concern and hurt staring back at me. It was so unexpected that my anger towards Leta weakened momentarily.

Refusing to be moved by her emotion, I looked down quickly and fiddled with the pen and paper in front of me. She took the seat opposite Sarah.

Leaning over the table, she whispered in a voice that everyone at the table heard, "Elena, how are you?"

I looked up at the gentleness in her tone. Then I saw her face and a brief wave of temper passed before I felt the eyes of everyone at the table on me. Then I was just embarrassed. Much to my dismay...and irritation... Leta's concern attracted the attention of the whole room.

"I'm fine." I tried for cheer, but it came out like a snarl.

Leta's concerned expression deepened to an almost comical depth. I might have laughed had I not been squirming under the intense gazes of my coworkers.

"Really, I'm fine." That sounded far from convincing but more civil.

Selene rushed into the room at that moment and fiddled with the laptop. Finishing her task, she faced the room, a smile forming on her lips.

"Leta, you're back! Feeling better?"

Thank you, Selene! Her pleasant inquiry drew Leta's attention and those in the room began asking her questions and welcoming her back at all at once.

"You must have been so sick."

"We missed you so much."

"Glad to have you back."

"What did you have? Was it horrible?"

Leta patiently answered and thanked people one by one. I, for one, was thankful that she was no longer focusing on me. And she was sticking to the story I created. She explained in detail...well, in all the detail she could without mentioning the bark and the branches…just how awful it had been to be sick. The sympathy poured out for her, and she soaked it up like a thirsty plant soaked up water. She looked at me from time to time, praising my nursing abilities. I rolled my eyes. What else was I going to do with a wailing, pathetic tree monster co-habituating with me?

Ouch! Heartburn filled my chest with pain. I had never had heartburn before. It had to be the stress. The heartburn only seemed to intensify as I sat there listening to people coo over Leta. If only they had seen her a few days ago. They wouldn't be so attentive.

I was the one who had stayed up getting her every little thing she needed or wanted while she went psycho. I was the one missing vital hours of sleep because I had taken care of her, covering up her secret, all while trying to save the project at work. And, being lied to by the man I was dating.

And my selfish roommate who knew that said man was a werewolf the whole time.

Damn, I was going to have to invest in some Tums if this heartburn was a new constant in my life. Maybe once I got out of that apartment and away from Leta, I wouldn't be so stressed.

Sonia rushed into the room, her voice projecting over the others. "Leta, security just called; the clients are on their way up." She practically bounced with excitement as she left.

The room was ominously quiet as Leta stood. She smoothed her jacket and pasted that annoyingly perfect smile on her face. "Here we go," she said cheerfully as she went to greet the clients.

That was when it happened. The pain erupted…and not just the heartburn.

I felt myself gasp at the enormity of it. The gasp was followed by faster and faster breaths. Soon, I was starting to feel a little lightheaded. Thankfully, no one seemed to notice.

In a daze, I could hear Leta's voice coming down the hall.

Think slow, deep breaths, Elena. Slow, deep breaths. I closed my eyes and felt the tears that started to gather.

No crying, I ordered myself. But the tears kept building, and my chest felt burdened with deep, stabbing pain. Maybe this was a heart attack.

I tried to think of happy things...kittens and dewdrops or such things...but the pain was so much more than I had imagined it would be. I had known it was going to be bad, I just had no idea it was going to be this bad.

Those damn tears were sneaky. I felt them slipping out, so I opened my eyes just as Micah and Nolan walked into the room. Leta guided them with a smile, and Glenda followed with a neutral expression. There was no point in any of us trying to charm the clients; that was what Leta was for. I slouched in my chair, thankful that no one was watching me. The tears still threatened, but my breathing was better.

Micah and Nolan looked mesmerizingly beautiful in their tailored suits, yet all I could think of was Miguel.

And, how he was a werewolf.

A few renegade tears escaped. I quickly brushed the back of my hand across my eyes.

I vaguely heard the voices around me as the clients sat, and Selene took charge of the presentation. She was sleek in her black low-cut V-neck that never seemed too risqué on her. *There you go*, I encouraged myself. *Focus on the details, Elena.*

Her wide-legged pin-stripe pants were paired with sensible flats. Her short black hair was flat-ironed and accented by a jeweled hairpin that looked vintage. None of the elements of the ensemble should have gone together, but they did.

She was telling the story now. Our story. The story that we desperately wanted the clients to buy. It was the story of a woman, confined by the city and the daily hassles of her life.

She's walking down the sidewalk past a glass front and suddenly, the reflection of buildings melds into trees, and we see an enchanted forest in the reflection. A man across the street sees her and the forest. The two make eye contact, but she continues walking. A breeze stirs her hair; it falls in a cascade of soft waves. The business suit begins to fall away and the sensual, wild, purely feminine woman beneath is revealed in a flowing dress of delicate ivory fabric. She looks behind her and smiles invitingly at the man before entering the forest reflection. He smiles though he has no choice but to follow this nymph-like creature. He is entranced.

My hearing was muffled, but I could hear Selene's smooth voice telling the story. I was vaguely aware when she pulled the mock-up up on the big screen, revealing a very rough illustration of what the ad would look like. A woman pressed against the glass by the man behind her and the reflection of her nymph self looking back with a seductive smile and the fantasy forest behind her.

The room was deathly silent. I closed my eyes and focused on breathing.

"I love it," Nolan said the words so softly that I almost didn't hear them. I opened my eyes to see the gaping faces around me. All eyes twitched from Nolan to Micah.

He stared at the mock-up with hard eyes, leaning back in his chair while one hand stroked his chin. We all waited in tense silence.

"Brilliant." That one word, said in a bored tone, released a collective breath of relief. "This is what I expected from your team all along, Glenda. When can I see a more finalized version?"

Glenda smiled with satisfaction. "We'll get working on it right away," she said smoothly.

"I believe there was a bottle of champagne, was there not?" Micah said as he stood, his voice dripped with snobbery.

People stood and began congratulating each other while they gathered around the clients. I struggled to get out of my chair. My eyes leaked like broken facets now, and I wasn't a plumber. I had no idea how to fix it other than to just let the source run dry. Someone popped the cork on the champagne, and I jumped in surprise. As I scooted past people, cheers went up and glasses were filled.

I retreated from the room, seeking a safe place to lose it. In an office like this, there was no safe place. I thought of the bathroom, but the pain and exhaustion were too much. Unable to bear it even a moment longer, I ducked into the other conference room. The door closed behind me...or I thought did.

Leaning against the table, I stopped trying to hold back the emotion that buried me. Tears gushed down my face as I made those horrible gasping, sobbing noises, unable to give a damn about how bad I sounded or how bad I looked.

How could this hurt so much? It wasn't like I had never been lied to before. Small-town living didn't protect you against that. Miguel was not the first man to withhold the truth in an effort to get laid. What man hadn't done that at least once in his life?

Why was this any different? Why was the betrayal I felt over Leta and Miguel so much more hurtful than past offenses? I didn't know the answer to it. All I knew was that it hurt, and I was too exhausted to fight it.

I couldn't remember the last time I had had a full night's sleep. Never in my life I had walked the line between truth and lies so closely as when I had been covering for Leta. I didn't like lying. Never had. The guilt was too much for me.

I didn't want Leta's secret. Life was hard enough without trying to keep something that big safe.

And of course that was part of it. My little bubble of a normal, happy world was busted. Never again would I be able to see or hear about some fictional monster and not wonder if it was real. Or wonder if the person on the subway next to me was a creature from my nightmares. Granted, Leta was completely harmless as far as I could tell, despite the shape-shifting strangeness that had occurred when she was sick. And Miguel had never acted like a horror flick monster with enlarged canines and sharp claws, but I hadn't seen him during a full moon. How was I supposed to know if he would turn into a people-devouring hulk of fur or not?

Having an illusion taken away, no matter how big or small, was devastating. So many beliefs were built on those illusions. Feelings of home and safety were cemented with them. Illusions kept us safe in the darkest places where things go bump in the night. I could no longer deny that magic and mythical creatures were real, and that realization rocked my foundation so hard that I felt myself falling into an unknown abyss.

"Tears of joy?"

Nolan's voice was so unexpected that I hiccupped as I swallowed a shriek.

"I thought I closed the door."

"No, it was open just a hair, but enough that I could hear the most... saddening noise," he frowned.

I cringed. Great. So maybe I did care how bad I sounded.

"I...just, I...needed some..." I babbled as I tried to wipe the tears from my face, which was probably a splotchy mess with black streaks of mascara. I was so busy scrubbing my face that I didn't see him approach. Nope. I felt him before I saw him. His hand gently pushed my tremulous one away.

I froze, unsure of what that gentle touch meant to him. Unsure of what it meant to me.

"Either you are very upset at the idea of having to see me more," he flashed that sexy smile, "or this has nothing to do with work." His fingers softly tucked a strand of hair behind my ear.

"I..." That was all I could breathe as the man stood over me, genuine concern in his eyes.

I don't know why. To this day, I'm still not sure why looking into those blue eyes, unfamiliar as they were, made me feel safe and comforted.

I gave up. I stopped trying to pretend that I was okay. Here was a man gently stroking my wet cheek waiting patiently for me to answer, and I was just so tired.

"It's been a really rough week," I said with a strained voice, trying to hold back the tears. "My roommate is crazy, the guy I was seeing is a beast, and I..." full-blown tears at this point, "haven't slept in so long, and-"

I stopped crying as strong arms enveloped me. One minute, his hand was on my cheek and the next my cheek was pressed against his chest. I didn't fight it. Here was that comfort that had been stolen away from me. This was familiar to me. Just one person giving another person in an obvious need a hug.

There was nothing sexual about it. It was just warm and reassuring. I felt myself melt into it as the tears started coming again.

With a gasp of horror, I tried to pull back. I was ruining his expensive suit. "Oh, your suit, I'm so sorry!"

He looked down at the tearstains and laughed. "Do not worry. What is a mere piece of clothing compared to a woman's tears? It is inconsequential."

He pulled me back into his embrace, and I cried without guilt for what felt like a long time.

"So," a voice from the doorway drawled, "is this your definition of a handshake?"

I pulled away from Nolan immediately, knowing how bad this would look.

"This is not what you think," I explained before I realized the person standing in the doorway was Micah.

"Oh, I think it is. A lovely woman in distress, and a man comforting her. And since we have already discussed the appropriate ways for a man to comfort a woman, I can only conclude that that was a handshake. It was a handshake that you said was appropriate, was it not?" His tone was snide, and his smile was smug.

Something about him made me feel all fired up inside and not in a good way.

"Did you need something?" Nolan asked his partner with a certain coolness.

"Contracts. Your signature is needed."

Micah looked so satisfied by the scene in front of him that I was a bit worried. He might report us to Glenda, and then I would be off the project. I didn't want to be off the project.

The two men stood in silence eying each other, a silent argument going on between them. I figured it was time to get out of this situation.

"I, ah, I should get back to the meeting." I looked at Nolan one last time. His eyes were warm, and before I got lost in that concerned gaze again, I stepped away.

He caught my elbow as I turned to leave. "Are you better now?" His voice was as low as a whisper.

I managed a weak smile. "Yes, thank you."

He let me go, and I headed towards the door with my head down. I tried to slip around Micah without touching him. But he leaned towards me just as I entered the doorway. I drew back and bumped into the doorframe.

"Do you need another handshake?" he asked with clear amusement.

"No, thank you."

As I moved past him, I felt a series of chills creep down my back. There was something about that man, other than his oversized ego, that I just couldn't stand.

I took quick steps down the hall, looking back only once to see Micah and Nolan standing in the doorway together, having what looked like a very heated argument. Nolan's chiseled face was tense with what looked like anger. Micah, though, wore the same smug look, posturing as if he were superior to all around him.

I was so focused on the scene with the two men that I collided with Selene.

"There you are," she said with a smile. "I went to pour you a glass of champagne, and you were gone." She paused and leaned down to get a better look at my face. "You don't look so good. Are you okay?"

Something drew her attention to the men down the hall. I watched as her eyes narrowed on the scene before she looked back at me with more concern. "Did something-"

"I don't feel good," I interrupted quickly. I was not going to have a conversation about what had just happened in the other conference room. "I think I'm coming down with something. Do you think I could leave early today? I know that it just started, but I don't think that I would be very productive today."

Her dark eyes stared at me for several seconds before she said in a careful voice, "Of course. It will most likely be a lax day anyway, and we need you in top condition when things get rolling. Are you sure that's all? You aren't upset about anything?"

Yes, I was upset. Mad at the whole world was more like it, but I was not getting into that either right now. "Nope. I just don't feel good." I was learning that it was better not to say too much.

"Okay, well, you go home and get some rest. Call us if you need anything."

She squeezed my shoulder even as she kept her eyes on Nolan and Micah, who seemed to have come to some agreement. Walking around me, she headed towards them, and I continued heading in the opposite direction. I grabbed my purse from my cubicle and headed towards the elevators.

I waited a few minutes for the elevator. When I heard it ding and saw the doors open in front of me, I breathed a sigh of relief. If I could just make it back to the apartment. I would cry, sleep, shower, and begin to look for a new living arrangement. Maybe not in that order, but it was a good to-do list.

Leaning against the back of the elevator, I watched the steel doors move in front of me. They were nearly closed when a hand shot through the opening. Slowly, they reversed course, and the hand entered the elevator followed by an arm and then a body. Leta's body actually.

"I heard you were going home. That you weren't feeling well." She stood between the doors.

"Yep."

"Elena, about last night..."

"No," I said more forcefully than I intended. "We are not talking about last night." I crossed my arms over my chest, hoping that she was reading my body language. Which clearly said, leave me alone.

Clearly, there was a miscommunication because she stepped into the elevator, allowing the doors to close. "I know this week has been hard on you," she began.

"Hard!" I exclaimed. It was only the two of us in the elevator. "This past week has been hell, Leta."

She looked struck by the volume of my voice. "I'm sorry."

"Sorry? Really? You think that makes up for everything?" I was yelling at her. I seldom yelled at people, but I was just so full of rage.

Her features hardened. "I can't help what I am, Elena. There are just some things that we can't change about ourselves."

"Oh, what things would that be? The selfishness, the complete lack of self-respect, or your lying, betraying-"

"I did not lie to you," she objected.

"You just didn't tell me the truth. I suppose you don't think of that as lying, do you?"

"I don't just go around telling people that I'm a nymph, Elena. They don't usually react well." She looked at me pointedly as if to imply I was an example of that.

"I think I took it pretty darn well. Even after you started growing branches and bark," I shot back.

Her anger dimmed slightly. "That doesn't usually happen. It's never happened before. I wasn't lying when I said I never get sick."

"Thank goodness for that! I don't think any of us could survive if you did."

The comment seemed to wound her. "I wasn't that bad."

"You were delusional, needy, demanding, and at times suicidal. Do you realize that I haven't slept in over a week? I was so busy taking care of you and trying to keep your secret with all that was going on at work."

"I didn't ask you to keep it."

I squeezed my aching temples and stared at her in disbelief. "So, you're saying I should have just told people about your tree and the bark and the pustules?"

"No, of course not." Leta was at a loss for words. Wow, who knew!

"I mean why wouldn't you want me to protect your secret when you had gone to such lengths to protect Miguel's secret? Is that some kind of code among people like you?"

"That's why you're mad because things didn't go well with Miguel last night," she said with an air of victory.

"No, Leta. I'm mad...because the person that I trusted and considered my closest friend let me get involved with a wolf in sheep's clothing. I thought you were my friend. How could you not tell me?" Those damn tears came back.

Leta looked as torn as I felt, and her voice was gentler when she said, "How was I going to tell you? Would you have believed me if I said, 'Hey, Elena, that hottie you like is a werewolf.' Until you saw me sick, you wouldn't have believed any of this. Besides, I didn't see any danger in you getting involved with him." She paused as the elevator dinged. "I wouldn't have let anything hurt you. I swear."

She looked so sincere, so upset by the argument that I wanted to cry more. But I refused to break down again until I was buried under a pile of blankets.

I released a loud sigh, letting some of the anger go. Being angry wasn't going to fix anything. Getting out of this crazy situation was. "Listen, Leta, it doesn't really matter."

She narrowed her eyes and asked cautiously, "It doesn't?"

"No, because...I'm moving out." The elevator doors opened. I took advantage of her surprise and stepped around her gasping form.

However, it didn't take long for her to catch up with me as I walked towards the exit. "You're moving out?" She asked softly, still in shock.

"I think it's for the best." I kept walking, looking longingly at the doors ahead.

"You're moving out!"

Her shock did not last long. She stepped in front of me to block my escape.

"What do you mean you are moving out?" I had heard that shrieking voice before; the last few times she had gotten in a fight with Corbett. I guess I would have to be watching for lice and fleas. Infestations seemed to be Leta's favorite form of revenge.

Her raised voice attracted the attention of the few people in the lobby. I looked around, giving them a reassuring smile. Leta was oblivious to them. She stared at me expectantly, as if her outburst was going to change my answer.

I stepped close and said in a calming voice, "Leta, I don't think we want the entire lobby to know our business, do we?"

She didn't even look around to see what I was talking about. Instead, she put her hands on her hips and continued to stare me down.

Fine. It's not like I had a secret to protect. We could air all our dirty laundry if she wanted. "I can't take any more of this...weirdness." I gestured to her.

She at least had the sense to understand it was not a compliment. Looking slightly taken aback, "Weirdness? Are you calling me weird?"

I just stared at her. That didn't need an answer.

"I am one of the sanest," she leaned forward to whisper, "nymphs you will ever meet."

I continued to stare at her.

"I am," she said indignantly.

"That's the thing, I don't want to meet any more nymphs or werewolves or any other make-believe creatures out there. I just want to go back to my normal life where the closest I come to werewolves and vampires is *Underworld*."

"You think Miguel and I are the only 'weird' people out there?" she asked with less heat.

"I don't care if there are more like you guys; I just don't want to know about it." I stepped around her and walked away.

"Normal doesn't exist, Elena," Leta said in that matter-of-a-fact tone.

I kept walking but called out over my shoulder, "It did at one time, so it can again."

Leta did not follow me out onto the street.

I ordered Chinese. After bingeing on some of the greasiest food on earth, I fell into a carb/exhaustion coma that was preceded by a bout of crying. I didn't care how long I slept; I figured my body would know when enough was enough, which was about eight hours later.

Rolling out of bed, I stretched my arms over my head. For the first time in a week, there was no tension. Rest had been so needed, yet I had been so deprived that I forgot what adequate sleep felt like. Glancing at the clock, I winced to realize that Leta would be on her way home if not already home. I had a feeling that our argument was not over yet. No way she was leaving it where we had.

Well, she could bring it. I was rested and recharged and could handle any Leta-illogic that she came up with.

But first I was going to take a shower. I peeked into the hall. Just because I was ready to confront my roommate again did not mean was going looking for a fight. The apartment seemed to be empty though a faint mumbling voice sounded from behind Leta's door. I assumed she was on the phone. I proceeded to the bathroom.

It was a glorious shower. Amazing how things seemed so much better with enough sleep. And a firm resolve.

I exited the bathroom, towel drying my hair when I noticed that Leta sat at the kitchen table. She sat silently, staring deeply into the cup she held. Momentarily, I thought of asking her if everything was okay, but I decided not.

I knew that she wouldn't take the news of my moving out well, but I worried for a moment that she might take it badly...really, badly. After all, I had been a witness to at least two fights with her boyfriend. Leta was mentally unbalanced after each.

Perhaps, I should be more worried about her.

Nope, I'm not going to worry, I told myself. I had exhausted myself worrying about Leta the past week. Better to just turn away and bunk down in my room for the rest of the night. I turned to go but paused as I heard a knock on the door. Leta would get it, I assured myself.

But as I took a few more steps towards my room and heard another knock, I began to wonder if she really would get the door.

Turning back, I saw that she still sat there looking into the depths of the cup.

"Okay, I'll get the door," I muttered to myself. Giving her a scrutinizing look as I passed the kitchen, Leta appeared so wrapped up in her own thoughts that she wasn't aware of the knocking.

But I wasn't going to worry about her.

I had my hand on the doorknob when I heard Leta say from the kitchen, "I called them while you were in the shower."

I leaned back to look at her. Still, she stared into the cup with an expression of grim resolve. What was that about? I was about to ask when there was a pounding on the door.

I decided to open it instead of trying to figure out Leta's cryptic comment. Whoever was out there was clearly impatient.

Opening the door, I found myself face-to-face with Farah and Selene. They shared the same grim look as Leta.

"Hey, what are you guys doing here?"

Selene took a deep breath, about to answer, when Farah said brusquely, "We heard you want to move out."

Farah then pushed her way into the apartment. Turning back to Selene, I saw her sigh heavily.

"Mind if we come in?" she asked nicely.

Since Farah was already in, there was no point in refusing Selene. So, I stood aside and gestured for Selene to enter. She smiled at me with something that looked a lot like pity.

I closed the door, turned back to them, and was hit by the first verbal missile.

"You cannot move out." Farah's command was said so simply as if she didn't expect anyone to dispute it.

"Excuse me?"

Selene stepped in front of Farah before she could speak again.

"We think that your decision to move out was made when you weren't thinking clearly. Leta said that you haven't been sleeping well this week. Sleep deprivation can make us think unclearly."

Were they here to talk me out of my plans? How had they even known?

I looked at Leta with a hard stare. *'I called them while you were in the shower,'* she had said. And of course, having been her friends longer, they were here to protect her interests. The problem was they couldn't possibly know all the facts, because if they did, they'd be helping me find a new place and offering to pack my stuff.

"I know that you guys are concerned about Leta, but you don't know what's going on here. This should stay between me and Leta."

"We're concerned about you," Farah said with the same abruptness that left me momentarily speechless.

Me? "I'm fine."

I felt a little defensive. Farah stood with hands on hips, thoroughly assessing me. Selene hovered near the door as if I might run at any moment. Leta hadn't moved. Something was going on here. Something weird.

"What the hell is this?" I asked, instinctually feeling like I should prepare for flight.

"This is an intervention," Farah and Selene said at the same time.

"An intervention for what?" I demanded.

"For you," Leta said softly coming up behind me.

I realized I was surrounded. "Look, you guys don't understand. I have good reasons for leaving," I tried to explain to Farah and Selene. I had a feeling that I would be trapped if that's what they wanted. "Leta is not what...who you think-"

"I'm a werewolf," Farah announced point blank. "And she's a djinn," she said with a head nod towards Selene.

The edges of my vision started to go black. Oh, hell.

Chapter 14

"**I** think she might faint." Leta's voice seemed far away even though I knew she was only a couple of feet away.

"Nah, she'll be fine," Farah said in front of me.

I wasn't fine; I was falling. Somehow my brain just shut down, and the parts that controlled balance and standing were now offline. I suddenly couldn't feel my legs. I knew they were there, but they were beyond my control. I couldn't have made them do anything even if I had wanted them to. Vaguely, I was aware of the view changing. One moment Farah was in front of me with her hands on her hips and eyes narrowed, and the next I was rapidly encountering the floor.

To my further embarrassment, Farah caught me before I could hit the floor.

She helped me stand. As I became more erect, my head started to spin. My hands clasped it in a death grip as if that would stop the spinning. I think I groaned as the dizziness forced me to close my eyes.

"I think she should probably sit down for this," Selene said.

Oh, God! Now what?

I felt myself being hefted into the chair in the living room. My head rolled back, cushioned by the back of the chair. Slowly, the dizziness passed as I listened to the voices around me.

"I can't believe she fainted like that," Farah said.

"I told you she was not taking it well," Leta said calmly.

"All week I watched her, and she seemed okay. I mean, she was exhausted but didn't let a word slip about you, Leta," Selene added.

"You know, I think it was Wolf-boy that did it."

"What did he do?"

"He's a werewolf," that pointing-out-the-obvious tone of Leta's.

A soft growl, "And? What's wrong with werewolves?"

"Nothing, besides the fur that gets everywhere on a full moon. I have no problem with them. Some of my favorite partners were wolfies," Leta reflected.

"You know, there was that one," Selene said slowly as if she was trying to remember something, "Oh, what was his name?"

"Was that the red-haired one?"

"No, not him."

"Anyway, he was fantastic in bed. He did this thing…"

That was enough, spinning head or not, I couldn't take anymore. "Please stop! Please, please just stop."

I opened my eyes to find Leta, Farah, and Selene standing over me, all looking at me like I had just interrupted a perfectly normal conversation. There was nothing normal about sleeping with werewolves!

Werewolves! Scary, uncontrollable creatures out to kill us all!

I didn't realize I had shouted that last bit until three sets of eyes narrowed in on me.

"She's losing it," Leta said sadly.

"I am not losing it," I shouted again. My volume button was broken.

Farah leaned in with what could have been called a mischievous smile, and I shrank back.

"Let me ask you this: do you find me scary, and uncontrollable, and think that I might be out to kill you?"

Before finding out she was a werewolf, I had found Farah intimidating. Upon finding out what she was, I was naturally terrified. So, I answered, "Yes."

She seemed to consider that for a moment before giving a soft grunt of satisfaction and pulling away. "A little fear's healthy."

I was healthy then.

"Maybe we should get her a shot of something," Leta suggested.

"No, let's start with tea. We can always move to the alcohol later," Farah recommended.

"Oh, good idea," Leta bounced off to the kitchen.

Selene leaned forward, and I drew back from her. She seemed to notice the withdrawal and paused. "Are you comfortable, Elena?"

"I'm not sure I could be comfortable at this moment," I said honestly.

Farah turned away and went to join Leta in the kitchen. "Do you have any of those cookies?" I heard her call as she left the room.

Selene and I watched her go. I jumped slightly when Selene took a seat on the ottoman. "I know this is a lot to take in. Farah and I thought it would be good for you to know the truth though."

Her eyes were kind and understanding. I allowed myself to relax a bit.

"I don't know how I'm supposed to deal with this. All the friends I've made in the city have turned out not to be real."

Selene smirked, and her eyes twinkled. "I don't seem real to you? Farah and Leta don't seem real? If you think that you are dreaming, I'll have Farah come in and nip you." Mischief glowed in her eyes.

"No," I said more forcefully than I intended. "No, I don't think that I'm dreaming. I know this isn't a dream. What I meant was that you're not people, you're fairy tale characters."

Selene considered that. "No, we're still people. We're just people who happen to also be fairy tale characters." I was not sold, and she laughed at my expression. "I don't think you understand the benefits of having unique friends like us."

"I have seen the 'benefits' of having a nymph friend, and honestly, I think I could do without them."

She laughed. "Okay, I admit that was not a great introduction to Leta's nymph side." She leaned forward and whispered, "Was she really covered in bark with branches popping out?"

I nodded.

"Oh, I would have loved to see that," she sighed.

"You've never seen Leta with bark skin?" I asked doubtfully.

"Nope. Leta had never seen Leta in bark-skin before. Truthfully, this was the first time she's ever been sick." She looked thoughtful for a moment. "When you found out that Leta was a nymph, you didn't immediately panic. You took care of her. What's different now?"

I thought about that. What Selene said was true; I hadn't panicked when I had first found out. Yet, somewhere between first finding out and now, I feared all of it.

"I didn't have any other choice. She was sick, and I just went into crisis management mode, I guess."

And then, I had just been stressed out, exhausted, and overwhelmed.

"Would it help you take this all in if I created a disaster?"

I know my eyes were big as I asked slowly, "You can do that?"

Selene just shrugged as if it was an everyday thing, but her eyes still glowed with amusement. They literally glowed. I leaned forward, suddenly driven by my curiosity, and stared into her eyes. "Your eyes are glowing; do you know that?"

Before she could answer, Leta and Farah rejoined us.

"They do that a lot," Leta said as she set a cup of steaming liquid on the coffee table. She handed me the other cup she carried. "It took me a while to get used to it."

I raised an eyebrow at that, but she didn't seem to notice. Instead, she joined Farah on the couch. The three of them sipped the tea. I started to take a sip but paused, taking a hard look at the creamed tea as if I could visually detect a poison. I even sniffed it.

Leta's gasp drew my attention, and I looked up. "Do you think I would poison you, Elena? Have I poisoned you with tea before?" She was hurt by the implication.

Farah's laughter saved me from having to answer though. "She has been living with you long enough to know that you would at least consider if not actually poison someone...especially if you thought they deserved it." She raised her cup to me. "Don't worry, I watched her make it. It's not poisoned."

She took a long sip to prove the point.

Leta huffed in indignation. "I would not poison you, Elena." We stared at each other, she waiting for me to take a drink and me waiting for her to admit to the poison. She won the staring contest, and I took a drink.

I waited but nothing happened. If she had poisoned me, it might be a slow-acting one. I took another sip as the four of us enjoyed our tea in silence.

"So, where should we start?" Leta perked up, obviously over my insulting insinuation.

"Start with what?" I asked. I cradled the cup to me, trying to absorb all the warmth. The heat was amazingly comforting.

"We thought that we should clear up any misconceptions that you have about nymphs, werewolves, and djinns. That way, maybe you wouldn't feel the need to run away," Leta explained.

"I'm pretty sure I have an idea of what goes on with nymphs," I muttered to myself, but they heard it.

"That was one week, Elena," Leta sighed. "That does not happen often."

"I wasn't just talking about that."

"I was born in Greece," she started while settling into the sofa, "One hundred and seven years ago. I'm still so young." She laughed at my gapping expression. "We spend the first hundred years or so of our life in our mother's tree before we connect with our own.

"Anyway, I lived there for most of my life..."

She described her hometown as a village on one of the islands in loving detail. Of course, it was paradise; everything that you would imagine a Greek island to be. Listening to her describe the surrounding beauty made me want to pack up and go on vacation where I could lay on a white sand beach as the Mediterranean sun warmed my skin.

It was a place that still clung to old beliefs though little old ladies chatted on cell phones to their grandchildren as they roamed the streets on a sunny afternoon. The buildings were old but cherished. The people were superstitious but friendly. Her family had been there for centuries. It was a place that had seemed to find the secret that allowed for a melding of the old and modern. And Leta loved it with every bit of her soul. You could hear it in the way she described it.

Nymph-ism, as I learned from Leta, was passed down from mother to daughter. Sometimes a daughter would not inherit, but the line was strong in her family for the past four generations. According to Leta, her pox wasn't all that uncommon. Nymphs were so connected to their trees that they suffered when the trees suffered. Leta's tree had been sick after its malnourished existence in the park and the stressful transplantation. Thus, Leta had been sick as a result.

Young nymphs, well dryads to be specific, went through a special ceremony at adolescence that involved finding their tree soul mates. Apparently, a dryad's soul could not survive in the human body for too many years after coming to age. Leta explained that a dryad would connect with a tree, a special tree. After finding that special tree, Leta placed her soul into the tree where it would be safe and grow. In return for the housing of her soul, it was the dryad's duty to protect and nourish the tree, for her soul could only thrive if the tree did and vice versa.

"So, your soul is in that tree," I pointed to the tree, "right now?" I heard the disbelief in my tone.

"Yep."

"Huh." What else do you say to that? "That doesn't make any sense."

"The science behind souls and soul transference is very complicated." As if that was going to help me.

"I was brought up with the idea that a soul resides in the body, that it gives life to the body. Maybe that's what I'm having a hard time with. Is this," I indicated her body with the waving of my hand, "just a shell? I mean, is command central over there, relaying orders to this?"

I pointed to the tree and back at her. Leaning forward, I took a closer look, "Are you in there?"

Leta laughed. "This isn't science fiction."

Nope, just fantasy.

"Think of it this way," Selene volunteered. "A part of Leta's soul is in her body. She isn't just an animated corpse."

Leta made a sound of disgust with a matching expression of disgust. "Eh, zombies."

I felt my heart pound and my eyes go wide. I looked over my shoulder as if one might be sneaking up as we spoke. "Oh, please tell me zombies aren't real. I can't take that."

Selene shook her head. "There are no zombies...here." Not very reassuring. I would have preferred a definitive, no, they do not exist.

"Anyway," Selene continued in that voice she used for meetings, the one that politely demanded my attention. "Leta's soul is a little too much for her body. She can't contain all of it in a human form; thus, she stores some of it in a tree. Does that make more sense?"

It kind of did. Leta was such a dynamic personality I could imagine her soul being a little too much.

"Will you age?" I couldn't contain the thought that just popped into my head.

"Of course. I do not look the same way I did twenty years ago."

Twenty years...I found a new reason to hate Leta. Seventy-five years in her body and she looked the same age as me. Again, I realized how unfair life was.

"It's like doggie years," Farah remarked with a stretch.

"Except about three dryad years for every human year." Leave it to Leta to quantify it for us.

"When did you come here?"

She thought about it. "Six years ago. I spent twenty-some years just traveling around and exploring. Then when I was in my sixties, I decided it was time to think about a career."

"Sixties...good time to think to start thinking about careers," I said.

Leta smiled and nodded in agreement. "Exactly."

I watched the sarcasm fly straight over her head. However, Selene and Farah's snickering told me that they got it.

"So, you decided it was time for a job, came to the city and just packed up your tree and brought it over here?"

Again, the sarcasm was missed, as Leta nodded her head in all seriousness. "What? You really just packed up the tree and brought it from Greece, across an ocean and planted it in the park?"

She nodded again, seemingly unaware of why this would seem strange.

"How did you get a tree over here? Fed-ex? No, wait, do you have some special power that you used?" I eyed her suspiciously. If we were going to co-habit even for just a few more days, I needed to know this sort of thing.

"Leta doesn't have THAT kind of power," Farah responded. I looked from her to Leta.

"What kind of power does Leta have?" I asked cautiously.

"Well, she can make anything grow just by touching it. Man, beast, and plant." Farah took a long sip of her tea, completely unperturbed by this.

"Like grow taller?" I asked.

"Plants, yes. Men and beast...more like growing out," Farah circled her hand around the area of her crotch and indicated a movement that did indeed go out. I stared at her in confusion. Realizing that I needed a bit more, Farah gave a little pelvic thrust. "You know, grow..."

Okay, now I had it. "Uhh, I don't want to know. I don't want to know." I raised my hands to my ears as the three of them started to laugh.

"Leta does this thing when she enters a room," Selene started to explain. "She infuses the air with, well, sex."

"Yes, I've seen. The men fall all over themselves when she is near."

Selene stared at me questioningly.

"Oh, come on." I looked to Leta to verify this. She too just looked at me without understanding. "Have we not all been going to the same meetings?" They continued to stare at me. "Never mind." Maybe they were so used to it that they didn't see it anymore. "Anyway, how did you get the tree here?"

"Selene brought it over," Leta said as if that explained it all.

I stared at her with wide eyes then slowly turned my gaze to Selene. "Okay, how did you get the tree here?"

"Magic," she said with a laugh and accompanying jazz hands.

"I don't think you're joking."

"She's a djinn, Elena. Of course, she can do magic," Leta retorted.

"I don't know what a djinn is!"

Heartburn accompanied the frustration. I really needed to get some Tums. I rubbed my chest and took a calming breath. "First the djinn, then the tree," I said firmly.

"Okay, Elena," Leta said in a placating tone.

"You probably already know what a djinn is; you just know it by another name. In most Western cultures, djinns are known as genies."

"You're a genie!" I exclaimed.

Selene laughed. "Sort of. I'm not the kind that you think of. First of all, I don't live in a lamp or bottle. I do not wear midriff-bearing outfits with parachute pants. And I do not call anyone master."

"Do you grant wishes?"

She narrowed her eyes at my eagerness. Like any normal person wouldn't have been excited by that.

"Only when I feel like it."

"Or if someone has trapped her into it," Farah added.

Selene did not appear happy with that information exchange as she glared at Farah. Not that it did any good. Farah just glared back.

"What? You don't honestly think that Elena would try to trap you into giving her a wish, do you? She'd have to figure it out first."

I nodded. Getting on a genie's, I mean, djinn's bad side was not something I wanted to risk. Selene seemed to be satisfied with that logic and continued with her story.

"I used magic to get Leta's tree here. I visualized what I wanted and then snapped my fingers."

Oh, so many questions...I wasn't sure where to start. Shaking my head, I hoped the jumbled mess of thoughts would fall into place. It didn't.

"Why...How...wait a minute." I turned on Leta. "If Selene can just snap her fingers, and make your tree appear wherever, why didn't you get her to save your tree? Why did I have to help you cart it from the park in a toy wagon?"

Leta shrugged. "There wasn't time."

"You carted the tree here in a toy wagon?" Farah managed to ask in disbelief despite the laughter.

"In the rain," I added grumpily. Farah laughed harder. I shook my head and looked back at Selene, who was smiling with amusement. "So, your magic, does it have limits?"

She seemed surprised by the question. Maybe it was the harshness of my tone as I asked. It was out of concern for my safety.

She read my thoughts when she answered slightly offended, "I don't use it against people. And, yes, there is a limit. Using magic is exhausting. Doing little things, here and there isn't a problem. But bigger things can leave me without magic for days. It was almost a month after moving Leta's tree here that I was able to do even something small."

That was a little comforting. But I thought of another alarming thing I had noticed about Selene. "No, I do not read minds," she answered before I could ask. "Sometimes though I get little flashes of the future."

I was not convinced. However, before I could say anything about it, Farah stood and stretched with a loud sigh.

"Time for more tea," she said. Selene helped her gather the cups. I was surprised to find that my cup was empty. I allowed Selene to take it from me. Farah and Selene left me alone in the living room with Leta.

"How you doing?" she asked me softly.

A sarcastic comment rose to my lips, but I held it back. When had I become so catty? Instead of saying something toxic that was sure to hurt Leta's feelings, I sighed and told her the truth instead.

"I'm not sure. I know I just jumped into action when you got sick, and I even told myself that I was okay with you being a nymph. I might have been if it weren't for all this." I waved my hand in the air. "Werewolves and djinns who snap their fingers and make things happen...it's a lot." I debated whether or not to add another bit of truth, but decided it was better to just be upfront.

"I don't know if I want to be a part of this. It might still be best for me to move out because I have a feeling that staying here will just bring more chaos into my life."

Leta looked sympathetic and understanding. She reached over to squeeze my hand. "I can't understand what you are going through because this chaos has been a normal part of life for me. But I could see why it would be hard for you. Listen to what else they have to say and then give it a few days to settle in. If you still want to move out,

I'll help you find a place...free of supernatural roommates." She gave me a reassuring smile that I couldn't help but return.

"Okay." It sounded like a reasonable request.

Selene and Farah returned with more tea, and the story of the tree was told. It turned out that Leta did not need to live close to her tree. As long as it was healthy, so was she. After moving to the city, she knew that she would be there for a while and felt that it was important to have her tree close. Having become friends with Selene, she found a way to easily make that possible. And until a week ago, her tree had been quite safe in the park. I looked over to the tree in the corner as Selene and Leta told the tale of transplanting the tree and wondered what we would do with it. It couldn't just stay in the apartment. However, that was a worry for another day. I wasn't going to be here to worry about it.

Selene had been a city girl her entire life. Her family had originally been from the Middle East, where I learned djinns were born, but had lived in the U.S. for many generations. Like Leta, Selene was born as her supernatural self. The "curse" as it was called ran in the family but did not affect every member. Apparently, there were usually only two members of a family at a time born as djinns, most often separated by generation or two. Selene's grandmother was a djinn born with powers. The magic had skipped her mother, though Selene swore her mother could "pull a trick" now and then.

The family's birthright was then passed to Selene, who didn't fully develop powers until she had passed into her twenties. She admitted a bit reluctantly that she hadn't mastered them as well as she wanted. Using magic was something she was still working on. Much to my horror, she told me that occasionally things went very wrong. I did not want to be around when any of that happened.

With another round of tea, Farah told me her story. She explained that werewolves came in two types: those born as werewolves and those who had been bitten by one in werewolf form.

She had been born into a family of werewolves. However, she was the only one in her family of four brothers to be a werewolf.

"Wait, you have four brothers, and none of them are werewolves?"

Farah smiled. "That's right, and they were none too happy about it, either. I wasn't your typical little sister. I saved my brothers from being beaten up a few times." She beamed with pride at the memory.

Her father was a werewolf. There were many theories among werewolves as to why some offspring inherited the gene and some didn't. One of the theories suggested that children conceived in wolf form came out as werewolves. Considering that Farah's mom was not a werewolf, she didn't give too much credit to that idea. Some theorized that it was a recessive gene. Another theory stated that if a woman ate raw meat during her pregnancy, she would have a wolf baby. I had to stop Farah as the theories became stranger. It was enough to know that she was a fully functioning werewolf.

Which meant that once a month, around the full moon, she would suffer what she called the change. Selene and Leta assured me that it was best to avoid Farah at those times. After stocking her fridge with yummy, bloody meat, they locked Farah in her apartment for a night. She only changed form on one night, though 'moody' had been used to describe her company the couple days leading up to and after the full moon.

I assured her that I was okay giving her plenty of space when the full moon came around. I needed to pay attention to that from now on. Getting a calendar with the moon phases would be a good investment. Even if I didn't stay with Leta, there were other werewolves in the city, and it would be good to know when the full moon was. I'd be sure to stay inside on those nights. With the door locked.

I finished my cooling tea in one long swig, only to find the three of them looking at me expectantly. I stared back in confusion, unsure of what they were expecting.

"Do you feel better?" Leta asked.

I thought before answering. Surprisingly, I did feel a little better. I still wasn't sure that I wanted to stay, but I didn't feel as angry as I had earlier in the day.

I'm better," I saw their faces light up and continued quickly, "but I still need some time to think about this."

"I don't think she fully understands the benefits of having us as friends," Farah said seriously to Leta and Selene.

"No, no, I think I do. Selene," I turned to her, "can do the occasional magical favor. I think that she's already done one or two for me." She made a noncommittal noise. "And she is a wonderful caller ID."

She snorted at that.

I turned to Leta, "You are the go-to girl if I want to grow a garden or flowers or something plantlike. You also put some kind of lust buzz in the air." Leta preened a bit as she nodded in agreement.

"And you, Farah," I didn't know what to say. I was still stuck on the full moon problem.

"Farah," Selene was quick to supply the answer, "is like a bloodhound. She can sniff out anything. And she's stronger than most men. That is a useful thing to have." Selene nodded enthusiastically.

"And she can scare the shit out of anyone," Leta added.

"And someone has to keep catching your ass. Otherwise, that face of yours is going to get misshapen in no time," Farah added helpfully.

"Right, those are all the great things about having Farah as a friend." I leaned towards Farah. "Thanks for that, by the way. I believe you may have saved me from a concussion."

They looked moderately pleased.

"Give me a couple of days. Just let me sort it all out."

The three of them readily agreed though Leta looked a little more reluctant than the other two. The mugs were gathered and taken to the kitchen. I murmured good night to them and headed back to my room. I plugged my phone into the charger, and the display showed the time was well past midnight. The meeting or "intervention" as they had called it had lasted much longer than I realized.

I set my phone down just as it beeped. Looking at the display again, I saw that Miguel had sent another text.

We need to talk. Soon. Please.

It was a variation on the other texts and messages he had left throughout the day. I wasn't ready to confront that particular beast yet, but when I was, I knew that I would be better prepared after talking with Farah. I knew more about werewolves now. Werewolves and dryads and djinns...oh, my!

I shook my head. When had my life turned into this tragic comedy? Deciding to deal with it tomorrow, I crawled into bed and turned out the light. Cuddled under the blankets, I quickly fell to sleep and dreamed of warm flames and comforting embers.

Chapter 15

Leta and I spent the weekend tiptoeing around each other with an awkwardness that had never been there before. She seemed eager for confirmation that I was not going to leave, and I was anxious that she would ask. I didn't have an answer to give her. I feared having to tell her that even after the well-intentioned talk with her and the others, I was still tempted to just run away.

My anxiety was pointless though because she never asked.

I refused to think about Selene and Farah, at least until I saw them again. Something I was not looking forward to, but for now out of sight, out of mind. I didn't have that escape with Leta.

Instead, we developed a strange way of interacting with each other. Leta went out of her way to be considerate. She offered to make me breakfast and asked if I wanted a sandwich. I was secretly delighted by the smell of her pot roast on Sunday night.

For my part, I tried to politely refuse, making excuses about why I didn't need something. I already ate, even though I hadn't. I don't have any laundry, even though I hadn't done it in over a week. However, my self-imposed distance was weakened by the sight of her cutting the perfectly done roast and the smell of garlic mashed potatoes. No matter how hard I wanted to distance myself, I couldn't resist the heavenly feast she prepared that night.

She smiled when I cautiously entered the kitchen. "You want some? I made plenty." We had enough to eat leftovers for the next few days.

"Sure," I tried to sound uninterested even though my mouth was watering.

"Great." I know she tried to sound less excited, but it was the first offering of hers I had accepted all weekend. She was excited.

I sat at the table and watched as she finished carving the meat. It reminded me of when she had been sick and had attempted to cut the strange bumps from her bark skin with that same knife. I laughed at how that image contrasted with the current image of her: a domestic goddess dressed in a flowered dress and pink apron with her long hair pulled back in a neat bun.

She turned to me with a questioning look. Her head tilted and her perfectly made-up lips formed a small pout. She was the 1950s housewife now, but she had been a dryad who had looked more like a tree monster just a few days ago.

How did the two meld together? I wondered how the two images were perfectly Leta in my head.

"Nothing, sorry," I murmured as she continued to look at me.

She decided it was better not to pursue it and went back to cutting. When she finished, she wiped her hands on the ruffled apron. The knife was set in the sink, and two plates were piled with meat, creamy potatoes, and a vegetable-filled salad. She set a plate in front of me before removing her apron and sitting down across the table.

We ate in silence. I had developed a strange habit as a child of eating my least favorite food first. Vegetables were a requirement in my house, and without eating them, there was no chance of getting dessert. Even as I developed a liking for them as an adult, I still ate them first. I bit into the crisp lettuce and shredded carrots as a thought popped into my head and out of my mouth before I could process it.

"Is this considered cannibalism?"

Leta paused in the act of raising a fork full of salad to her mouth. Her wide eyes stared at me.

"For you, I mean," I added to clarify. Not that it really clarified anything for Leta as she continued to stare at me with her fork frozen in midair.

"I mean you're kind of a tree and that's a plant, and you're about to eat another plant."

This was why it would have been better if my brain had processed that thought first. It had made more sense in my head.

Leta stared at me in silence for a moment longer before bursting into laughter. She dropped her fork and laughed uncontrollably. It was infectious, and I soon joined her. The image of a tree munching on a carrot popped into my head, and I had to grab my side. She tried to say something a few times, but every time was overcome by more snorting giggles. And the laughter continued to escalate until we sat at the table grabbing our sides and gasping for breath. It felt good to relax as if I hadn't done it for a long time.

It was several more minutes before either of us could breathe normally. She was the first to speak.

"You know I never thought of it like that, but…" she paused for another giggle and wiped a tear from her eye. "No, I don't consider it cannibalism." She picked up the fork and eyed the salad.

"But if it is, just call me Hannibal Lector because, damn, I love salad!" She took a big bite and made a loud and satisfied yum, yum sound as she chewed.

That sent both of us into another fit of laughter. When the laughing subsided, we continued to eat our meal in silence, though the tension was gone this time. We made satisfied sounds while consuming our food in a relaxed silence. Like the laughter, it felt good to be comfortable with Leta again.

I devoured everything on my plate, and my stomach was on the verge of bursting. I didn't care. Emotionally, I was perfectly sated. Pushing back from the table slightly, I slouched in my chair to accommodate my full belly.

Leta followed suit, and we sat there as mirror images; feet planted wide on the floor, our backs slouched, and our hands folded across our bellies. We even gave a deep, contented sigh at the same time. I chuckled, and Leta followed.

"Oh, please, don't make me laugh. Please."

"I think I might bust if I laugh too hard."

"I hear you there." Leta's laughter had subsided. "I think I'm going to crawl onto the sofa for the next few days as my body digests this." She struggled to get up.

"That was great, Leta. Thank you. I'll do the dishes," I managed to get to my feet and looked towards the sink full of dishes.

"Leave it for now. You ate as much as I did. Come, let us digest," she commanded in a lofty tone as I followed her into the other room. She did just as she said she would and collapsed on the sofa. I reclined on the big chair.

I felt drowsy and content. My eyes drifted shut, and I started to fall asleep. The apartment was quiet, so I assumed Leta was doing the same. Sleep had almost taken me when I was startled awake by the vibrating ring of my phone on the coffee table. I jumped a bit and looked over at the lit screen. It had woken Leta up too. She reached over from the sofa and lifted the screen to where she could see it.

Giving me a concerned look, she simply said, "Miguel."

I shook my head and snuggled deeper into the cushions. Leta nodded and rejected the call, sending it to voicemail. *If there's room*, I thought. I hadn't checked my voicemail in a long time. The multiple messages from Miguel were getting to me.

"I know I'm the last person who should say anything about your relationship with Miguel." I heard Leta say from the sofa. She sat up, looking at me.

"Yeah, and?" I mumbled. Not exactly a go-ahead on the advice, but she took it.

"I don't think he meant to lie to you."

"Kind of like how you didn't mean to lie to me?"

"No, I did mean to lie to you," she said thoughtfully. I narrowed my eyes at her, and she continued quickly. "I knew that you didn't know what I was, and I decided not to tell you. I think Miguel might have thought that you knew. Farah said that they both knew each other was a werewolf and maybe he thought..." her voice trailed off as she looked at me.

Undoubtedly, I had a sour expression that she took as a warning to shut up. When in fact, it was an expression of stubborn reluctance. Miguel had said that very same thing. He had thought that I had known because of my friends. If I looked back on that night, I'd have to admit that it could be easy to interpret the situation that way.

"No, I don't think he did either," I admitted. With the revelations of the weekend, I had had a lot of time to think about things.

"So, why are you still so angry with him?" Leta asked gently.

I didn't answer because I didn't know the answer. For some reason, finding out that Miguel was supernatural had been too much. It was harder to accept than the dryad, djinn, and female werewolf altogether.

"Maybe," Leta ventured, recapturing my attention, "being with Miguel or any guy makes you feel too vulnerable."

When I just continued to stare at her, she decided it was okay to continue. "You were alone for a long time. I know you were busy with school and the internship, but as a woman with a lot of relationship experience, I'm pretty sure there was some other reason you were single."

"Not everyone has to be in a relationship, Leta. Some of us are quite happy alone." I hadn't meant it as an insult, but as the words came out, it sounded like one even to my ears. I cringed a little, but before I could apologize, Leta replied.

"You're right." She didn't sound offended but nodded thoughtfully. In that serious Leta tone, "I physically cannot be single. I have needs, and well, they're not like the average person's needs. I would start to wilt and wither away without a physical relationship. I might need constant sex because I'm a nymph, but I crave a connection with another person because I'm also human."

She leaned forward with her hands clasped in front of her.

"Despite all the baggage and insecurities we carry with us, we all need to connect with another person. We all want it on some level even if we are completely content with our lives."

I nodded in acknowledgment of what she was saying, though I didn't necessarily agree.

"I think that you took a chance for the first time in a long time with something that made you feel vulnerable. Because of those feelings of vulnerability, the truth felt like an even harsher betrayal. I bet it hit a nerve, though I don't know which one or why. There was a reason that it took you so long to take the leap again, and now you're telling yourself you shouldn't have because you got hurt."

I mumbled a 'maybe' and changed the subject.

We decided to watch a movie, and the night passed pleasantly. The tension between us was gone, but I could feel the building discomfort from her words earlier.

I hated that someone pegged me so well and pointed out the things that I couldn't see about myself. Or maybe the things that I didn't want to see about myself. I didn't want to think about it. And, though I tried hard to concentrate on the movie, I kept coming back to what Leta said.

Nothing was traumatizing about my last relationship. We had parted with a mutual agreement that things weren't working. He had been a nice guy with many of the same interests. And even though I knew early in the relationship that I was bored by being with someone who loved the same movies, books, and ice cream I did, I didn't do anything about it. Instead, I let the relationship continue and became a girlfriend that was only mildly interested. He stuck with it because he believed that it would get better; I stuck with it because I was waiting for something better. But better never came, and eventually, neither one of us could deny it just wasn't working.

With Miguel, I wondered if I had done the same thing I did with my last boyfriend. My feelings for him had never been more than lukewarm, but I hadn't found better yet.

I remembered the feeling of Nolan's arms closing in around me as I had fallen apart. Maybe the problem was that I had found better.

But it was so far out of my reach. I wouldn't ...and shouldn't...be able to obtain it, so why not settle for something just good enough?

Leta had suggested that I was afraid to be vulnerable. Was that why I hung on to men who could never touch the depths of my heart? If Nolan wasn't a client and interested, would I pursue him? Would I ignore the knowledge that he had the potential to penetrate that wall and get closer than anyone else ever had? Would I let him in?

Or would I run away from it because I was fully aware of the damage he could do?

I didn't want to be a coward, but I didn't want to be hurt either. Sadly, the thought of being a coward when it came to love was easier to accept than the thought of being hurt. I didn't want to face Miguel because I was hurt that he wasn't the nice normal guy I thought he should be. But I also didn't want to face that I was the worst person in this situation. I had used him to avoid forming any deeper feelings for a man who could invade my safe little bubble.

The credits rolled, and Leta turned off the TV. She yawned as she stretched her arms in the air. "I think I'm ready for bed."

I pushed aside my uncomfortable thoughts. "Sleep well," I said as I stood. "I'll do the dishes and put away the food, then head to bed."

"Oh, do you want me to help?"

"No," I said with a shake of my head. "Dishes are sort of meditative for me."

She nodded in understanding.

I entered the kitchen when I heard her say softly from behind me. "You'll have to confront the Miguel thing sooner or later, Elena."

I didn't turn around, just sighed. "I know. I just don't want to deal with it yet." I was good at being a coward.

"Okay," she said soothingly. "You just let me know when you're ready. Until then, I'll run interference. Good night."

She retired to her room.

I turned around and watched her close the door. I smiled. If anyone could run interference, it would be Leta. I shook my head as I realized that she would probably recruit Selene and Farah to run interference also.

I almost felt sorry for Miguel.

Almost.

Chapter 16

The atmosphere at work had changed markedly. There was still the impression of busy bees buzzing around, but they were happy worker bees. My team was still excited about impressing our clients. I high-fived a couple of people in the hall as I made my way to the tiny cubicle I occupied. Despite the drama of the weekend, I was in better spirits, well-rested, and ready to dive into work again. Nothing like the job to avoid the problems in your life. And now that work was no longer a stressor, I fully intended to use it as a distraction from all the other things happening in my life.

I got to my desk and saw the huge bouquet of roses in a thick glass vase. There was a small, ivory card. Though I already knew who they were from, I opened it.

I'm sorry, it read. It was from Miguel, of course.

They were pretty flowers, but I briefly considered just throwing them away.

"Ugh!"

I turned around and found Leta looking over the partition.

"You don't like flowers?" I asked skeptically.

She made a face of disgust. "Of course, I do...when they're still alive."

I could see how a tree spirit would feel about picked flowers.

"What is romantic about murdering those beauties and then sending them wrapped up in a bow? As if that makes up for the fact that they are dying?"

I tried to hide a smile. "So, you don't like when men send you flowers?"

She shook her head. "No, but if they give me flowers in a pot, I get very excited. That is romantic."

I smiled. "Now that you put it that way, I'm not sure I can enjoy being sent flowers again." I looked at the flowers. "I don't think I like apology flowers."

"You don't think?"

"Well, I've never gotten them before, but I'm becoming more certain that I don't like them."

"Apology sex is so much better." I gave her a look. "If you're into that sort of thing."

"Into what sort of thing?" Selene asked as she rounded the corner. I unintentionally pulled away from the partition. If she noticed the space I put between us, she chose not to react or comment.

"Apology sex," Leta answered.

Selene seemed to consider it. "It depends on who is apologizing."

I shook my head. "I don't think I would like apology sex either."

"You're missing out," Leta informed me.

I smiled intending to make an excuse about needing to get back to work, when I noticed Selene holding her head. "Are you okay?"

She took a few minutes to answer as I stared at her with concern. "I've been having these strange headaches. They started last night."

"Great," I said dryly. "What do you turn into when you're sick?"

She felt good enough to be amused. "Smoke," she said with a mischievous smile.

"Oh, well that's more manageable than a tree monster."

"That's what you think," Leta said pointedly. "Just wait until you're choking on all that smoke. You'll be begging to have the tree monster back."

I wasn't sure about that as I had a feeling Selene would be much less dramatic in her sickened state.

"I'll be fine. I don't think I'm getting sick. This sort of thing happens to..." she looked around, "my sort from time to time. Every so often, we have to fight off bouts of insanity. We have periods of hallucinations and hearing voices, sometimes followed by power surges resembling psychic breaks on a magical level."

Leta and I stood there staring at Selene, both of us at a loss for words. I wasn't exactly sure what she was talking about, but it did not sound good.

"Not every one of us has a break," Selene tried to reassure us. "And it's not permanent. My grandmother had one that only lasted a few hours. The power in a twenty-block radius was out for those few hours, but she recovered just fine. She never had another one."

Stunned silence.

"See, tree monster is looking better every minute," Leta muttered as she walked away in the direction of her office.

"Just out of curiosity, what are you experiencing right now?"

Selene raised an eyebrow and gave me a sly smile. "Do you really want to know?"

I considered that for a moment. My life was not going back to normal if I kept getting involved in things like this. Yet...I couldn't help but be curious. And Selene did look uncomfortable.

"Yeah, I'm sure."

She seemed pleased with my answer. "I'm hearing a very faint chanting every so often. I can't make out what the chant is, but it's irritating, like a fly buzzing in my ear."

"That would be irritating." I paused. "I'm sorry. I hope it goes away, and that you don't suffer a magically psychotic break."

Selene was amused by my answer. "Thank you. I hope to avoid it as well." She looked down at the flowers. "Miguel, huh?"

"Yeah. Leta says I'll have to face him eventually, but I'm trying to put it off for a little while longer."

She nodded slowly as if in thought. "For a little while longer, I think." With that cryptic comment, she continued down the hall.

"Thanks for that, Selene. That tells me so much," I muttered to myself.

• • • •

WORK WAS GOOD. THE week passed steadily. I found myself content to be absorbed in the design aspects of the ad.

However, not everyone around the office was doing as well as I was. It seemed a few of the girls, including Sarah, had come done with colds. I bumped into her one morning, and she coughed vigorously as I apologized. With a gasping breath, she tried to apologize but just ended up coughing more.

"Are you okay?" I asked as I steadied her. She coughed so hard it looked painful.

She stared over my shoulder as she reached into her pocket and pulled out a cough drop. Her movements were slow and heavy. She looked like a zombie.

"I'm fine," she said with a raspy voice.

"There must be something going around the office. I saw Lisa yesterday, and she looked just like you."

Yes, lately the whole office had been filled with zombie women. Maybe I needed to clarify with Selene again that zombies were not here.

"I was feeling fine yesterday. I even stayed late to finish up a few things I was excited about. But when I woke up this morning, I just felt so weak and achy all over. The cough came on about an hour ago." Her voice was dull and flat.

"That is a pretty harsh cough," I said.

"Yeah," Sarah sighed. "Anyway, Glenda took one look at me and ordered me to go home for the day. She said she didn't want any more infected." She looked sad and hurt.

"It's not your fault that everyone is getting sick." It was probably Leta's. "It's flu season. You know how people always get sick this time of the year. The temperature changing and all."

She looked mildly relieved. "Thanks, Elena. I guess I should be on my way." She continued past me with her shuffling zombie steps.

"I hope you feel better." She waved weakly in acknowledgment.

"It's horrible how so many people are getting sick."

I nearly jumped out of my skin. Turning to the side, I found Selene watching Sarah leave.

"Are you really that sneaky, or did you just... poof in?"

She smiled at my mild irritation. "I don't just go around poofing. You're just easy to sneak up on."

"That does not say anything good about me," I muttered. "Please tell me once and for all that zombies are not real."

"As far as I know, zombies are not real." That was good enough. "Why? Do you suspect anyone in particular of being one?"

I looked at where Sarah had just been.

"Sarah is not a zombie. She's a perfectly normal person."

"As far as you know." Selene laughed as I repeated her wording from earlier. "It's that there's been so many of the girls here looking like the walking dead."

She shrugged. "Flu season."

"Yeah, I guess. Speaking of being sick, how are you feeling?"

She grimaced. "I still hear that damn chanting now and then. And now I'm getting these weird feelings." Selene looked disturbed by that, which could not be good for the rest of us.

"Like you want to harm those around you sort of feelings?" I asked cautiously, taking a step back.

She smiled. "No, I'm not homicidal...yet." Her smile faded. "I feel like I'm being pulled in a different direction, almost like a different plane."

I nodded. The only experience I had with planes was with the kind that jetted from place to place, but I'm sure that was not the kind she was talking about.

"I've never had sensations like this before." She leaned in, "I'm a little worried, to be honest."

Before I could answer that, Christina called from down the hall. "There you are." She power-walked her way down the hall toward us. I looked over to Selene.

Yet, we had barely made eye contact, when she just disappeared. There one second and gone the next. I could feel my eyes popping out of my head in amazement.

I couldn't stand there and gape though because Christina had reached me.

"Where did she go? I saw her. Selene was just here."

I made a show of looking around as my brain quickly tried to put together a convincing lie.

"No, she wasn't." I'm not always brilliant under pressure.

Christina's face went from confused to mildly annoyed.

"She was just here, Elena," she said slowly as if the words were beyond my comprehension.

"No, she wasn't," I said just as slowly. It effectively irritated her further.

We stared at each other. She eyed me with confusion but eventually just shook her head.

"I'm going to go find Selene."

"You do that." Good luck. Selene was probably on another plane right now.

Christina stared at me a moment longer before turning away.

I turned on my heel and headed towards Selene's office. However, she wasn't there, and I didn't see her until the next day at work.

"What happened to you yesterday?" I whispered. After seeing her walking the hall towards me, I quickly grabbed her arm and pulled her into the break room.

She looked around nervously, took a deep breath, and was about to speak when Leta popped into the room, surprising us both.

"What's going on?" She eyed us closely before smiling mischievously. "Oh, secret meeting, huh? I love secret meetings."

With a look over her shoulder, she slipped into the room, looking eagerly from me to Selene.

Selene took a deep breath and released it with a heavy sigh. "I don't know." She seemed truly upset by that.

"You don't know what?" Leta asked.

"Selene just disappeared yesterday. I had to argue with Christina, who saw her disappear, that Selene wasn't there."

Leta's big eyes got bigger as she switched her gaze to Selene. "You disappeared in front of people? But you never do that. I've never seen you disappear before."

"I don't know what happened."

I'd never heard Selene so aggravated before. Her usual calm was missing, and she looked around frequently with obvious paranoia.

"One second, I was in the hall talking with Elena about the chanting and these new feelings of being pulled in another direction, and then I was pulled in another direction. It was like I was being summoned somewhere but halfway there, the force pulling me just stopped, and I was stuck in an interplanar space. It took me a while to figure out where I was. Around midnight, I was able to bring myself back to **THIS** plane." She looked at the door again.

"That is so not good," Leta stated.

"What would have the power to pull you into the...interplanar space?" I asked though I had no idea what the interplanar space was.

"Ugh," Selene started as she rubbed her temples. "I don't know, and it's freaking me out."

"That is not good," matter-of-fact Leta.

I gave her a look that said, you're not helping, and took a step towards Selene. "Could another djinn do this to you?"

"I suppose," she stopped and looked past me as if she was talking to someone else. "But I don't know why they would want to. I've never heard of a djinn doing that, have you?"

I was surprised by the question and about to answer when she answered herself. "No, I didn't think so. No, no, no. What else? What else?"

Again, I tried to respond and again she beat me to it. "Warlock? No, I would know. Mystic? Maybe. Have I upset any shamans lately? Well, there was that one...but it was six months ago. Would have come after me sooner."

I realized that Selene was talking to neither of us. I gave the dryad a look over my shoulder, but she merely shrugged. "It's her process."

Maybe she was talking to a friend on another...plane or something. At this point, I wouldn't be surprised by anything. We let Selene talk to herself for a few more minutes just silently watching. She became silent and turned to us.

"I have to get back to work." With a nod, she walked past us and down the hall.

"Well, that answered none of my questions," I said exasperated.

Leta put an arm around me as we exited the room. In the tone of a teacher imparting an important lesson to a student, "You will learn that you rarely get answers from Selene, just more questions and riddles."

That I could believe.

By the end of the second week, Selene had had twelve unexpected disappearances, with five of them happening in front of other people. Leta and I did our best to cover for her. It's amazing how willing people are to believe that they didn't just see something strange happen. They might not believe it on a subconscious level; but on the surface, they jumped at the opportunity to have someone explain it away for them.

After reassuring another round of co-workers that Selene had not disappeared in front of them, for the third time, I headed home. It was surprisingly easy to accept Selene's disappearances, probably because I was reassured that soon Leta, Farah, Selene and I would only be coworkers. I would move out, and my life would be normal again. I could just conveniently forget that they were mythological creatures.

I pushed that thought aside just as I continued to push aside the guilt I felt over not calling Miguel back. His texts and calls had stopped. I realized that the flowers were probably his last attempt, and yes, I was immature enough to be relieved by that.

Surprisingly, I felt relaxed as I unlocked the door to the apartment. Leta curled up in the corner of the sofa, talking softly into her phone, smiling and giggling. She nodded in my direction as I came in.

"Okay, I'll see you later. Ooooh, you know I do." The soft moan that followed indicated that something in this conversation was about sex. I didn't want to know. I really didn't want to know. Soon, I wouldn't have to know. "I'll talk to you later, big boy."

Big boy? Nope, I didn't want to know.

Leta hung up and gave me a warm hello as I stepped out of my shoes. "I'm guessing you were talking to Corbett? It's been a while since you guys have seen each other."

She was shaking her head. "Nope, Corbett and I broke up."

"Before or after you gave him ticks?"

She laughed. "You're so funny sometimes, Elena. I didn't give him ticks."

"But you were thinking about it."

She thought about that. "I can't remember if I had or not." She pondered it for a few more seconds as I hung my coat on the hook. "Anyway, that was Billy."

"Who is Billy?"

"He's this really sweet guy I met a few days ago."

"What happened with Corbett?"

Her face scrunched up. "He was an unsupportive, egotistical jerk. I called him a few times when I was sick and you were at work, but he could never find the time to come and see me. He came up with all sorts of stupid excuses. But as soon as I was better, I met with him and told him it was over. I can do better, and I have. Billy is so wonderful, and he has the biggest-"

Thankfully, a loud banging on the door interrupted that statement. Leta and I looked at each other and then back at the door. She got up quietly and slipped into her bedroom, coming back out with a bat. She gave me the go-ahead nod as we both edged towards the door.

I returned the nod and undid the lock. I had barely turned the handle, when Farah barged through, almost mowing me down.

"What the hell is going on?" she said in a voice filled with worry.

"I don't know; you're the one who barged in here," I said as I closed the door behind her. Leta lowered her bat.

"Selene just popped into my place, told me she needed help and then just disappeared...what is going on?"

She was fuming and frightened. Leta and I were just confused.

"She's been disappearing a lot at work this week. Uncontrollably," Leta stated as her face tightened with concern.

"I saw her maybe two hours ago. We were wrapping up at work, and she just disappeared in front of some co-workers."

"She's just been disappearing, in front of people? That doesn't sound like Selene. She is very careful at not showing off her magic, especially not in front of people she doesn't trust," Farah said.

"She was quite upset about it. Said something about a possible psychic break, but more recently, she said it was like she was being summoned, but she didn't know of anything that would be summoning her."

Farah looked even more concerned. "I don't know of anything that could summon her. She's immune to a lot of magic." Farah directed the comment at Leta.

"I don't know of anything off the top of my head. I looked into it a few days ago, but Selene told me not to worry about it. That she was taking care of it. She said that she wasn't going anywhere when she unexpectedly disappeared."

"Something is going on," Farah growled. Leta nodded, and they both looked at me.

I held my hands up. "I didn't even know what a djinn was a few weeks ago. I have no answers here." They both nodded.

"We have to figure out where she is and what is going on," Farah said. "I already checked her place, but she wasn't there."

"I might know some people who could help us track her. It may take them a few days though," Leta responded grimly.

A burst of wind blew from the kitchen, and we all turned towards it. Things swirled around, but as they settled, Selene stood in the middle of the mess. She looked strained as she bent forward with heavy breathing.

"Witch...trapped me...high priestess of Twilight Raven Coven...help...please help." She looked up at us with her dark eyes before disappearing once again.

"What the f-" Farah exclaimed.

"Oh, this isn't good," Leta said.

So much for normal.

Chapter 17

I wanted to pretend that I wasn't interested, that I didn't care. Hadn't I told Leta that I was still contemplating moving out just to get away from all this? This was craziness, yet I couldn't look away, couldn't pretend that I didn't care about what happened to Selene. Rationalizing, I told myself that I was only going to give moral support and was not going to let them pull me into anything strange.

We waited patiently on Saturday for Selene to reappear. Well, some of us waited patiently. Farah alternated between pacing our living room and rushing to check her apartment and Selene's. I was sure that by nightfall, Selene would show up again, telling us that the situation was not as dire as she had thought.

Problem solved. Nothing to worry about.

That's what you call wishful thinking.

Selene did not reappear by nightfall.

"That's it," Farah roared as she burst through the door. "No more sitting around. It's time that we did something."

I sat on the couch with my laptop in hand. Leta exited her room as Farah loomed in the doorway and slammed the door behind her.

"What would you like to do?" Leta asked in a tone that was mildly placating.

Farah glared, but Leta seemed unaffected. "We need to find her and get her out."

"And where are we going?" Leta asked in the same tone.

Farah stared at her then with a huff of defeat, she collapsed into the chair, obviously exhausted.

"Okay," Leta said happily with a clap of her hands. "Let's get to work," as if all she had been waiting for was Farah's collapse.

Leta's cheer immediately dissolved into military commander mode. She slowly walked the space between Farah and me with her hands clasped behind her back barking out orders.

"Elena, tell me what we know." I hadn't noted the riding crop in her hand until it was snapped just inches from my face. Maybe dictator mode was more appropriate.

Here is what we knew: Selene had been experiencing strange symptoms that led to uncontrollable disappearances. She had explained that she felt like she was being pulled in a particular direction each time, and with her last known appearance she had mentioned being trapped and the words "twilight raven coven" and "high priestess."

"Are you taking notes?" Leta asked as she tapped my laptop with the crop. I took the hint and opened a new Word document, quickly typing out the information.

"So," our commander began slowly walking the space again. "What can we deduce from this?" I prepared to answer but jumped as Leta brought the riding crop down on the arm of the chair. Farah jumped, but Leta didn't seem to notice.

"Farah," was all she said in that no-nonsense tone.

The werewolf rolled her eyes and pinched the bridge of her nose. "It is most likely that this high priestess of the twilight whatever coven has her, and that she has been trying to get her for a while. That would explain the other disappearances."

"Very good. And?" The crop was pointed at me.

"The high priestess is very powerful?"

Leta nodded. "Yes, she must be a very powerful witch. Hmmm," she continued to walk. "Now, a witch that powerful would no doubt be known by people in the community."

Farah perked up at that. "You have some contacts in the community, Leta. You should call around and see if anyone has heard of this woman."

"Exactly." She shared Farah's enthusiasm as she pointed the crop at her friend. "No one's heard of her."

That deflated all of us.

"Wait a minute. Maybe she's not local," I said. Pulling up the Internet, I Googled the Twilight Raven Coven. And got a hit. "I got something."

Within seconds I was an Elena sandwich, squeezed between Farah and Leta.

"What are they? Black arts?" Farah asked as we waited for the sight to load.

The black background loaded first, followed by pictures of stars, moons, and galaxy swirls. "What is this?" Farah asked with confusion.

"This" was the website for the Twilight Raven Coven. As a graphic artist, I was offended by the mismatch of images cut and pasted onto the site with its twinkling stars and flute music. It caused me eye strain.

"It's just a message board. You must have a login to see anything useful." The Twilight Raven Coven might have proclaimed "All are Welcome," but you had to share your information before they were willing to let you through the door.

"Elena, register as a member," Leta said.

"What?" The last thing I needed was to get involved with a coven. Hell, I was trying not to be involved in this.

"That's a good idea," Farah said from the other side of me.

"Let's register you as a member," I said irritably to Leta.

"Elena, what is the problem?" That damn placating tone again.

"When this whole thing goes bad, I don't want them to track it back to me."

And I was sure this was going to go bad. Funnily, before I met Leta, I had been such an optimist. "I don't want an angry swarm of witches after me. I think I have enough going on that I don't need to be cursed."

"Oh, Elena," Leta said in the tone you use for a confused child. "You are not going to get cursed."

"Yeah, can you guarantee that?"

She didn't answer.

"I don't think that you have anything to worry about, E. I doubt they could curse you. They look a little floopy to me," Farah said reassuringly.

I turned my irritation on her. "What makes you think that?" She pointed to the website.

"They could be the real thing!"

She raised an eyebrow. Okay, I admit the website didn't indicate that we were dealing with the serious power players. But somehow this group was connected to Selene's disappearance.

"Is it possible that Selene told us the wrong thing?" Two doubtful looks answered that.

In the end, I created a fake email to register to the site. Despite all their reassurances, neither Farah nor Leta wanted to use their emails. Once the fake email was created, I created a login that then led to a page worth of questions.

When had I come to realize my spiritual path?

What experience did I have with the Craft?

Had I reached enlightenment?

What deities did I pray to?

Did I have any spirit animals?

With the help of Leta and Farah, I filled in the questionnaire with answers that sounded ridiculous. However, Leta reassured me that they sounded authentic. At some point, she switched from commander mode to secret agent mode. She excitedly declared that we were infiltrating the enemy. I didn't ask where her secret agent experience came from.

Finally, we were at the site. It was just as offensive to my standards of aesthetic design as the previous one. There was a calendar with events, various reference links, and icons for Facebook, Pinterest, Twitter, and Instagram.

"Jackpot," Leta said as we looked at the picture of the High Priestess, Joyous Daughter. I'm guessing that wasn't her real name.

"We know who the High Priestess is, but how do we find her?" Farah asked.

"We go undercover," Leta replied.

"Nope." They both looked at me. "I am not getting any more involved in this. That fake email can be traced back to me, and that is as much as I am willing to risk."

They continued to look at me.

"No." I shifted the laptop onto the coffee table and stood. Their stares made me twitchy.

"I'm trying to get away from all of this, remember? I'm still thinking about moving out. Normal, that's what I want. Getting involved with a coven of witches, real or not, does not fit into the category of normal."

"Life is not normal," Farah stated simply shaking her head at my apparent ignorance.

"Life is not paranormal either," I retorted. "Listen, if you guys want to 'infiltrate' the enemy camp and all that, go for it. I'll help where I can, but I am not getting involved with witches."

Leta straightened with a grave look on her face.

"Elena, it's time to decide if you're in or not. If you are in, then you're all in. You don't get to pick and choose what life brings you, just like you can't pick the weather. We don't get clear, sunny days all the time. And, before you answer that, I just want you to know that Selene would do this for you."

Oh, the guilt treatment. A classic, but a good one. Despite my resentment that Leta would use such a low-handed tactic, I had to admit that she was right. I couldn't keep doing this in and out stuff. And not just because it wasn't fair to them. I'd continue to feel torn if I didn't make a decision.

Momentarily, I thought about just backing out completely. Return to my normal life, but as I looked at Leta's firm but patient expression, and Farah's inquisitive raised eyebrow, I realized that I didn't want to say goodbye for good.

Undoubtedly, these women were going to get me in a lot of trouble, not just now, but most likely in the future. However, I remembered how Leta had been there for me through all the tears with pot roast nights and movies. I remembered how Farah had growled protectively when I had first met Miguel, and that was oddly touching. Thoughts of Selene's logical patience and the lurking playfulness came to mind.

They were crazy people, but they were my crazy people. And every group dynamic needed a grounding influence. I would just have to be the anchor of normalcy amongst the supernatural.

"I'm in," I said with a big sigh. It was like jumping off a cliff even though you knew there was a bungee cord tied to you. Letting go and embracing something that you should instinctual fear was difficult.

Leta smiled brilliantly, and Farah cheered her approval. I gave them a weak smile and tried to quiet the panicked voice that said life would never be normal again.

Chapter 18

L eta insisted that when planning a rescue mission, it is important to consult reputable sources. Hers consisted of *The Craft*, *Practical Magic*, *Man on Fire*, and the *The Wizard of Oz*.

The plan came together in about an hour. Now that we had the name of the high priestess, and thankfully there was only one, Leta called up a friend of hers who was "into computers." I'm sure what she meant to say was that he was an accomplished hacker.

Billy, her new boy toy and hacker, assured us that he would have an address for us by no later than the end of the week. With that taken care of, we next discussed how to deal with the witch. It turned out that my dryad and werewolf didn't have a lot of experience with witches, and you could hardly ask a witchy friend the best way to defeat another witch. People didn't readily reveal their Achilles heels.

This discussion of course led to the discussion of whether or not we needed to "take out the witch." I argued that we could reason with her and ask that she release our friend. My suggestion was met the identical looks of incredulity.

"What?" I said defensively. "Why does this have to end in violence?"

"That witch stole our friend! She is not getting away with it!" Farah growled.

"Besides, just think of how much fun it could be," Leta said cheerily.

It was my turn to give a look of incredulity. "Maybe we should clarify. When you say take out, what exactly do you mean?"

I was met by a moment of silence followed by simultaneous responses:

"Kill, of course."

"Neutralize."

They looked at each other. "I like 'neutralize,'" Farah said with a nod of approval.

"Neutralize?" I repeated with a bit of shock as I rose from the couch to stare down at them in disbelief. "You intend to kill someone?" My voice rose with disbelief and panic.

Leta responded calmly. "Neutralize."

"Which means kill, right?"

"It means," Leta said matter-of-factly, "do whatever we have to, to take care of the problem. We will make it so that she won't cause any more harm."

Obviously, I'd committed way too early. Next time, I'd have to make sure I knew all the particulars first.

"I still insist that we try to reason with her first." Silence. "I want you two to promise me that we will try reasoning first."

More silence.

"Now!" I shouted. "If I'm a part of this then I get a say in what the plan is. This is my say."

"Okay, Elena," Farah said with a smile. "We will try to 'reason' with her first. When that doesn't work, then we neutralize her however we think is best. Are we all agreed on that?"

Dear Lord, please let this witch be reasonable.

"Agreed." I felt like it was a surrender, but I had gained the only ground I was going to get.

"Oh, I like this plan," Leta said with excitement.

"Do you guys even know how to take on a witch?" When they just stared at me, I added, "I'm new to all of this, remember?"

This was where *The Craft, Practical Magic,* and *The Wizard of Oz* came in, though none of us thought that any of the films provided a realistic way of dealing with a witch. *Man on Fire* was simply an overview of various neutralizing methods.

We stayed up late into the night, hoping that Leta's hacker friend would call while we watched the research. Farah's favorite was

Practical Magic; she felt it gave the most useful information. Leta's was *Man on Fire*. Something about the violence appealed to her.

The night finally ended with *The Wizard of Oz*, at which time Leta declared that Operation Red Shoes was on hold as we awaited information. Farah growled her displeasure but stalked out of the apartment threatening Leta if she was not immediately notified of any new information. I crawled into bed, aware that I was yet again starting the week with very little sleep.

The next day at work dragged. Leta had explained to everyone that Selene was sick with whatever the office bug was. At least Selene wouldn't have to worry about her job.

No matter how hard I tried to concentrate on my project, I couldn't focus. Too many things vied for attention in my head.

I was antsy and nervous about Selene, terrified that we wouldn't find her and terrified that we would. Telling myself that they didn't really intend to kill anyone was like putting a Band-Aid on a gushing artery of worry. I didn't want to kill anyone. Up until moving to the city, people would have described me as sweet and easy-going.

Lately, though, I felt my temper catching much quicker than before, and preserving someone else's feelings wasn't a priority for me anymore. My thoughts were darker than they had ever been, and though a part of me was freaked out by that, another more deeply buried part felt that things were just right. Perhaps this was the result of hanging out with my new crowd; I was becoming mentally unstable.

So lost in thought, I didn't notice Nolan's presence until he whispered in my ear.

"Thinking of anyone in particular?"

The voice was low and smooth, but I jumped anyway.

"Hi."

He smiled and leaned a hip against my desk, arms crossed over his chest. Like every other time I had seen him, his suit fit perfectly.

At this distance and without tears blurring my vision, I was aware of his broad chest and muscled arms.

"Of me, perhaps?" He studied me with a playful smile. When I didn't respond, "You look better."

"Thank you." I suddenly remembered how nice it had felt to be wrapped up in his arms. The warmth and understanding that had enveloped me as the world seemed to be falling apart. Here I was, feeling like I was on the verge of another crisis, and he stood there offering his comforting presence. This man had great timing...or horrible timing.

"Yes, I feel better." I blushed as he continued to gaze at me. "About last time, I just want to apologize."

He waved away my apology. "For what? What do you apologize for? It was not your fault your roommate was ill, or that a man you trusted turned out to be not what you thought." He reached out and tucked a stray strand of hair behind my ear. "Though I do prefer your eyes without the tears. They are such a stunning color."

I had never heard someone describe my brown eyes as stunning and immediately distrusted a man who did. I laughed. "I'm sorry, but my eyes are brown."

He looked amused. "Yes, so is a stone called tiger's eye. Lustrous reddish brown with hints of gold just like your eyes."

I was stunned; it was a good line.

"Are you flirting with me, Nolan?" My tone implied that I might be flirting with him, which I reminded myself was a bad idea. I didn't flirt with men like this, but something about him.

He laughed softly and leaned towards me. "No."

Ouch! Way to crush a girl.

"I do not flirt. I pursue. Flirting is a cat playing with a mouse. Pursuing is a lion running down a gazelle."

The temperature went up a few degrees in my cubicle.

"When I pursue, you will not doubt it." The back of his fingers brushed my cheek. "Tomorrow night, I'm taking you to dinner."

Oooooo, heat spread throughout my body in a really good way... "Wait, tomorrow night? No, I can't do tomorrow night." I might be hunting down a witch. "I'm not sure I can do any night this week."

He blinked a few times, looking stunned. I'm sure no woman ever had turned down an offer from him. Honestly, I was shocked that I hadn't melted into a puddle on the floor. Oddly, I felt fairly in control of my wits, unlike some of the other times we had met.

Surprisingly, he didn't seem offended by my refusal. Instead, he looked amused, probably, one of those, 'the more a challenge, the more the fun,' sort of things. I wasn't being a challenge; I just couldn't commit to dinner.

"Oh, I think you're more than just a challenge." He stood over me, considering me thoughtfully. Apparently, I had said that last bit out loud. "Evade for now. But I'll be back tomorrow."

He pushed off from my desk. As he turned the corner of my little cubicle, I called out. When he turned to me with a look of inquiry, I said, "You really shouldn't be pursuing me."

Again, he looked intrigued as he took a step forward. "Why is that?"

"You're a client, and I'm working on your marketing campaign."

"Are there rules against it in your office code of conduct?"

"I'm sure there are."

"However, you are not sure."

I raised an eyebrow at that. "Even if there isn't, I'm not sure getting involved with you is a good idea. I'm just coming off a..." what to call the Miguel thing?

"The last guy I dated wasn't really who I thought he was, and I'm not ready to get involved with anyone. Also, I don't think it would be appropriate to go out with a client. Getting into any kind of relationship with you would be a bad idea."

"I have no intention of this going badly for you."

He got two raised eyebrows for that. "Oh, really?"

"Really."

"Right, and the lion doesn't intend to eat the gazelle either."

"Perhaps, the lion is just looking for something to lie down next to." He turned to go, but not before throwing over his shoulder, "Tomorrow."

He did return the next day and the day after. Though I turned him down each time, he never seemed defeated. Must be such a fun game for him I thought, as I stood in line to get coffee at a place close to work. I arrived early, not wanting to hear Leta and Billy say good morning to each other in a very physical way.

I was flattered and amused by Nolan's attention, but I didn't want to be another notch on the belt or just an amusing pastime. Hell, with the immature way I handled the Miguel situation, I wasn't even sure I should be allowed to have a relationship. Of course, that was if I even wanted one, which I wasn't sure of either.

"Decisions, decisions," a voice said from behind me that had warm fuzzies going up my spine. I may not have wanted a relationship with him, but my body wanted his attention. Which was why, it responded so cheerfully every time Nolan was around.

I turned away from studying the menu to look at him. No fancy business suit today. Instead, he wore jeans and a thick sweater that looked so soft I wanted to touch him. The sweater, not the man- I wanted to touch the sweater. Not Nolan.

Well, maybe.

"Have you come to a decision?" For some reason, I wasn't sure we were talking about coffee.

"I think I'm just going to get my usual." I smiled and tried to look casual as I moved up in the long line.

"Ah, a white chocolate mocha then."

I turned back to him. "How did you know that?"

He laughed at my wary expression. "You had a drink from this café last week that smelled like white chocolate." He eyed the menu. "And the only thing I see with white chocolate is the mocha."

"Excellent powers of deduction."

He smiled. "Thank you." His stare was warm and appraising, but I felt uncomfortable with our silence.

"So, not going to the office today?" He raised an eyebrow. "I haven't seen the jeans at the office before." And my, did they look good.

When he thanked me with an even bigger smile, I realized that the last part had been said aloud, and I covered my eyes with my hands.

"I'm so sorry, that was so inappropriate." I removed my hand to find that he was standing even closer to me.

"It was not," he said with a look that seemed to sympathize with my embarrassment.

"I am always making a fool out of myself when you're around."

"I don't think so."

I gave him a stern look. "Of course, you don't think so." I paused to step forward in line again. "Men love having women throw themselves at them."

"I didn't realize you were throwing yourself at me. American women do it so differently," he teased.

"Think about our first meeting, the first day."

"Ah, if I had known, I would have done a better job catching you." He put a hand to his chest with mock concern, "I thought that you had simply tripped. Had I only known that you were showing the depth of your feelings for me..."

I laughed as his hand on my elbow gently moved me forward. "It was the heels that made me trip."

"Not my eyes?"

"The heels," I stated firmly.

"Of course." Amusement made his eyes shine.

"Besides, you're used to having women throw themselves at you."

"Am I?"

I paused in front of the cashier to stare at him incredulously. His smile challenged me to elaborate.

"Attractive men like you are always the center of attention and expect to get that attention." I ignored the cattiness in my tone as I dug into my purse. I felt heat flood my cheeks as I struggled to locate my wallet. I pulled it triumphantly from the depths of my bag as he nudged me away from the counter. His arm came around my waist as I started to resist.

"Wait, I have to order."

"You did order."

I looked up at him. "No, I didn't."

"You told me you wanted a white chocolate mocha, so I got you one."

When he nudged me again, I didn't resist. We joined the men and women who waited on the other side of the counter for their drinks, and though we still faced each other, his arm fell away. I started to protest that he had bought my drink, but he turned the conversation. "Back to attractive men and attention. You sound as if you resent it. Why is that?"

Sometimes I wanted a pretty boy to just be a pretty boy. I didn't need a man who looked like a god and was insightful too. "I don't resent it."

"It is in your tone." He considered me for a moment before thoughtfully adding, "I do not resent you."

"Why would you?" I asked with honest confusion.

His smile widened until it turned to soft laughter. "Why would I," he repeated the question to himself as if he didn't understand it. His attention was stolen from me when the barista called out his name. He returned from the counter, handing me one of the drinks.

"You are a beautiful woman."

It was stated as a fact. I paused with the cup at my lips.

"Undeniably beautiful." He took a drink of his coffee, which allowed me to take a drink of mine. "Men must constantly be throwing themselves at you."

Again, he was teasing me.

I responded with a firm no while I checked the time on my watch. I was still early despite the wait in line, so I turned towards a table with two chairs. We sat down together as people continued to come and go in a mad rush for their morning caffeine hit.

"I didn't hear you deny it." I eyed him over the rim of my cup.

"That I like women throwing themselves at me, being the center of attention?" He took a drink of his coffee while he chuckled to himself. "I do like it. Why would I not?" He leaned forward placing his cup on the table. "The question is why is that a bad thing?"

"It's not," I tried to sound reasonable, but it came out as a sigh. "I just don't want to be one of your adoring fans or your latest conquest." I stood up to leave, but his hand on my wrist stayed me. Looking down at him, his expression seemed so sincere.

"That is not what this is." He stood with me, his cup in the other hand.

"So, it's just a flirtation?" I don't know why I needed the clarification.

"It is until you say yes to dinner."

"You're still a client."

He held his hand out for me to lead the way. We didn't say anything else as we walked out of the coffee shop.

I was trying to figure out what I was going to say next when I felt his hand on my arm. He gently turned me to face him.

"Elena, I'm not always going to be a client, and I do not go to the trouble of learning what kind of coffee a woman drinks and where she gets it if she's just a challenge."

I had no idea how to respond to that.

"Details are important. Knowing them is important." He leaned down to kiss my cheek. It was quick and sweet. Softly next to my ear, he said, "I enjoyed our coffee date."

He pulled away. His smile was briefly triumphant but turned slightly sad as he stepped away. "I hope you have a pleasant day."

He started to walk away but stopped to look at me when I called out his name.

"That first day you had your coffee black. Is that what you always drink?"

I don't know why I was so affected by his sad smile, but I wanted to change it, to make it happy and playful again. What he had said about details was true; they were important.

His smile was almost breathtaking when he responded. "Always." Then he turned away, and I headed to work with a smile of my own.

My attraction to Nolan was one of the strangest attractions I had ever experienced. I had tried describing it to Leta on our way to work.

Sometimes in his presence, my senses seemed so overloaded that I couldn't think or function clearly, doing things like almost falling on my face. Other times, he seemed just like any other attractive man. The kind that would initially make my heart flutter but after the first encounter the appeal would wear off to just an appreciation of good breeding.

At times, I was flushed and filled with pleasurable heat that arose from his mere presence with sexual fantasies filling my head. At another time, I had been wrapped in his arms and thought only of how comforting it was. Was it normal to be so turned on intermittently by a man I had no interest in other than a working relationship?

Leta explained that it was stress and hormones. I willingly accepted that answer for now.

I didn't see Nolan again until Thursday. Wearing that smile of pure confidence, he again told me that we were going to dinner. Thankfully, Leta's friend had come through that morning, and we were finalizing our plan for that very evening. That left me so preoccupied that I didn't think twice about turning him down.

Nolan leaned over my desk eying me with confusion. "So, you are not going out with me tonight?" He said it slowly as if that would give more meaning to the words.

"I can't."

I stared at my computer screen, looking for the quickest way to our suburbia destination tonight. When there was only silence, I looked up.

"I told you this was not a good week for me." I started to look back at the screen when I thought of something else. "And I still think it would be a bad idea to get involved with a client. I could get fired for it, you know."

His face became serious. "I would not let Glenda fire you."

"That might work while we are working on your ad but once that is done, and you are out of here, nothing will keep her from tossing me out for inappropriate conduct."

His self-deprecating laugh startled me, completely unexpected from this man. "You aren't interested."

"Doesn't happen often, does it?" I asked gently.

"Never." He was eying me with interest. Not in the hunting lion way, but in another way altogether.

"Are you okay? Will you recover?" I was concerned that it might be a blow to his ego.

"I think I will survive, but I am stunned by the novelty of this experience."

I smiled at him.

"However, I think I will continue to enjoy working with you, and I look forward to any moments we spend together."

"Thanks." I wanted to refocus on the mission at hand but felt it was rude to look away. "So, I'll see you around."

"Yes, see you around." He stared at me for a moment longer before leaving.

I emerged from my room later that night, dressed in practical dark clothing. Leta had ordered me to dress in black as we entered our apartment after work. The plan was to change quickly while we waited for Farah to pick us up in her car. I was surprised that she owned one in the city, but she explained that sometimes she just had to get away and surround herself with wilderness. I didn't need any further explanation.

My jeans were a dark wash, my black sweater was warm, and my black boots were comfortable, especially if I needed to run at some point tonight. Which was a distinct possibility. My peacoat would complete the look, as the autumn temperatures were beginning to drop significantly at night.

The sound of objects dropping indicated Leta was still in her room. I realized as I stared at her closed door, that I had only seen Leta's room a couple of times, one of those being when she had destroyed it in a rage. The other had been when I had first moved in. Otherwise, I had avoided Leta's room mostly out of respect and then out of fear that I might walk in on something. As more sounds filtered through the closed door, I wondered if her room was in a permanent state of organized disorder.

Kind of like the occupant.

The front door was thrown open with such force that I jumped as I turned towards it. When I saw what came through the door, I gave a half scream and fell off the sofa.

The figure turned quickly to the hall in a battle-ready crouch. A growl permeated the air.

"Farah?" I whispered in disbelief.

The figure turned to me, still looming just inside the doorway. "Are you alright?"

The fear in my chest flared into a roaring flame. "Am I okay? You barged in here and scared me to death." I yelled at her as I struggled to my feet.

She straightened and closed the door, satisfied that there was no threat lurking in the hall. "You look alive to me."

That flame flared again, and I had a brief thought of setting something on fire, which was just strange. Instead of exploring that impulse, I took a slow, calming breath. When I felt less like a dragon about to breathe fire, I said, "What are you supposed to be? Black ops?"

Farah looked down at herself, apparently finding nothing wrong with what she was wearing. She wore a black tee tucked into gray camo pants accented by a utility belt and knee-high Doc Martins. The belt held a sheathed knife, a small cordless drill, a bit of rope, a small hatchet, and a flashlight.

Just as I was about to comment on the amount of artillery she was carrying on her belt alone- who knows what was hidden- Leta's door opened. The nymph sauntered out in a skintight black body suit and stiletto black knee-high boots. Her hair was pulled back into a tight bun, and her eyes were done up with smoky black make-up. Well, they matched the boots at least, I thought as I looked from one to the other.

"What are you wearing?" The question just escaped my mouth without a thought.

Leta gave herself the same self-appraising look, finding nothing wrong. "What are you wearing? I told you to wear black."

"I am wearing black."

"You are going to stand out like a weed in a rose garden," she said with a tsk.

I was going to stand out?

Leta looked to Farah as I stood there in silent disbelief.

"Did you bring any cuffs?"

"No, I couldn't find any."

"Don't worry about it; I have a few pairs we can take." Leta walked back into her room, returning with two pairs of cuffs. One steel pair gleamed in the light coming from the kitchen. The other was covered in pink fur.

"Now these are bigger," the steel ones, "but the lock is not as good. They come open more easily than these." She held up the other pair. "No one has ever gotten these open before," she said proudly of the pink ones.

Farah considered it. "Let's take both." Leta threw the cuffs to Farah who fitted them to her belt.

"Unbelievable," I muttered.

"You know the last time I wore this," Leta said as she ran her hands down the super tight clothing.

"No, and I don't want to know," I said with my hands pressed to my ears.

That successfully got Leta's attention again. "We need to do something about you, Elena." I thought she was referring to my aversion to hearing about her sex life, but she returned from her bedroom with a black ski cap. "Here, this will help."

It was one of those knitted ones with the eyes and mouth cut out. I stared at her in disbelief. She was worried that someone might see my face and pay attention because I was dressed like a normal person, while she and Farah were going to blaze in with those outfits?

"Thanks, Leta," I took the cap without argument.

"Okay, are we all good with the plan?" Farah asked impatiently.

Leta nodded.

"Can we go over it once more?"

They seemed mildly annoyed with my question, but Farah went over the plan again. We had the address thanks to Leta's friend, Billy. With Farah's car, we were going to drive to the suburbs, park a few blocks away, and approach the house. Farah said we would have to assess the situation before deciding if it was a stealth or full assault attack. I was hoping for stealth.

The drive to the suburbs took forty-five minutes, which was good time despite the evening traffic out of the city. The drive was mostly silent with Leta and Farah making idle chit-chat here and there. I sat in the back, listening to GI Jane and Cat Burglar Barbie. My nervousness grew with every mile, but my resolve was strong. I had made my choice to be all in, so I was going to see this through to the end. We were going to rescue Selene from the witch. Operation

Red Shoes would be successful. There was no turning back until we had our ruby slippers, and the witch was defeated. Secretly, I was still hoping to reason with her, and if that didn't work, I was hoping that she would melt with a bucket of water.

Farah parked next to a park. The sun had already set, and the houses across from the park were lit with cozy warm lights. They were the type of houses that you see in newer developments, all similar in structure and material. Only slight differences in accents set the houses apart. Even the well-trimmed grassy, manicured lawns all looked the same. I was sure as we meandered down the sidewalk attempting to look casual that even the flowers in the flowerbeds matched from one house to the next.

Thankfully, looking obvious became less of a problem when Leta and Farah put on their coats, which managed to cover up the catsuit and well-equipped utility belt. However, as I walked behind them, watching as they nodded to one man who was putting out his trash and to another who was going for a late evening jog, I realized that no matter what they wore, they would always stand out.

Farah didn't exactly stomp down the street, though she had the boots for it, but there was something in her walk that made people alert to her presence. It wasn't menacing or even threatening, which she could easily do on occasion, but it was the walk of a woman who knew she could kick your ass.

Leta, of course, sauntered and swung those full hips of hers every time she took a step. As the men's eyes rolled off Farah, they paused to appreciate Leta. The friendly smile and little wave that she sent each one of them didn't hurt either.

I had the benefit of being able to observe all of this because people's eyes just seemed to pass over me. Not that I was surprised. Walking with a werewolf and a nymph, where do you think people's eyes were going to go?

However, I was glad when we turned the block, now only one street away from the witch's house. A skeptical part of me had been sure that we would never have made it this far with the get-ups Leta and Farah had on, but we were almost at our target.

It was 6754 Moss Grove Street, the fourth house on the left. This house we could have found without the address Leta's friend Billy had looked up for us. Unlike all the other quaint houses that conformed, this one did not.

The front was a bit of a mess with flowers and plants popping out everywhere, and if there was a lawn, I couldn't see it. Trees and bushes grew on either side of the house, and the shrubs lacked the cleanly trimmed lines of the neighbors. Tapestries hung where curtains should have been and were backlit by the light inside. The door had been painted a dark hunter green with a slightly skewed cross hanging at eye level and a wreath of dried flowers over the knocker. There was a stone gargoyle in the messy flora and a cheery gnome by the front door.

Farah gave a faint grunt and motioned us to the side of the house. She and Leta sneaked away silently. I looked up and down the street to see if anyone was looking before I followed. We carefully treaded through the plants as silently as we could. I followed closely on Leta's heels as the plants seemed to open and bend, making a clear path for her. Farah had disappeared ahead of us at some point.

We headed to one of the front windows blocked from the street by a tree. The tapestry had been pulled back from one corner, and we all crowded together to peer inside.

The interior was lit by glowing candles on every surface. The main room was small, and a kitchen could be seen just off to the side. Obscure and random objects filled the shelves that lined two of the walls. A bronze bowl and chalice were on top of the red and orange woven rug that covered the hardwood floor. A dagger rested on the bowl.

"What is the dagger for?" I whispered.

"It is usually just for ritual. Sometimes cutting herbs or sacrifices," Leta whispered back to me.

Farah swore softly, and I asked, "What kind of sacrifices?"

"Most witches are nature-based and give sacrifices of herbs, oils, flowers, that sort of thing. Only a certain kind sacrifices a living thing."

"Does she look like that 'certain kind'?"

"No, I don't think so. She just looks like your standard wiccan witch, not a dark arts type."

That was good. The thought of taking on someone who practiced the dark arts was much scarier than taking out the standard type.

A woman in blue and purple robes entered the room from a hallway that was out of view. She was of average height and a little on the plump side. Her graying blond hair and the faint wrinkles on her face led me to guess that she was in her mid to late fifties. She had a pair of thin rectangular glasses perched on the tip of her nose, for reading most likely. Multiple necklaces hung from her neck and rings glittered from every other finger.

She bent down and placed something in the bronze bowl. Then she went to the shelf and pulled out a jar of salt. With the salt, she started to trace out a star on the floor.

"What is she doing?"

"Drawing a pentacle with salt for protection," Leta explained.

I was about to ask Leta how she knew so much, but I remembered that she had mentioned having a witch friend when Selene had first gone missing.

"I don't see Selene anywhere," Farah said. Her body pushed mine to the side as she tried to get a better view of the room. "We'll have to question her."

"Oh, I looked up a few good interrogation techniques earlier," Leta whispered gleefully.

The amount of joy GI Jane and Burglar Barbie took from this whole thing was a bit sick. Couldn't we try to talk with her first? Did we really have to jump to the bond and torture?

Leta pushed against me to get a better view. Being the shortest, I had been sandwiched between the two of them. I tried to duck down more so they both could get the views they wanted without losing my own. Instead, I lost my view and my balance and fell back on my butt with a crash as I took out a hidden gnome.

I groaned loudly without thinking. The gnome's pointy tip hat stabbed me before it crumpled to the side. Farah and Leta went deathly still, looking from me to the window. Then without a word, I heard the front door open, and a cautious voice call out, "Is someone there?"

Farah dropped to the ground and rolled out of site. Leta gave a little squeak, and flora moved to cover her behind a screen of leaves and flowers.

I sat on the ground, momentarily dazed by the pain of my fall. The porch light turning on brought me out of the daze.

"Who are you?" that voice called again.

I looked around, realizing that Leta and Farah were completely out of sight, and the High Priestess stood just a few feet away scowling, phone ready in one hand and bat ready in the other.

Well, here was my chance to talk.

"Hi," I said lamely as I stood. "My name is Elena. I'm sorry to startle you."

She continued to stand there tensely. "What are you doing lurking outside my window?"

That was a good question.

"I'm sorry, I tried knocking at the front door but there was no answer." Oh, that was good. "I was sure that someone was home because of all the lights, so I thought I would try knocking on one of the windows. I tripped on the gnome," I pointed to the fallen yard ornament, "and fell."

She continued to eye me suspiciously. "Why didn't you just use the doorbell?"

I'm sure I looked at a complete loss. "There's a doorbell?" was all I could think to say.

"It's the small lion's head just to the left of the door."

"I thought that was a decoration. I'm sorry."

She watched me for a few moments. "What do you want?"

I heard a soft sigh behind me, but it was too soft for the other woman to hear. "You are the High Priestess of the Twilight Raven Coven, right?" Might as well make sure we had the right woman before the troops stormed the house.

"Yes, I'm Joyous Daughter, High Priestess of the Twilight Raven Coven." She stood taller and her voice became regal as she repeated the title. I decided to play to her pride.

"Oh, thank go-...goodness, thank goodness." It was probably not a good idea to take a deity's name in vain in front of any spiritual leader. "You are who I have been looking for. You are the only person who can help." I tried to fill my voice with relief and a bit of anguish.

She immediately looked proud and concerned. "What are you talking about? Why would you come to me?"

"I just joined the coven, and I was told by everyone I've met that you are a powerful and wise witch and a true leader...of our people." I'm not sure who I thought our people were, but she seemed pleased by it.

"Well, come in, child. Come in. Let us see if we can fix this problem that you have."

I smiled inwardly. I knew talking would work. If you appealed to people in just the right way, you could get what you wanted from them. With the high priestess, it was appealing to her role as a spiritual leader.

As I walked to the door, I heard the leaves rustle behind me and a soft 'yay' from by my feet.

Joyous Daughter welcomed me into the cozy living room of her house. It was cluttered but welcoming. Books of various sizes and colors, some looking quite aged, lined up neatly on the shelves. Mason jars of water and other liquids, dried herbs and dirt lined another. There were gold and bronze statues of different sizes, feathers, bells, and chimes.

A sofa was pushed against the window I had been looking through. She gestured towards it with a solemn face. I took a seat quickly with my hands folded in my lap.

"As you can see, I was about to start a ritual, and usually I would not interrupt that for anything," her tone was lecturing, "but I see that you are a soul in great need."

I nodded.

She closed her eyes and circled her arms in front of me. "There is a great change coming over you now. A fire has been lit inside your soul."

I stared at her with big eyes. She circled her hands in silence, and I felt compelled to respond somehow. "Okay."

That was all she needed.

"A cleansing for rebirth. Yes, that's what's needed. Basil and rosemary for fire. Maybe," she paused in her motions and opened her eyes. Without a word, she got up and went to the shelves. She held two stones in her hand as she came back to the couch. One was a glassy black stone and the other looked like amber.

"Lie back," she instructed.

"What?" I blurted with alarm.

"We need to bring the fire to the surface. We need to release it."

"I'm not sure I want the fire released," I said timidly.

"Shush, this is best." She placed a hand on my forehead and exerted gentle pressure.

I started to submit but stopped. "Maybe I could tell you about my real problem, and then we could do this. It's important."

"This is your real problem," she said soothingly.

I didn't even know what 'this' was, but I found myself leaning back again, stretching out on the couch. Great, just great.

I knew I was going to get cursed. I just knew it.

Her fingers coaxed my eyes shut. She started chanting over me. I peeked with one eye open and watched as she ran the stones up and down my body, hovering just above touch. She turned her head toward me, and I closed my eye.

I waited for the cavalry to come. What were they waiting for? The woman was obviously doing magic on me. Even if Farah and Leta didn't take her magical abilities seriously, this was not something to be messing around with.

Especially since it was me.

They might have magical immunity. That would explain why they hadn't been as concerned. I didn't have any immunity.

"You must clear your mind, your heart, and relax your body."

Yeah, that was not going to happen, but I did take a deep breath and then another, and the panic seemed manageable again.

"So much fire," she said in awe.

I opened both eyes and looked at her. "Is that bad?"

She gave me a pointed look, and I rested my head against the sofa once more with closed eyes. "What does it mean that I have a lot of fire?"

Maybe it was the heartburn she was picking up on. I felt it rising in my chest with a fury. I hadn't really eaten anything before we left; hadn't really had an appetite. Usually, it came when I was angry or stressed. Though I wasn't angry at the moment, panic was likely the cause.

The pain increased drastically as she continued to chant. If I hadn't been having heartburn for the past few weeks, I would have believed that she was cursing me with it.

The pain spread from my chest down into my abdomen and legs and out to my arms. It burned and grew hotter with every radiating pulse of pain. I felt it pulsing up my neck and into my cheeks. I was flushed and hot, but my body couldn't break into a sweat. The heat was trapped inside, with no way for it to be released.

"Oh, god, I think I need a Tums," I managed to mutter. "Please tell me you have a Tums!" My body was on fire. A Tums might not be enough.

"I've never felt so much fire," she said in awe again.

I couldn't take anymore. Sitting up, I gasped.

Joyous Daughter took a step back, taking the stones with her. The burning faded to a light fever and then to a gentle warmth. The warmth I could bear. It was comforting, like the feeling of a favorite blanket wrapped around you on a cold night, only I had that feeling on the inside. The warmth receded to the base of my chest and felt like the heartburn I knew. Now, a Tums might work.

"Antacid," I whispered.

She stared at me in wonder. I couldn't understand her fascination. It was how I would look at Leta or Selene at times. That made no sense. There was nothing supernatural about me.

"Let me get you some water," she rushed into the kitchen.

I'd take the water. It was better than nothing. I could hear her opening and closing cabinets. A glass was set on the counter, and the refrigerator was opened. Water filled the glass. She talked about the potential and how a thorough cleansing would be needed. The excitement leaked into her voice, but I only heard a few words.

Fire, rebirth, surface.

My breathing calmed. However as the pain began to clear, I felt my anger growing.

Where the hell was my backup?

I stood and took a step towards the kitchen so I could watch Joyous Daughter and see the spot where the tapestry was pulled back. Maybe they needed a signal.

Though I didn't believe that the woman had meant me harm, I didn't like whatever had just happened. The heat had been strange and familiar at the same time. I didn't want to go any deeper into that. I didn't want to know what that meant.

However, as I took a second step, I felt my toes touch the edge of the bronze bowl. I looked down and saw that a jeweled brooch rested at the bottom. And in the clear facets of the jewel, I saw a familiar face.

"Selene!"

In the center jewel of the brooch, Selene cried out soundlessly for help.

Chapter 20

Any moment now, Leta and Farah were going to burst through that door and this situation was going to go from very bad to horrible.

Any moment now...

Where the hell were they?

I leaned down to look more closely at the brooch containing Selene's image. The center stone was a translucent golden yellow and about the size of my thumb but egg-shaped. The metalwork containing the stone was antique gold done in a delicate scroll pattern.

Selene looked up and down, right and left, seemingly unable to see me. I crouched closer, and recognition showed in her face as our eyes locked. A brief expression of relief passed over her face before it was replaced with worry. I'm not sure if she was worried about my safety or the apparent lack of backup.

I could sympathize with both of those concerns.

My fingers reached for the brooch when Joyous Daughter reentered the room. "Oh, be careful. That is a very powerfully charged stone."

I stood up as she handed me the glass of water, watching her warily. "What do you mean 'powerfully charged'?" Like charged with the magic of a kidnapped djinn?

"There is a great deal of energy in that stone, more than I have ever felt in a stone before. It's almost as if there is a life force in there." She gestured for me to sit.

We sat on opposite sides of the sofa. She held a cup of steaming tea in her hand. I hadn't heard a kettle whistle, so I assumed she had made it before I entered the house.

"Do you mind if I ask where you got it?"

She pursed her lips at me. "I'm not sure you're ready to work with any outside energy yet. There is a whole lot inside," she pointed to my chest, "that needs to be worked through."

No kidding. I was thinking that I might just have to make an appointment with a doctor to talk about all this heartburn.

"Oh, you misunderstood. I'm not looking to work with any outside energies right now," or ever. "I was just curious, that's all."

She considered me a moment before smiling and leaning forward with excitement. "Strangely enough, I found that at a yard sale a few weeks ago. I didn't realize that it was charged at the time, but I did think that it would look good with my ceremonial robes. Anyway, I brought it home and forgot about it. Then last week I found it again and decided to clean it. As I was rubbing it with a soft cloth..."

This just got better by the second.

I thought it was lamps that genies came out of. In Selene's case, it was apparently old brooches... which oddly seemed appropriate for her. Joyous Daughter described to me the surges of energy that she felt every time she touched the center stone of the brooch. She explained that it had psychically connected with her. That was how she knew it wanted to be stroked and that by warming it with her body heat, the energy in the stone seemed to grow.

On Friday, she had begun a meditation with it, rubbing a sacred silk cloth over it, because silk was a good conductor of energy she told me. This particular time, the energy grew, and a golden mist rose from the center and briefly filled her living room before withdrawing back into the stone. It had left her stunned. Nothing so amazing had ever occurred in all her years of practice.

Tonight, she had planned to attempt the meditation again, to draw out the energy.

"You are seriously crazy." That...I did not intend to say.

"I beg your pardon," Joyous Daughter's excitement changed to confusion.

"You don't even know what is in there. It could be good energy, or it could be really bad. Maybe something destructive was imprisoned in there."

Great, now I was an expert on the supernatural. I could add it to my list of interests. First date conversation could go something like this...so, I like long walks on the beach, breaking and entering, and discussing monsters under the bed.

I seriously needed a break from them after this. The mythical was taking over my life. First a sick dryad and now a djinn rescue mission. What was next?

"But it was such a warm and welcoming energy," Joyous Daughter objected.

"Yeah, if I was an evil creature trapped in there, I'd be warm and welcoming too especially to someone who might be able to get me out."

What was I talking about? If I was an evil creature trapped...what! I was starting to think like them now.

"That is beside the point." She started to say something, but I continued before she could, "The point is, you don't know what is in there, and you should be more careful about what you do with things you don't know about."

Wasn't that just common sense?

She stared at me in silence before shaking her head. With a huff of indignation, "I would have taken the necessary precautions if I had not been so sure of the source of the energy, and I will remind you that I am a High Priestess. I have been doing this for...Aaaahhh!"

She didn't get to finish her sentence because that was the moment that backup decided to show up.

They were well choreographed; I'll give them that, even though they were late. Farah kicked the door in with her Doc Martin. It hadn't been locked, and I wondered if either of them had tried turning the handle, but I highly doubted it. Her foot hung in the air, the door partially torn from its hinges and leaning meekly against the wall. Leta somersaulted through the now open door landing on her feet in an Olympic gold-medalist pose before lowering into a karate stance. Her smoky eyes narrowed fiercely as she looked around the room.

Farah, having successfully opened the door with her foot, sprinted across the room towards the high priestess. Joyous Daughter tried to scream, but it came out as a squeak just before Farah grabbed her by the shoulders, lifting her from the couch. Farah then proceeded to shake the woman senseless before forcing her into the chair that Leta had placed nearby. The priestess was so shocked that when she was plopped down by a snarling woman dressed in camo, she could barely manage a few incoherent cries. Leta covered her mouth with a strip of duct tape.

Farah leaned over her and growled, "Where is Selene?" It was a low growl, soft as a whisper, and terrifying.

Joyous Daughter's eyes got even bigger, and she tried to talk despite the tape, which of course didn't work.

"What are you doing?" I asked in horror.

I did not remember this being discussed as part of the actual plan. We had just joked about torture and interrogation...at least, I had been joking.

"I don't think that any of this is necessary-"

"If she won't talk, we'll have to move on to the torture," Leta said. She had just finished applying the pink handcuffs and stood behind the chair with her hands on her hips.

Joyous Daughter, of course, began to cry. She looked to Farah, shaking her head when asked again where Selene was, trying to convey her thoughts through her tearing eyes.

"Now, we just want to know where the djinn is," Leta said in a soothing voice. "Just tell us what we want to know."

This was their good cop/ bad cop technique.

"Leta, Farah, I don't think this is necessary." They weren't listening to me. "She doesn't know anything."

They still didn't hear me.

I stood up and took several steps towards them. Farah leaned over the priestess on one side while Leta crowded her on the other.

"I was intrigued by the water techniques," Leta said to Farah. "Do you think we could start with those?"

Farah just growled in response.

This was just getting to be ridiculous.

"Are you both crazy?" I yelled at them. I must have projected quite a bit because the candles in the room seemed to flicker a bit. Good lung capacity, I guess.

That got their attention.

They stared at me; the room utterly silent. Even Joyous Daughter stared at me.

"This is not necessary! She doesn't know anything!" I took a deep breath to calm myself; the heartburn was starting again. "She found the brooch a few weeks ago at a yard sale and thought it was pretty. It was apparent to her only a week ago that the stone was something more."

"What brooch? How do you know this?" Leta asked.

"She told me."

"She could be lying to-"

"She thought I was a new convert. She didn't have any reason to lie to me."

"Maybe she's an evil mastermind who has been planning this all along," Leta suggested.

We all looked at Joyous Daughter with her confused and scared eyes full of tears. Even Farah raised a skeptical eyebrow when Leta insisted that it was possible. After that, the two of them stepped away from the priestess though they continued to eye her suspiciously.

"Where were you guys? Didn't you hear us talking?"

Leta and Farah exchanged a look. Farah looked irritated, and Leta gave a shoulder shrug. I learned later that Farah had gotten tangled in the flora outside...after Leta had inadvertently made it attack her.

When Joyous Daughter had come out to investigate the noises in her yard, Farah had done a drop and roll while Leta had willed the plants around her to provide cover. She hadn't thought that it would work; actually, she hadn't thought about it at all. Leta explained that commanding plants was a skill that came with maturity in dryads. It varied from one to the other, but Leta was quite pleased to discover that night that she had achieved enough "personal growth" to now have the power.

Unfortunately for Farah, Leta had no way of knowing how to control it. In her panicked response, Leta managed to communicate to the nearby plants that she needed cover, and they had covered her. When Farah grabbed Leta's leg in an attempt to pull her to the ground, a surprised Leta unconsciously transmitted to the plants that she was being attacked... by Farah.

So, they did what any loyal, obedient plants do...they attacked Farah. The werewolf found herself tied down by the overgrown grasses while the shrubs attempted suffocation, and a rose bush threatened her with its thorny limb. The more she struggled, the tougher the plants got. The more alarmed Leta got, the more threatening the plants got.

I was surprised that we hadn't heard any of this, but I remembered the mediation thing Joyous Daughter had done to me and realized that I'd been distracted at the time.

Eventually, Leta managed to convince her defenders to stand down, though she wasn't sure how. The already hostile Farah was even more so after the grasses released her. She had growled briefly at Leta but had been more concerned about me inside with the witch. Thus, the kicking in of the door.

"Anyway, Joyous daughter found a brooch at a yard sale."

"What does that have to do with Selene?" Farah demanded.

"I'm trying to tell you that." The candles flickered slightly. "Selene is trapped in the brooch."

That set Farah off. She was in Joyous Daughter's face demanding to know how she trapped a djinn and how we could get her out.

Leta said something about wanting to do "all this the easy way", and I rolled my eyes.

I tried in vain to get their attention. Finally, I just gave up and picked up the brooch. It was warmer than I had expected and somehow it...felt like Selene. I rubbed it with my finger, and it glowed slightly, but nothing else happened. I remembered all the stories I knew about genies. Getting one out of a lamp always seemed to require rubbing. Figuring that I wasn't rubbing hard enough, I rubbed both thumbs vigorously over the stone. The golden mist that Joyous Daughter had described rose out of the stone. I kept rubbing, and the mist filled the room and formed a swirling column in front of me.

A sudden pop and blinding light from the column forced me to cover my eyes with a hand. When I dared to open them, I saw Selene standing in front of me.

"Selene?" Farah had paused in her intimidation act to stare disbelievingly at Selene.

Leta looked from me to Selene and then back. "How did you free her?"

"I rubbed the stone," I said, holding it for them to see. They stared at me. "Haven't you ever heard of Aladdin?" Still, nothing but blank stares. "Genie in a bottle? You know, you have to rub it to get the genie out. Oh, never mind."

Farah had come over to sniff Selene, to confirm it was her. She appeared satisfied that it was Selene. "I thought that whole genie in a bottle was just a fairy tale."

Said the werewolf to the djinn.

"I wish it was," Selene said. She stretched as she looked around. "That," she pointed to the brooch in my hand, "is not very spacious."

"I wouldn't think so," I said.

"What the hell happened?" Farah growled with a look back at the priestess.

"It turns out all the stories my grandmother told me when I was younger are true." We looked expectantly at her. "I'll explain that later, but essentially the stories about djinns or genies are true and that brooch," she pointed, looking apprehensive to touch it, "is my lamp or bottle."

"So, that makes you the djinn in the brooch?" Farah asked skeptically.

Selene just shrugged.

"And what do we do about her?" Leta said from beside the priestess.

"She is just an innocent bystander in all this. She had no idea what she was getting into."

Selene looked at Farah and Leta carefully for the first time. "Obviously, she had NO idea what she was getting into." A hint of amusement colored her voice, though her face was wary with exhaustion.

"So, we don't need to take her out?" Leta asked with a considerable amount of disappointment.

Selene's eyes got big. "Take her out?" She sounded confused but understanding seemed to dawn as she looked at Jane and Barbie again. "No, definitely not! She is clueless."

"Yeah, I would agree with that," I added.

The priestess tried to object.

"Can we get out of here, and I'll tell you about the rest on the way home? I'm presuming, well more hoping, that you brought a car because I am too tired to get myself out of here."

"What about her?" Leta asked.

"Well, I think we can start by taking the handcuffs and tape off," Selene said as she took a step, and bones somewhere in her body popped. She made a sound of satisfaction.

"We're just going to let her go after what she did?" Farah asked.

"She didn't do anything other than find an enchanted object and think that it was benign. No offense, Selene." The djinn just smiled at me. "And, then she ends up being assaulted, handcuffed, and scared to death by a werewolf and a nymph."

The priestess muttered something about an elemental as Leta tore off the tape.

"Frankly, I think this experience has been as traumatic for her as it has for Selene."

Joyous Daughter nodded as Leta released her from the handcuffs. "A djinn, a werewolf, a nymph," she said in awe as she took a step back from Leta.

"A dryad actually," Leta corrected. "And, just so you know, you could put a little more nitrogen in your soil. The plants would be very appreciative."

The priestess nodded slowly, still in a daze. Poor woman.

"I'm sorry about all this. It was just a huge misunderstanding, and these two," I pointed to Farah and Leta, "are too enthusiastic. We didn't mean you any harm."

Even without Farah's growl, I'm sure she would not have believed me.

"And you," she said as she pointed to me.

"And me, yes, I was regrettably a part of this whole thing. Like I said-"

"So much fire," she muttered.

"Okay." My brow wrinkled in bewilderment. I was the least hot-headed of the three of us, and she accused me of having the most fire?

"Fire, huh?" Selene said bedside me as she studied me with those knowing eyes. "Interesting."

I was about to ask Selene what she meant by that, but a movement across the room attracted my attention instead.

Joyous Daughter slowly retreated to the set of shelves opposite the window facing us with terrified eyes. From one of the shelves, she grabbed a small dish of salt and sprinkled it in a circle around her. She noticed us staring at her and did another circle, even heavier this time. Grabbing a tied-up bunch of dried leaves, she lit it with one of the candles nearby. Once a good portion of it had caught, she blew it out, and it smoked. Waving the smoking bundle in the air, she started softly praying to a deity of some sort.

"What is she doing?" I asked.

"I believe she is trying to ward herself against us," Selene said.

"That poor, poor woman. I wish that she would forget all of this."

"Done," Selene said beside me.

I turned to ask what she meant, but I heard a thump. The priestess had collapsed on the floor. She didn't look dead from where I was standing, but Leta was the one closest to her.

"Leta, what did you do!" I exclaimed.

She looked at me with surprise. "I didn't do anything. She just closed her eyes and fell to the floor."

"Is she dead?" Farah asked. Leta leaned closer to find out.

"No, she's not dead. She's just asleep. When she wakes up, she will not remember being terrorized by a werewolf/dryad duo," Selene explained. "Now, can we go? I feel like crap, and I don't want to be here when she wakes up."

"You just made her forget? Just like that? I didn't know that you could do stuff like that." I was slightly disturbed by the fact that she could.

"Well, normally I can't, but when it's part of a wish, then yes, I can." Selene started to head towards the door.

"Wish?"

She turned back to me. "Yeah, you're the one who rubbed the brooch. That means you get three wishes."

I was beginning to understand that most of the things that I had always thought of as fairy tales were in fact real, but reality wasn't always true to the stories.

Selene explained more on the way back to the city. Of course, that was after we blew out all Joyous Daughter's candles, and made Farah fix the door. Her cordless drill was good for something.

There was truth to the tale that genies, or djinns, could be summoned for the granting of three wishes. Unlike the stories, djinns did not live in the object that summoned them, at least not all the time. They were only bound to the object while it was active. Frequent summoning trapped the djinn in their "lamp" until all the wishes were made.

It turns out that the summoning vessel would occasionally go into energy-conserving mode and trap the djinn as frequent summoning took a lot of power. And, when the djinn resisted the summoning, it took even more power. The "lamp", therefore, would just keep the djinn easily accessible. Each time that Joyous Daughter had rubbed the brooch, she had unknowingly been summoning Selene.

However, now Selene was bound to me because I had rubbed the brooch and officially summoned her out of it. Had Joyous finished summoning her out of the brooch, Selene would have been stuck with her for the duration of three wishes.

I volunteered to free Selene from the brooch with a wish, but she just laughed at me and said that didn't work. She also explained that there were few limits to what she could do in wish-granting mode. Resurrecting the dead and making people fall in love were all allowed; though those particular wishes stopped once the djinn was out of the wisher's service. Many a person found their true loves not so true once the wishing transaction had been completed, and the occasional dead body was found in random places.

Also, djinns often interpreted vague wishes. For example, a wish of "I wish that person dead," could result in that person being dead...for about a minute. If details like that weren't stated in the wish, the djinn was able to fill in the gaps however they saw fit. So, the important thing to remember when making a wish was to be very clear about what you wanted and how you wanted it. It was a little disclaimer that they didn't mention to most wishers.

But Selene did not want me to use my wishes. As long as my wishes were incomplete, she could not be summoned by anyone else even if they had the brooch. And, once a person had used all her wishes, she could not summon the djinn for more. So, as long as I didn't use all my wishes and didn't use the brooch to summon Selene, she could not be summoned by another, nor would she have to reside in the brooch.

Selene had passed out as soon as we tucked her into bed that night. After another day, she was back at work, though it was obvious that she was distracted. She told me over tea the evening on her first day back that she had called her mother the day after getting home.

She had always known that djinns could be summoned for wish granting. Selene just didn't think that she would ever be summoned, especially not by an unknowing witch of no real power. I assumed that she had always imagined it would be a powerful warlock or something, and they would have an epic battle. Whatever she thought would happen though was nowhere close to what really had. Some djinns went their whole lives without being summoned, and some like Selene's grandmother were summoned multiple times throughout their lifetimes.

I asked what made the brooch so special and why it was linked to her, but she politely told me that it was not my business. I suggested putting the brooch into a safety deposit box so that no one could use it. She laughed and explained that the brooch was supposed to be in a safety deposit box in some very old and secure bank in Europe. Yet, it was currently lying on my nightstand.

When I looked at her in confusion, Selene further explained that magical items had a will of their own and did things that couldn't always be explained. She also added with emphasis that just as magical items couldn't be denied their purpose, people couldn't deny who they were.

A djinn was a creature of striking contrasts, all-powerful but subject to the wishes of others. As much as part of that disturbed her, Selene could not deny it. To do so, caused more trouble and pain than needed, she said pointedly. I'm sure there was something I was meant to take from that, but I couldn't figure out exactly what it was.

The whole event, harmless though it was, seemed to affect Selene. She was more cautious and quieter the first few days she was back. I wondered if she had ever felt that helpless before. Either way, she had not liked it one bit.

I kept the brooch on my nightstand for the first few days but packed it away in a box that held my most treasured mementos. I told myself I did it to keep the brooch safe. In truth, I couldn't stop thinking about it, Selene, and the possibility of wishes. Not looking at it every day helped a little.

But it seemed to be on my mind all the time.

Finally, I asked Selene if she wanted me to just make all my wishes so that she could have the brooch back. Again, she assured me that she very much did not want that. I argued that I could just make my wishes, and she could give the brooch to someone like Farah who would undoubtedly be able to protect it. I also secretly thought to myself that Farah didn't seem the type to be tempted by wishes.

Though I had no intention of mentioning it to Selene, I was very much tempted by the wishes. Not that I knew what I would wish for, but when you knew that could have anything that you wanted, you started thinking about all the things that you wanted. Which led down paths that wouldn't have been explored otherwise. I didn't want to go down those paths, but I couldn't help but be distracted by the possibilities. That was the great and evil temptation of wishes.

Though I never confessed my fears to Selene, she seemed to know anyway. Despite her assurance to the contrary, I still sort of thought she could read minds.

"I don't expect you to not be tempted. Wishes are tempting. That is their nature," she said one night after work. We were sitting at a low-key bar, though it was packed. A blues band played in the corner and the lights were dim and intimate.

She suggested the place and the drink, citing this as one of her favorite places to unwind. I had thought it a good idea; Selene had been tense all week. Now, I was wondering if the place had been picked for this very conversation.

We sat in the middle of the bar, but the people crowding the bar weren't interested in us. The music invited soft conversations that couldn't be heard by others over the piano and sax. It was surprisingly a good place to have a private chat while enjoying a good atmosphere.

I wasn't sure how to respond. Should I tell her I was tempted? Would she understand?

"Yes," she said as she took a sip of her cocktail. "I may be the one who's supposed to grant the wishes, but I also know what it's like to be enticed by the attainment of my greatest desires." She smiled.

I took a drink, giving myself time to think of a response. Selene silently sipped her drink, as always cognizant of my thoughts.

"So, you know that I'm tempted. But you trust me anyway?"

She thought about her response, her eyes fixed on the shelf of high-priced liquors behind the bar. Her lips pressed together.

"Yes, I do trust you," she answered slowly. "Not because I believe that you'll resist temptation. One day, you will make a wish; you won't be able to help yourself."

She turned to me. Her dark eyes peered so intensely at me that I felt that she was looking into my soul. "But I also know that every time you think about making a wish, you'll think about me, and how that decision would affect me. The thing people don't understand about wishing is that there are consequences to every wish. Not always bad, but always unavoidable.

"I trust that you understand that and will consider the consequences of any wish you're tempted to make." She turned away and took a drink.

I wanted to tell her how much her trust meant to me. It felt like our friendship had been taken to another level.

"I know that Farah and Leta would be the same. They would be just as tempted as you, but they would also understand, the way I know you do." She turned back to me before I could respond. "So, though I trust you, it's not the only reason I don't want you to make the wishes."

She set her drink down with a shudder.

"When you wished for the priestess to forget that night, I wanted the same thing. I probably would have tried to find a way to make her forget even if you hadn't wished for it. Nevertheless, I made her forget. Even though I wanted it, I had to do it because you wished it."

I couldn't speak in her moment of silence but simply watched as she turned her drink in her hand.

"And I can't help but consider how different it would have been had I not wanted to do it. You know what the difference is, Elena?" Her eyes focused on me. I shook my head. "Nothing."

We stared at each other. "Nothing is different. I would have still done it. Not because I wanted it or agreed with it or willed it. I would have done it because it was what you wanted. What I want doesn't matter." She took another drink.

"My limits when it comes to wishes is...scary, and when I think of all the things that I could be made to do, even if it was against everything I believed in, is even scarier. When I grant a wish, I'm all-powerful and completely powerless." She turned to me.

"Just so we are clear on this; I'm staying your 'genie' because while you're worrying about all the shoulds and shouldn'ts, I'm only concerned about me. I don't want the brooch to go to anyone else, not because you're a paragon of restraint, but because it would mean I would have to grant you two wishes. I've only granted one wish. Though it was something I wanted to do, it didn't change the feeling of complete subjugation. I don't like the way I felt when I had to grant a wish, and I don't want to have to do it again for a very long time." She paused. "Do you feel better?"

I nodded, unable to formulate a response to anything that she'd said. I knew that I couldn't possibly understand what Selene experienced when she granted a wish. Knowing that Selene accepted my inevitable succumb to temptation was surprisingly relieving. The pressure was off because we both knew that I was going to lose the battle at some point; it wasn't a failing, just a fact. The tremendous weight of never falling into temptation had been replaced by a more manageable weight of postponing the inevitable.

With the relief also came a more practical sense of responsibility. I knew that I would only put Selene through the wish-granting for something very important. I was devoted to that promise.

We didn't talk about the brooch or wishes after that. I knew where she stood, and she knew where I stood. The slight distance that had developed between us after the rescue mission seemed to close with that conversation. Selene relaxed and was more her usual self.

Things had been resolved with two of my closest friends, and it seemed that life would be peaceful for a while.

I was not so fortunate.

Chapter 22

L eta's tree hated me.

The tree started it.

I couldn't help but feel just as hostile in return. The attacks were small at first. I didn't even notice them for what they were. Sometimes I would walk out of my room, face first into a screen of leaves. Leta said that sometimes trees had to stretch especially when they were trapped indoors. It made sense so I thought nothing of it.

Then there were the occasional flicks I would feel against my arm or cheek. Nothing that hurt more than a quick sting, but I just assumed that I had run into a branch or that the tree was stretching again.

About a week after Operation Red Shoes, I was walking to my bedroom when I felt something smack the back of my head. I cried out and turned to see the cause. No one in sight. Leta hummed contentedly in the kitchen. It was just me in the living room...and the tree, which occupied the corner furthest from the front door and closest to my room.

It was oddly still.

I had been observing it closely since Leta told me it stretched now and then. Not because I was suspicious at the time, but because I found her tree fascinating. It was the first sentient tree I had ever met. Of course, it was interesting!

From my observations, I knew that the tree was always moving. Sometimes it was so slight that a person wouldn't notice unless they were watching for movement. The leaves would rattle at times as if a wind was blowing through or it would shift to expose more surface area to the sunlight. At other times, the tree did actually stretch.

But on this night, the tree was still. It was choosing to be still. It was tense...battle-ready tense. Eyeing the tree warily, I turned back towards my room.

And felt another smack to the back of my head. "What the he-"

I turned just quick enough to dodge the third attack.

"Leta!" I yelled as I maneuvered away from the tree into the living room.

Leta poked her head out of the kitchen. "What is it? Are you okay?"

I pointed to the tree. "Your tree is trying to kill me."

Leta stared at me and then at the tree. Then at me again. "Huh." She looked back to the tree. "Yeah, it might be."

I stood with my mouth hanging open in disbelief. "Your tree is trying to kill me?" The volume of my voice was somewhere between normal and shouting.

"Yep," she said as she wiped her hands on her ruffled pink apron and stepped into the room. "I think it is." She stood beside me with her hands on her hips, staring at the tree.

"Why?"

"I don't think that it likes you very much."

"Why? I saved that tree!" I pointed at it. "I towed it through the pouring rain in a little red wagon. I faced down a disgruntled city employee. I endured you with the tree pox because of my efforts to save your tree. And now, you're telling me it doesn't like me?"

"Yep."

Words were beyond me at that moment. I made a noise that sounded something like Farah's growls. How could a tree hate me? What had I ever done to it?

I had even watered it when Leta was sick. I had trimmed off all the dead leaves and branches when it had first arrived in the apartment. I was the one who always remembered to open the curtains in the morning so the tree could have the best light possible. And now, it wanted to kill me!

"Something has to be done, Leta."

She turned to stare at me with wide eyes. "What do you mean?"

"Your tree has inflicted bodily harm on me, intentionally."

At that moment, the tree, or The Tree as it would be known from now on, decided to join in the discussion. The leaves on the branches shook furiously.

"See, malicious intent," I said indicating the tree.

"I'm not sure that is malicious," Leta said in a placating voice.

"Let me tell you what malicious is," I took a few steps towards the tree.

My chest felt like it was on fire but didn't hurt nearly as much as it had in the past. I could feel the heat of my anger warming me from the inside.

"This tree hit me in the head twice and tried for a third time, but I dodged just in time. What else would you call that?"

I felt on fire now. Heat radiated out of my pores like I had a fever.

I looked at Leta, my back to the tree, telling her that intentionally trying to harm something was malicious.

Suddenly, she cried out, "Elena, watch out!"

The Tree shook even more violently than before. The branches swayed eerily and menacingly.

I took a step back. "See," I said to Leta.

A branch came at me like a boxer's right jab. I saw it coming in time to jump back with a pathetic squeak. The branch missed me, but I got a face full of leaves. Taking a few more steps out of branch reach, I gulped in sudden fear.

For the most part, I had been mostly just irritated. I still was irritated, but I also realized that The Tree was a lot bigger than I was and could easily take me out. It could clobber me to death with its branches. Suffocate me with its leaves. There was no telling all the horrible deaths that tree could devise.

It continued to shake angrily.

Leta stood between me and the tree holding a hand out to each of us, as if we were fighters in a ring. "I think that the two of you need some space. A little separation might be good."

"I am not leaving the apartment," I stated strongly.

"Well, the tree isn't leaving."

"Leta!"

"What? All I am suggesting is that the two of you hang out in different rooms. Unfortunately for you, the tree gets the living room."

"I would gladly go to my room. In fact, I was on my way to my room when it attacked me."

"Okay, Elena." That infuriatingly calm voice! "I will distract the tree while you go to your room."

"What about when I need to come out of my room? Are you going to hold it back every time I come and go?"

Leta looked thoughtful. "I will take care of it."

That was all she said on the subject, and I wasn't in the mood to wait around for more of her peacemaker mode. I eyed The Tree as I cautiously walked past it to my room. Leta stood between us, making soothing noises to the shaking leaves. I made it to my room without further injury.

I didn't leave my room for the rest of the night, not wanting to have another encounter with The Tree. However, I could not avoid the living room in the morning. Walking out of my room, I was on the defensive, ready for any possible attack. I kept my back to the opposite wall as I peered around the corner where The Tree was.

It wasn't there though. Stepping cautiously into the living room, I looked around. It wasn't hard to find The Tree; it was a tree after all. The sofa had been pulled out, and The Tree had been put in front of the window. Its branches shaded the sofa but could not reach me as I walked through the room. The Tree shook slightly as I walked by. It wasn't the greatest thing to live with a hostile tree, but the situation was at least survivable.

The Tree's hostility seemed to lessen after a few days had passed, but there continued to be tension between us. I glared, and The Tree shook its leaves. Selene, who had been spending more time at our apartment since Operation Red Shoes, found the whole situation highly amusing though she refused to explain why. I, of course, was no longer able to sit on the couch. The Tree would undoubtedly smother me with the cushions if I tried.

Leta was not as amused as Selene. She seemed genuinely confused by what was causing the animosity. She muttered a time or two that it could be "all that fire," but she never explained what that meant. I began to think that she and Selene were sharing a secret and keeping it from me. That thought irritated me and gave me heartburn. I was convinced that my friendship with them was causing me stomach ulcers.

Besides the violent plant occupying my living room, the next two weeks brought an array of even more disturbing sights.

It seemed that Leta was recovering from her breakup in a very nymph way. She was having sex; lots and lots of sex.

At first, I wasn't that concerned.

I came home late one night after having drinks with Farah and Selene. The noises coming from Leta's room needed no explanation. I was just happy that they sounded normal. No animal noises. The next morning, I met the man who had helped us find Selene.

Billy was everything you would expect a genius/computer geek/ hacker to be. He was tall and thin. Though he was obviously in his late twenties, he looked like his body had not grown into his arms or his legs yet. He was gangly and awkward. His hair was a dull brown, messy, and had outgrown its last cut. Baggy clothes hung off his thin frame and a pair of oval glasses sat slightly lopsided on his nose.

He appeared to be sneaking out, as though I hadn't heard his performance the night before. I sat in the kitchen with a cup of tea watching as he tried and failed to be quiet. First, he knocked over the umbrella by the door. As he was trying to catch it before it hit the ground, he ended up hitting his head on the wall. A loud groan followed.

I quickly got up. "Are you okay?"

He jerked upright, his face flushing a bright red. "Uh..."

"Are you okay? It sounded like you hit your head hard. Do you want to sit down for a minute?" I hovered nearby in case he was dizzy, but I didn't make any attempt to touch him. His face flushed a deeper red by the minute.

"Oh, I'm fine, really fine," he stuttered a bit.

"Are you sure?"

He nodded ardently. I didn't believe him. He winced as he rubbed the top of his head.

"I'm Elena by the way. Leta's roommate."

I held out my hand but instead of shaking it, he just looked at it with panic. So, I withdrew it not wanting to cause him more distress.

"Anyway, can I just say thank you for helping us find Selene. I'm not sure how we would have done it without you."

"I'm fine. Bye."

And with that, he bumped into the door as he tried to pull it open and exit at the same time. He gave a weak laugh, flushed red again. With another mumbled goodbye, he managed to get out the door. I stood there for a while just staring at the door.

Leta came out in her royal blue silk robe that barely covered the essentials. "Is Billy still here?" She asked with a yawn and a stretch of her arms.

"I think that I scared him away."

She looked at the closed door. "He does scare easily. I should have warned you." Turning to go into the kitchen, I followed her.

"You could have warned me that you were bringing someone home."

Leta paused in the middle of pouring herself some hot water. "I'm sorry. Are you mad that I brought someone here?" She looked concerned so I quickly reassured her.

"No, of course not. It wasn't the first time, though I have to say that it was a relief not to hear animal noises." I gave her a mischievous smile as I took a sip of tea.

She looked confused. "Animal noises?"

"Corbett. Well, you know." Her expression didn't change. "You know?" Still looked confused. "Leta, he bleated like a sheep or something."

The light went on. "Oh, well he is a satyr."

"Right." I didn't want to get any further into that topic. "I'm just relieved that this guy was normal."

"I don't think I would call Billy normal," she smiled as she emphasized 'normal.'

"Well, he's a bit of a nerd," I laughed a little, "and awkward."

"And a descendant of Priapus."

"Who? What?"

"You don't know who Priapus is?" Leta was highly amused.

Was he a politician? A movie star I had never heard of? "No, I don't."

She looked even more amused. "Google it." She turned from me with a wicked smile. "I'm starving."

I bet. Marathon sex did that.

"I'm going to make breakfast. Do you want any?" she said over her shoulder.

I was trying to remember where I had put my laptop and absently answered in the affirmative.

Remembering that I had left it in my room, I put my tea down on the end table next to the chair and rushed off to get it. I was going to find out who this Priapus person was. Leta was far too amused by my lack of recognition.

"You have got to be kidding me!" I cried out after the search results loaded.

I put the laptop on my bed and went back to the kitchen. "No," was all I said to Leta's back.

"Oh, yes," she purred as she placed a skillet on the stove.

"You have got to be kidding me!" I repeated.

She turned to look at me, smiling like the cat that got the cream. "No joke."

"But, but," I thought back to the guy I had just met, "he was so...tiny. A strong wind would blow him over."

"He's big where it counts. Spectacularly beautiful." She got that wistful look in her eyes, and I knew she was reliving the events of last night. I kept quiet. I didn't want the details.

But fate would have none of that. I saw Billy again, a few nights later. We had both sneaked out of our respective rooms on a mission to raid the kitchen. I was sneaking in an attempt not to wake The Tree; I decided that if it was sentient enough to dislike me it was sentient enough to need sleep. Billy was no doubt sneaking around in an attempt not to wake me.

Whether it was his unfamiliarity with the living room furniture or his lack of gracefulness, he bumped into the sofa, disrupted The Tree, and almost knocked Leta's Greek figurines off a nearby shelf. I almost screamed in surprise and reached out to turn on the nearby lamp.

I was in my PJs. Billy was in nothing. We stared at each other from across the room. I couldn't help it. I had to look.

After that night, I didn't question Leta's claim that he was the son of Priapus.

Chapter 23

"Mr. Tasev, Mr. Tasev! Nolan," I called after him. Was the man deaf?

It was a Friday afternoon and with the flu going around there were fewer people in the office than usual. Unfortunately, that meant that there was no one in the cubicles to stop him as I tried to run him down. Leta had charged me with the task of getting his signature on an important document that had to be faxed tonight.

Despite his casual gait, the man covered a lot of ground with each stride.

I burst through the glass door just as Nolan turned around inside the elevator. I raced in to join him, slightly breathless.

"You forgot to sign," I managed through my heavy breaths. Wow, I needed to work out more.

Standing up, I held the papers out to him, my breathing still labored.

"Are you well?" he asked as the doors closed us in.

Great, now I was stuck with him in an elevator after doing my very best to avoid him.

"I'm fine. I just need you to sign these." I shoved the documents in front of him.

His brow furrowed. "I just signed documents with Leta."

"I know and I'm very sorry-"

"You are going to wear out those words, and then you will have only actions to convey your apology."

That drew me up short. I looked him in the eyes.

"I'm sorry- excuse me? I don't understand." But I'm pretty sure I did understand. A sort of, "you'll have to prove it" challenge.

He simply laughed at me.

A flare of annoyance spread warmth throughout my body. "So, now I have to prove to you somehow that I really am sorry? Look, I came running after you because Leta ordered me to. I'm not here so that you can try to blackmail me into some sort of-"

I didn't finish the sentence because he touched me just then. A single finger against my lips. A slow smile spread across his face and a mischievous glint in his eyes. That was it. Fire burned through my abdomen and burned the few functioning brain cells in my head. That was all it took for me to lose the last bit of sanity I had.

I pushed away his hand...and launched myself at him.

With a leap of sorts, I wrapped my arms around his neck and eagerly pressed my lips against his. This had been building since the moment I saw him. I suddenly felt as if this had been destined to happen and that no excuse I made would have stopped it.

His lips were smooth as I figured they would be and slightly cool. But I was on fire, and the coolness of his skin felt so good. I wanted to press all my fevered skin against his if only to find some relief from the heat.

He must have been stunned because, for the first few moments, there was no reaction on his part. I began to pull away as the realization that he was not participating cooled my arousal. However, I didn't get the chance to break contact.

His hand swooped in and cradled my face. His mouth was insistent as his lips pushed greedily against mine.

And suddenly, I wasn't even touching the floor, literally. His other hand gripped my waist with his arm wrapped around my back. I had been lifted off my feet and carried to the side of the elevator. My back was pressed against the cool metal, and my front was flush with the coolness of his body.

His lips were amazing, his body taking mine past arousal and to a level that was almost orgasmic, it was so good.

"About time," he muttered against my lips after pulling away.

The lust daze took a moment to clear, but once I realized the reality of my current position, I was suddenly very clear-headed.

"Oh, no!" It came out as a whisper. "This is not good, not good."

"Really?" he nuzzled my neck. "I thought it was great."

"Yes, it was." Focus, Elena. "But it wasn't."

He smiled. "Do I need to kiss the sense back into you?"

"Apparently," I muttered to myself, but he took it as a serious response to his question, leaning down for another kiss.

"No, we can't do this. I still have my reasons." I really wished I could remember them at this moment.

He pulled back, his hands still holding me against the wall of the elevator.

"Ah, yes, the reasons. Because I am a client, and you are on my account? We could just have you taken off the account."

I had been nodding to the first part of his statement when the last part made me stop. "No, I want to stay on the account. This is huge, and so important for my career. You are not worth giving that up for."

He laughed when he should have been offended. "No, no one is worth giving up your dreams, but I still do not see why you cannot have dinner with me."

"That would constitute a date, would it not?"

"What if we talked about business the entire night?"

"Do you want to talk about business the entire night?"

"No."

"And, do you expect to have sex after dinner?" Oh, sex after dinner would be great...kind of like dessert.

His smile deepened. "I never expect it, but I am always thankful when it does happen."

"See, that is a date."

With sex at the end! *Oh, cool down, Elena, cool down.*

"What if we go to dinner, talk about work some of the time, and agree not to have sex?"

What! No sex?

"That's still a date."

"That is dinner between two adults who are allowed to eat and talk with other adults. Is it not?"

"Well, yes, but-"

"Then that is what we will do...tonight. I'll pick you up. What is your address?"

I felt my feet touch the ground before I could respond. What was I responding to?

"Your address, Elena," he reminded me politely, and I gave it to him.

The ding of the elevator surprised me, and I jumped. He gave me a soothing kiss on the cheek. "Eight o'clock," he said and walked out of the elevator.

I watched him in a daze until he was out of the building, and the elevator doors closed in front of me. I leaned against the back wall and let out a deep breath.

I had a date tonight.

I was nervous.

The apartment was oddly empty when I arrived home at six-thirty. I had idled away time at the office after returning the papers to Leta, who left shortly after faxing them. She asked if I wanted to catch the subway home with her, but I declined, claiming that I had a few things to finish before leaving. There were a few things that I had planned to leave undone for the weekend, but I wasn't in a hurry to leave the office.

One: I didn't want to face my roommate and admit to the date I had stupidly agreed to, and two: I just didn't need to be alone with my thoughts.

I didn't have a number for Nolan, and though I was tempted to look up his personal information in Leta's files, I decided against it. It wasn't like I didn't want to go on the date. I did, and that was the problem. I wanted dinner, a late-night kiss, and first-date sex. That was the problem. Nolan was not a man I could sleep with for professional reasons.

That knowledge did not, however, change the growing sexual need.

I put my keys in the bowl by the door and heaved a big sigh as I leaned against the door when I realized that Leta was staying the night at Billy's place.

I stood there for about five minutes and realized that I needed to take a shower and get ready. So, with a groan, I pushed forward.

After the steamy shower, I slathered myself with lotion and plucked a few stray hairs around my eyebrows. I figured if I was going on a date that was going to end in blissful disaster, I might as well go all out. I dried my hair and used a flat iron to give it some soft curls. I put on the sexiest pair of underwear I had. I considered a clingy, short black dress and a tailored black dress with a deep

V-neck, weighing the pros and cons of legs versus cleavage. Then the form-fitting, strapless, blue dress caught my eye.

It had been an impulse purchase. The kind that you make after breaking up with someone and you've moved through the nothing-but-PJs period followed by the wallowing-in-self-pity period and had emerged to the I-need-to-feel-alive-again period. The shade of blue was shocking.

I ran my fingers down it, feeling hopeful and wistful. Yes, that dress made me feel hopeful, which was part of the reason I had bought it. I wanted to be the woman who wore a shocking dress, who was alive and confident.

Without thinking about it any further, I pulled the dress off the hanger. If I thought about it, I would talk myself into one of the black ones instead. I couldn't do that. I needed to wear this dress tonight. I needed to prove to myself that I could be that woman if I wanted to be.

By the time I was dressed, it was seven forty-five. I rushed through my make-up, making my eyes just a little smoky. I went back and forth between a neutral gloss and a bold red lipstick. The knock on the door stopped me from changing my mind again, and the red lipstick won out.

Glancing at my phone, I realized it was eight on the dot. The man was punctual.

Smoothing my dress, I walked to the door and paused. There was no going back. He was here, I was dressed to kill, and there was no way I could fake sick.

So, I opened the door.

He looked amazing, standing with a single red rose in his hand. I can't remember the color of his suit or shirt. I don't even know if he was wearing shoes. I couldn't have cared less. He was beautiful, and the appreciation in his eyes that was almost soul-shattering. I'm not sure any man had ever looked at me like that.

"Hi," I croaked. Clearing my throat, I tried again, and it came out better the second time.

His smile deepened as his eyes roamed from the tip of my head to the peep-toe heels I wore and all the way back up.

"Hello." His voice was warm and smooth. "You look amazing."

Again, the awe was more than I had ever experienced.

"Thank you." I smiled and could feel the blood rushing to the surface of my skin.

"Ah, do not blush. I'm not sure I could breathe if you became any more beautiful right now."

And, of course, I only blushed more as he handed me the rose.

"I'll put this in some water before we leave."

I rushed into the kitchen, taking a brief moment to fan my face. Grabbing a tall glass, I filled it with water and stuck the rose in. I'd look for a vase later.

He stood just outside the doorway, smiling when our eyes met. "Shall we?" he offered his hand. I grabbed a purse, threw my keys inside, and took his hand.

His skin always seemed so cool, which was a relief to my burning skin.

"Your skin is so warm," he commented as we descended the stairs. "You are not getting sick I hope."

I shook my head, trying to remember the mechanics of speaking.

"That is good. I would not want you to be sick."

Nope, this was not an illness-induced fever. This was pure lust, and if I got any hotter, my smoking hot dress might just catch on fire.

We reached the sidewalk outside my building and waited. I looked to Nolan for some indication of where we were going and how we were going to get there. He guided me to the curb looking expectantly down the street.

"Are we waiting for something?"

He nodded. "Oh, yes, here it comes."

I turned my head in the same direction as his and saw a sleek black limo coming towards us. "No."

"Yes."

"You rented a limo?"

"I would not take you near the subway looking like that," he said with a suggestive smile.

Oh dear, I wasn't going to even last until dinner!

I did last until dinner. Though the three dozen red roses in the back of the limo almost had me jumping Nolan right then and there. But I didn't. Instead, I had settled for cozying up to him, letting the hem of my dress ride up my thigh just so slightly. He responded to everything, though it was with less enthusiasm than I would have liked.

He placed a soft hand on my exposed knee while complimenting the dress, the shoes, the hair, and my lips. He breathed in the perfume on my skin right where my neck meets my shoulder, everything so casual as if he had done this a hundred times. And who knows, maybe he had. I refused to think of that just now.

It was strange, I thought as we entered the restaurant. I had always gone on dates worrying that sex might happen at the end, that there would be an expectation. However, tonight I was worried that there might not be sex, and it would all be because he didn't want it. It was a silly worry. He wasn't giving off any signals that claimed he was otherwise disinterested. If anything, his eyes held that anticipation that told me he was just waiting for the preliminary stuff to be done. This was all just a complicated ritual that required certain things to happen in a certain order.

I would just have to be patient.

We went to a restaurant that I had heard of many times but had never been to, one of those restaurants that required a reservation months in advance. Somehow, he managed to get one in a few hours. And we weren't just seated at the table tucked into a corner by the kitchen. Our table by the windows overlooked the city, providing an amazing view. The lighting was soft and intimate. An opera, I imagined Italian, played in the background and the servers were dressed in crisply pressed vests of black and dress shirts of glowing white. Nothing was out of place, not the uniforms, the table settings, the volume of the music. Everything was carefully perfected so that not a single detail was overlooked.

"Does this please you?"

"Yes. This is a beautiful view, and so is the restaurant. I've heard of it before, always with the warning that it takes months to get into. Want to share with me the secret of how you got a reservation tonight?" I had leaned forward as if we were imparting confidential information to each other.

His glance briefly focused on my cleavage, before he too leaned forward. He glanced both ways. "I made a reservation months ago."

I laughed. "You made one, months ago for this very night?"

"My psychic told me this would be a good night. I put two and two together."

I laughed again. "I'm sure you have a lot of good nights. Did she tell you how good a night?"

"A very good night."

I smiled and sipped the water that had just been poured for me. Nolan ordered a bottle of wine, only pausing for any objections I might have. When I smiled and nodded, the waiter praised his choice and left to retrieve it.

"I don't believe that you have a psychic," I said.

"Would you believe that I made a reservation every night for the last few weeks, hoping that you would eventually say yes?"

It sounded sweet and romantic, but I couldn't help but wonder if he did have nightly reservations for whoever the flavor of the night was. Something of my thoughts must have shown on my face, for his expression became serious.

"I only had intentions of bringing you here."

"Sure, you did," I took another drink as he stared at me.

"You don't believe me," he seemed a little surprised. I shook my head, and he sat back, pondering me. "Why is that?"

I almost choked on the water. The waiter came back with our wine, giving me a reprieve from answering. I opened the menu, perusing over the appetizers and entrees while he described the evening's specials. The salmon dish sounded wonderful.

Nolan ordered an appetizer, again waiting for my nod of approval. After which he ordered the filet mignon, and I ordered the salmon. The waiter nodded in approval of both our choices before leaving us alone once more.

"Why is it that you do not believe me?"

He was determined to get an answer on this, so I gave him one.

"I imagine that I am not the only date that you have had this week. An immediate frown on his face, "Okay, not your only date in the last few months."

"Why do you imagine that?"

"Because you are a flirt," I said with an incredulous laugh.

"As are you. So, I should also assume that you have been on other dates this week...these past few weeks?"

I took a moment to be shocked. "No. I've been too busy to go on dates."

"So have I."

"But I'm not the type of woman who just casually dates." This date aside.

"Yet, you seem to think that I am... the causal date type?"

"Aren't you?"

"No." This topic seemed very important to him, and not at all the way I thought our sexy date conversation would start.

"I'm-" I was not going to say sorry. "I didn't mean to offend you."

"You haven't."

"You sure about that?"

"Yes."

Okay...we'd let this topic drop and find a new one.

"But why wouldn't you?" So much for dropping it. "I mean, you could have women lining up to go out with you. You could have a different one every night. And you seem to...appreciate women."

He laughed though it wasn't a hearty one. "I do...appreciate women. What man wouldn't? There are so many things to appreciate. And I enjoy flirting for the same reasons you do."

"But I only flirt with you."

Now, he genuinely laughed. "Is that so?"

"Yes," I said a bit defensively. "I think so."

His laugh was filled with amusement. "A woman as vital and alive as you cannot help but share that with others."

"You're saying I can't help but flirt?"

"I would guess that it does not always seem like flirting to you."

"Maybe not." I hadn't ever thought of myself as a flirt. "You must be even more vital and alive than I am. Because there is no doubt that you are flirting."

He smiled though it seemed a bit sad. "Friendly flirting puts people at ease. It is a way to make them more comfortable."

"It didn't make me more comfortable."

"That is because it was never just a friendly flirtation with you."

The appetizer arrived just then, and I was saved from responding to that. Nolan watched me with a smile as I took a bite of the appetizer and changed the subject to commentary on the food.

The food was worth talking about. It was amazing. The chef had been praised in many articles for his inventive mixings of flavors in traditional American staples. We moved into a conversation on favorite foods and least favorite foods, and reminisced of childhood foods that were now comfort foods.

He talked of Eastern European dishes that I had never heard of, explaining them through entertaining stories of his grandmother, who was the tiny dictator who ruled his family. The rolling pin was her weapon of choice. His stories of growing up in a small house filled to the brim with five other people had me laughing so hard that I felt the need to cover my mouth to contain some of the laughter in this fancy restaurant.

I told him about growing up in a typical American house. I had two siblings, a brother and a sister. Though my family could be traced back to Ireland and Scotland with one family member originating in Spain, we had been American for too long to remember any of our ancestors' customs. My family had been brought up on hot dogs at backyard barbecues, baked potatoes loaded with sour cream, cheese, and butter, and eggs and bacon with jammed toast for Sunday mornings. I told him about my ongoing love affair with ice cream. When he asked what my favorite flavor was, I professed that I loved them all, and he laughed.

I described summer picnics with fresh strawberry shortcakes piled with whipped cream, cold deli sandwiches, and potato salad. He knew what a picnic was, but the concept still seemed foreign to him. So, I described the old blanket that would fit all five of us, spread out on the ground with the food piled in the center. We would usually hike a short way to the spot and then gorge ourselves on food. After the feeding frenzy, we would lay out in the sun for an afternoon nap.

"I miss picnics. I can't remember the last time I was on one. Thank you," I said as the waiter placed my entrée in front of me. I had been so engrossed in our conversation that I hadn't even noticed his approach.

After placing the food in front of us and making sure that we had no other needs, the waiter disappeared. I took a sip of wine. It was a red, not usually my favorite, but still good. French, I guessed.

"There haven't been a lot of opportunities to go on a picnic lately."

"Perhaps you'll go when it gets warmer."

"Yes, they are so much better when it's warm. Otherwise, you're huddled in your coat trying not to freeze."

"Or you huddle with someone else."

I smiled at the suggestion. "There's an idea."

We were silent, each of us taking the first few bites of food. Mine proved to be as good as the appetizer, and I moaned with appreciation of the flavors.

"You like it?" he asked with a smirk.

"Yes, it is very good. And yours?"

He cut a piece of filet mignon, speared it with his fork, and held it out to me. "Here, try for yourself." When I hesitated, he asked, "You do not eat beef?"

"Oh, no, I do." I let him feed me the piece of meat, and it too was good. So was his look of pleasure as I took the bite.

The conversation switched to the normal first-date conversation. Politics came up at one point, and we both laughed when we realized that neither one of us was interested in the subject.

"I know only what I need to get by, but I do not have a passion for it. Unlike Micah. He has studied Machiavelli passionately."

I nodded. "I could see that. Are you two friends?"

He shrugged as the plates were cleared from the table. "We are business associates. I knew when I started the company that he would be valuable, and he has been."

"Wait, you own the company?"

He smiled as he swirled the wine in his glass. "You did not know that?"

I shook my head. "Micah takes the lead on so much that I just assumed it was his company."

Nolan took a drink and set his glass down. "No, it is indeed my company. Micah enjoys such things, so I let him do them. I enjoy sitting back and watching people react to his ways. It can be quite entertaining. However, I make all final decisions."

The waiter stopped by our table and asked Nolan, "Would you like coffee, perhaps look at the dessert menu?"

He sent me a smile. "Whatever the lady wants."

The waiter turned to me. "Yes, to both please." He nodded and returned shortly with a dessert menu.

I scanned the items, thinking that the chocolate hazelnut soufflé would be amazing, but the cheesecake was a classic. I was bent over the menu and did not realize that he had leaned towards me. When I looked up to ask for his opinion, I felt his hand envelop mine, and all the lust that had been on the back burner flared to a boil.

"See anything you want?"

Ah, yes, actually... you. I didn't say that, though I'm sure he read the thought in my eyes because he smiled. I told him about the soufflé and the cheesecake. He made a noise of agreement over the soufflé. So, when our served returned with the coffee, we ordered the soufflé.

I sipped my coffee. "What are some of the things that you love?"

"I love nights with a new moon when all the stars are visible."

It was such a small thing to love, yet knowing it made him seem more real and less the sexy god who entranced the office.

"Do you know the constellations?"

He looked a bit shy for a moment, the only time I had ever seen him look that way. "I used to. I'm not sure that I remember them anymore."

"Has it been that long?"

With a sigh, "It has."

"The new moon is coming soon. You should drive out of the city and spend an hour or two getting reacquainted with the stars."

His fingers rubbed little circles on my palm and wrist. "I think I will."

Dessert was another memorable affair for my taste buds though I couldn't enjoy any of it. My brain had switched back to sex. I tried coyly a time or two to rub my foot up the inside of his leg. He smiled, obviously aware of what I was doing. However, it was an amused smile and not one that asked, please do more. I eventually gave up as the conversation took off once more.

We finished the wine, coffee, and dessert. He escorted me from the restaurant with my hand tucked into his elbow, but when we reached the elevator to go down, his fingers entwined with mine and we walked that way to the car.

Assuming much the same position in the back of the limo as before, I snuggled up to him with his hand on my knee. He seemed distracted though. I wondered if his impression of the night differed that much from mine.

When we reached the apartment, he hauled two dozen of the roses up while I carried the other. I unlocked the door to my apartment and set the flowers on the table in the living room. He waited outside the door with the others, handing them to me so that I could carry them into my apartment. I placed the last vase by the door and turned back at him. He stared at me as if he couldn't figure out a problem.

"Is everything okay? Would you-"

"It is fine. I cannot make the driver wait for too long."

"Of course," I felt my hopes deflate. "My roommate isn't here tonight. I can't remember the last time the apartment was this quiet."

It was lame, I know. I needed to let him know that this could end with him in my apartment, but I didn't have the nerve to straight out ask if he wanted to spend the night.

He smiled; again, it seemed a little sad. "That is good. You will get the rest that you have been missing lately."

Oh, if there was ever a gentle letdown, that was it.

"Yes, that will be nice." I felt nothing but awkwardness. "Thank you so much for dinner. I had a great time." I stood inside the doorway, him just outside it. "Have a good night."

I started to turn away, when he said, "Come here."

I took a step forward. He wrapped me in his arms. "We did not talk about work. This will end with a kiss good night, so I'm afraid it was a date after all."

He did not wait for my response, but instead, proceeded to kiss me. It was a sweet kiss, lacking the heat and passion I needed. I tried to increase the intensity that I so desperately wanted, but he kept it mellow.

When he pulled away and whispered good night against my lips, I was still shocked at the lack of satisfaction. He left with me gaping in the door like an idiot.

I guess that answered some questions. I thought the night had gone well, but apparently, I had misinterpreted it. A good date did not end with a kiss like that, especially not with an invitation to come in.

With a great sigh, I closed the door and looked around my apartment. I was glad that Leta was not here to witness my rejection. Of course, I might have gotten a cake out of it if she had. She believed in treating bad emotions with good food. Can't say I was against the idea.

Right now, though, I wanted to crawl into bed and possibly cry.

The Tree must have sensed my mood because it shook gently as I walked towards the hall. "Thanks," I said, not sure what it was trying to convey but aware that it was meant to be comforting.

As I fell into sleep that night, I thought just briefly of the evening. The blue dress was in the closet pushed towards the back again. I didn't want to look at it. In fact, I thought of burning it right before sleep claimed me.

Chapter 25

I woke up the next day in pain. My head hurt, my abdomen hurt everywhere, and pulses of heartburn burned in my chest. Taking a handful of Tums, I contemplated staying in bed all day.

Leta arrived later in the night when I was in between flare-ups and the hot flashes that had started around midnight. Sometime around noon, I realized that I had not eaten all day and dragged my sad self out to the kitchen.

Leta was smelling the roses when I came out of my room. Turning to me, I saw the sympathy on her face. "Miguel," was all she said.

I shrugged. Sure, why not? That was a lot easier than explaining that I had been out on a date with our client.

Leta just shook her head. "I thought he would have given up by now, but I guess not. Did you talk to him yet?" I shook my head. "Elena, you have to start facing things. They won't just go away because you're not ready. You know?"

I had no idea and didn't even bother to respond as I walked through the living room, rubbing the center of my chest.

A harsh knock on the door caused me to jump.

"Leta, Elena. It's me, Farah."

I raised an eyebrow at Leta who just shrugged.

With a complete lack of enthusiasm, I opened the door and there stood Farah in her jeans, brown leather jacket, and calf-length Doc Martins.

"I'm surprised you didn't just come on in," I said.

"I didn't want to interrupt anything that might be going on."

Though I knew exactly what she meant, I found it amusing. "Hasn't stopped you before."

"Hi, Farah. Give me a minute to change," Leta called over her shoulder as she headed toward her room.

I had gone to the kitchen to scrounge for food without realizing Farah had followed me in until she spoke right next to my ear. "What is wrong with you?"

I nearly dropped the container of soup I was so surprised. "Nothing. Why?"

Farah leaned back on the counter, crossing one leg over the other, and her arms across her chest. "You seem different today," she said thoughtfully.

"I think I might be getting a stomach ulcer or something because I've had horrible heartburn all day."

"Oh, yeah. Have you been particularly upset or worked up over something recently?" When I just stared at her, she added, "Have you been experiencing a lot of emotion like anger or lust?"

"Stupid men," I muttered to myself as I put the soup in the microwave. Of course, I forgot Farah had the hearing of a wolf.

"Stupid men, huh?" she said with a smile. "One in particular or just the bunch in general?"

I straightened up. "They're all stupid, but one in particular." I glanced into the living room; Leta was still changing. Stepping closer, I confided in Farah. "I had a date with Nolan last night."

"Nolan...as in one of your clients Nolan?" she asked with raised brows.

I took a step closer. "I have to tell somebody, Farah, and since you don't work at the firm, you're the safest person to tell." She nodded nonchalantly in agreement. Taking a deep breath, I divulged all. "He's been flirting with me for weeks, like hard-core, aggressive flirting."

She nodded. "I had heard that." From Selene no doubt.

"Then the week that we made the second presentation, I was so stressed out and sleep-deprived from having taken care of Leta that I just broke down at work. He found me, and well, comforted me. It was nice. Then more flirting in the weeks after that, and he started asking me to dinner. The week we were waiting to hear back from Billy, we sort of had a coffee date."

"You and Nolan...sort of had a coffee date?"

"Yeah, we ran into each other at the place by work. He bought me coffee, and we talked. He called it a date, not me."

Farah nodded.

"And, then yesterday. I had to chase him down because Leta needed him to sign some papers. Anyway, we ended up in the elevator together, and I lost it."

"How so?"

I squirmed a bit just thinking about it. "I...kissed him, rather passionately."

I looked up to determine Farah's reaction. She smirked. "I know, it was stupidly impulsive, and not at all like me. I don't know where it came from."

Farah looked thoughtful again as she uncrossed her legs and headed towards the stove. "So, you're having really bad heartburn after emotional situations and experiencing bursts of impulsiveness?"

I nodded, not sure what the two had to do with each other.

"Interesting," she said as she filled the kettle with water. "Go on."

"I never would have kissed him if we hadn't been in that elevator."

"Here, hold this." She handed me the kettle. I looked at it in confusion. "You kissed Nolan," she prompted.

"I kissed Nolan, and then he tricked me into a date with him."

"Tricked you, huh?" her concentration seemed to be on the kettle. "Tricky McTricksterson."

"Yes, he was!" I felt anger building.

"But you wanted to go on that date."

The reminder of how much I had wanted to go was annoying. "Yeah, but I was set on not being seduced by him, and then he went and tricked me into a date."

"Sneaky bastard."

"Yes! So, I got dressed up for this date that I didn't want to go on. I mean I wore my blue dress, the Dress, the one I have never worn before. I'm talking about pulling out the best panties I own for this guy."

"That lousy son of bitch."

"Lousy, yes! He comes up here with a single red rose saying some nice crap about how great I looked."

"Can't trust a sneaky bastard though."

"No, you can't. Then this limo pulls up, and it's filled with dozens of roses."

"He was just trying to schmooze you."

"You think so?"

"Absolutely. Don't trust a schmoozer," she nodded sagely.

"That must have been it. Because I snuggled up to him in my amazing dress revealing a great bit of leg, and my cleavage practically pouring out of the dress, looking incredibly hot this entire time."

"Naturally."

"And do you know what I get? A pat on the knee and little neck action."

"You looked that hot, and he gave you nothing but neck action," Farah said in disgust.

"I know, right!" I could hear the volume of my voice rising, but I couldn't control it.

"Jerk."

"Yes, yes! Then we go to this great restaurant, have amazing conversation, and I'm playing footsy with him under the table, and he just looks amused."

"Total asshole."

"And, then he brings me back up here, I discreetly indicate that he should come in and have sex with me."

"Did he take you up on the offer?"

"No!"

I could hear the water in the kettle heating up. I felt just like it; any second now I was going to blow. "He says something about me needing rest. And, he has one last chance to fix it with a good night kiss, and all I get is a lame, soft lip pucker with no passion at all."

Farah's eyes were fixed downward. "Let it out, let it all out."

"That bastard!" I yelled as the whistle of the kettle filled the air.

"Thank you," Farah said as she took the kettle from my hands.

I had forgotten it was there.

"Wait, what just happened?"

The kettle had been in my hands, but I'd heard the whistle. Farah was pouring hot water from it into her cup.

"Wow, Leta," Farah called over her shoulder. "She's faster than the stove."

I looked behind me just as Leta entered the kitchen and proceeded to get herself a mug. "I know, right? I have her warm up my tea sometimes."

"What are you talking about?" I was seriously confused. "What just happened?"

"We'll tell you when you're older," Leta laughed at the joke while Farah smiled and doctored her tea.

I glared at Leta.

"You're not ready yet," she said more seriously.

"What does that mean?" I demanded, but she just shook her head. So, I turned to Farah, ready to demand that she answer me.

She shook her head and lifted her hands in a gesture of surrender.

I huffed and turned back to Leta. "Tell me what is going on."

My roommate stared at me with narrowed eyes. "I don't think that you are ready to hear this, Elena."

"I'm not five, Leta. Just tell me."

She set her mug down and stared directly at me. "Okay then. Elena, you are an elemental. A fire elemental, it would appear, and you are starting your transition."

I stared at her and shook my head to clear it. There was no way she had just told me that. I shook my head again just for good measure.

"I'm sorry," I said with a faint laugh, "I must not have heard right because...no, just no."

"I told you were not ready for this, but it's good. You had to hear it sooner rather than later because your change is going to hit soon."

"And what makes you an expert on these...sorts of things?" I asked indignantly though I couldn't figure out why I was getting so worked up.

"I'm an elemental-"

"I thought you were a nymph or dryad or whatever." I lost my temper again. "Oh, no!" I gasped as I took a step back from Leta. "IT'S CONTAGIOUS! This crazy mythical stuff is contagious? Did you cause something strange to happen to me?"

My voice was a mixture of anger and hysteria, my stare accusing. After all, I was the normal one in this group. That was the last little fact that kept me sane with everything that had happened.

Farah snorted a laugh at my reaction, and Leta looked torn between irritation and concern. "No, Elena, nothing is contagious." Leta used that patient tone of hers though I could see she was strained. "And just so you know, a nymph is an earth elemental."

"What does that even mean?" I was in shock, feeling lightheaded and queasy all of a sudden.

"You're not going to faint, are you?" Farah asked. I glared at her. "Just making sure in case I need to be ready to catch you."

"Elena," Leta's soothing tone was so irritating, "'This crazy mythical stuff' you're talking about is real. You know it's real. And yes, now you are a part of it. Not all elementals are the same.

Nymphs, dryads, in particular, are so dependent upon the bond with their trees that they are born into what they are, but not all the elements are the same. It can take years before that part of themselves emerges."

I was on the verge of interrupting, yelling at her that I didn't even know what an elemental was, but she quickly explained.

"An elemental is a person that is deeply connected to one of the elements: earth, air, water, and fire. Because of their connections, the elemental force becomes a part of who they are, like dryads and their trees, and they can learn to control that part of themselves. Do you see what I'm saying?"

She stared at me with her big eyes full of concern. Farah stood behind her also eyeing me with concern. It was like being in a fishbowl. Just when I thought I could handle how crazy things were, it got bumped up a level.

"This is too much." I turned to walk out of the room, but Leta stopped me with a gentle hand on my arm.

"I know, honey, but it's so important-"

"No, don't." I pulled my arm away. "You have no idea."

"See, these surges of temper; it's the fire trying to come out."

"The impulsiveness, the lust," Farah added. "All part of the fire."

Leta nodded ardently though I could tell she had no clue what Farah was talking about. We were not going to go there.

"I don't want to talk about this anymore," and again I tried to leave the kitchen.

"Elena, you can't be stuck in denial forever," Leta called out to me.

I turned on her in rage, my chest and abdomen burning. "Until I shoot fire out of my fingertips, I don't want to talk about it."

"Technically, salamanders, which are fire elementals, usually breathe fire, not shoot it from their fingers."

I growled and kept walking to my room. Even The Tree was smart enough to recognize that I was not in the mood. It pulled its branches in tight to its trunk as I passed it on my way down the hall.

Leta could say whatever she wanted, but I was not turning into a fire-breathing nut-job like her. I refused. Refused to believe it was possible. Refused to let it happen even if it did turn out to be possible. The anger, the impulsiveness, and the lust were all the result of stress. And I had had a lot of stress in my life recently, thanks mostly to that nymph.

There was absolutely no way I was ever becoming a fire elemental.

Chapter 26

The weekend left me cranky and mildly pissed off at the world. I was more than mildly ticked at my roommate even though she had respected my wishes and not mentioned the elemental thing again. However, just looking at her made me think of that conversation, and I would get enraged all over again. My temper was harder to control, though I refused to believe that it was because I was becoming some mythical creature.

The pain was also getting worse. I wasn't eating much, and I carried a bottle of Tums with me everywhere. I even contemplated seeing a doctor for what I was sure was an ulcer.

Not the elemental fire trying to find a way out.

On Sunday, while restricting my cranky self to my room, I did a little research on fire elementals. I figured I could argue with Leta better if I was more informed.

Fire elementals were indeed called salamanders, which was also a type of amphibian. There seemed to be no consensus on what this being looked like. One of my favorite descriptions was a "worm penetrating fire". What girl doesn't like thinking of herself as wormlike?

If I was a fire elemental, (according to the lexicon of Dungeons and Dragons) I would be unable to enter water or any other nonflammable liquid. Which was funny considering I was on the swim team in high school, almost winning the state competition my senior year.

But my absolute favorite was the legends that said salamanders were also poisonous, making everything they touched toxic. Because that seemed to be exactly what had happened to my love life.

I didn't want to be excited about seeing Nolan on Monday, but I was. I had difficulty concentrating as I kept an eye on the hall just in case he came to the office. And it was when I left my desk to get lunch that he appeared. I was returning to my desk, sandwich from the deli downstairs in hand when I saw him turn the corner. He walked with Selene, the two of them in deep conversation. I stood, like an idiot by my cubicle waiting for them.

I'm not sure what I was expecting. It's not like I wanted him to profess his undying love to me, especially not at work and not in front of my supervisor. But the casual smile I got as they passed was not what I was expecting. I couldn't help but feel defeated as I stood long after they had passed me.

Apparently, I had misread the date completely. No doubt, I had misread him completely. I collapsed into my chair wondering why it was that I couldn't read men at all. Miguel came to mind, but there was no way I could have known he was a werewolf before being told by Leta.

I pulled my antacids out; the heartburn was flaring even though I hadn't eaten yet. Rubbing my chest, I gave myself a silent pep talk. Nolan was not the only guy on the planet, and even though the date had underwhelmed him, it wasn't a reflection of me. Sometimes people just didn't click.

The pain flared. Damn it!

We had clicked though. There was an ease and comfort between us that didn't always come so easily. And there was chemistry.

One-sided, maybe, a cruel little part of me pointed out.

I was still rubbing my chest when I heard a soft laugh. "I know that look."

Micah stood in front of my cubicle, a look of false sympathy on his face.

"Can I help you with something, Mr. Renier?" I said as sweetly as I could.

"I think you are the one in need of assistance, and I might just be able to offer it to you." I wondered if the man knew how smarmy he was.

"Ah, no. I'm just fine, thank you."

"Elena, Elena," his voice dripped pity. "I've seen him do this countless times."

"I don't know what you're talking-"

"The flirtations, the dinner invitations. He does it all the time. Woos and seduces one sweet, naïve woman after another." It was amazing how he always seemed to embed an insult into every conversation we had. "It means nothing to him."

I stood, figuring that it was the only way out of the conversation. I tried to excuse myself, but he blocked my way. Leaning against the cubicle's partition on one side, he flung his blazer back, placing his hand on his hip. The top buttons of his white shirt were unbuttoned, and had he never spoken to me, I might have found him attractive. Fortunately, I had already heard him talk.

"Excuse me," I said again.

"Elena, why don't you let me console you?"

I stared into his confident face. "You're a client. That wouldn't be appropriate. Besides, there is nothing to console."

I tried to push past, but he stopped me again, this time placing his hand on my hip. I immediately stepped out of his reach. I tried to control the temper that boiled just under the surface. The last thing I needed was to blow up at Micah because he would undoubtedly take his complaint to Glenda, no doubt painting it in the worst possible light.

With a look over his shoulder, he said in a snide voice, "I don't think that has stopped you before."

Cheap shot, I almost yelled at him in fury. Instead, I managed a deep breath. "I am absolutely of the mindset that any interaction with clients outside of work is wrong and... inappropriate."

He seemed amused though I couldn't understand why. "I am sorry that you will suffer for him. He's not free to make such pursuits."

I wanted to question that, to ask what he meant, but I remained quiet instead. Micah seemed disappointed with my lack of reaction.

"I hope you will let me know if there is anything that I can do for you," he said with a self-satisfied smile before walking away.

I waited a few minutes to make sure that he was not coming back before dropping my forehead to my desk. I could stay like that all day I decided, just wallowing in self-pity.

"You feel okay?"

I looked up to find Selene eyeing me with concern. I was getting so tired of people looking at me with concern. "I'm fine. Just some heartburn." I straightened in my chair.

"Did you have something spicy for lunch?"

"No, I haven't eaten yet." I fussed with papers on my desk.

"Hmm."

My eyes shot right back up to her giving a clear warning. "Don't go there."

"You know, Leta's concerned."

"Leta is also crazy."

Selene smiled. "No argument. But out of curiosity, I did some research." She looked down both sides of the hall before continuing in a softer voice. "Transitions or changes can come on very quickly even if there have been weeks of symptoms. They tend to knock people out for a few days followed by a surge of...energy."

"Oh, that's interesting. I missed that when I did my internet search. What site were you looking at?"

Selene seemed unfazed by my acerbity. "I used primary resources." She looked thoughtful for a moment. "Elena, just be careful. Even if Leta is wrong, I feel like this is a very vulnerable time for you."

I waited for her to hint at more, to give some indication that she knew about the date with Nolan. But she didn't go any further.

Finally, I nodded and assured her that I would be careful. She seemed pleased with that and left my cubicle.

My appetite was gone so I pushed the wrapped sandwich to the corner of my desk and returned to working.

I woke with a groan and realized as I lifted my head that there was something slick plastered to my face. With a crinkly noise it fell off, and I stared down at my finished bottle design. Thankfully, the shiny print did not appear to be affected by being plastered to my face.

I blinked the sleep from my eyes while looking for my cell phone. The little screen was bright in my darkened cubicle as it flashed the time for me. It was way past normal work hours, but that was unsurprising. Ever since my date with Nolan, I had been working longer hours.

One: to avoid my roommate's very healthy sex life.

And two: to distract myself from thoughts of Nolan. Being at work reminded me why it was a good thing that Nolan wasn't interested in me. I didn't know what had gotten into me, but it had been a horrible idea to date a client. I knew better than that.

Fortunately, the clients had been gone all week, having returned to Europe.

Not seeing Nolan for a week had strengthened my resolve that there was not to be anything between us. Not that it mattered since his apparent lack of interest had been clearly made, and the week had not lessened any of my anger though, which was silly.

I forced myself to admit (often grudgingly) that I hadn't wanted to go on the date with him in the first place. I had only done it to end the incessant flirting. I hadn't expected myself to enjoy the date. I conveniently forgot that I had wanted to have sex with him.

Pushing thoughts of Nolan aside, I stretched my arms over my head and winced at the soreness. I must have fallen asleep in a weird position. Trying to stretch out the soreness, I stood and gathered the rest of my stuff. The other cubicles were dark and abandoned for the weekend.

I paused to make sure that the front glass door was closed behind me and rode the elevator down, wondering what I was going to do with the remainder of my Friday night and even more depressing, the rest of my weekend.

Idly scratching my neck, I exited into the lobby hoping to avoid Stan. No such luck though.

"What are you still doing here?" he asked as he came around the security desk to greet me.

"I had some work that I needed to finish up."

He raised a gray eyebrow at me. "You've been working late every night this week."

"Deadlines and all that," I responded lamely.

"You sure you're not just trying to avoid something?"

Of course, Stan would see through to the real problem. This was why I wanted to avoid seeing him.

"Nope, can't think of anything I would be avoiding," I said cheerfully; he didn't look convinced. I started walking towards the exit with Stan following. "Well, maybe just my roommate-"

"I thought you got that worked out," he interrupted with concern.

"Oh, we did, but she has a new boyfriend and..." He raised his hands and with a knowing look indicated that I did not need to finish explaining.

"Hmm, you might need to find another way of dealing with that. All this work isn't good for you. You're looking a little pale." As he leaned towards me, I reacted by leaning back. "Are you sure you're feeling okay?" Something strange in the look he gave me...as if I would sprout branches at any moment. No, that was my roommate. The intensity of his concern made me shift uncomfortably.

"I'm fine, Stan. Maybe just a little tired."

He continued to assess me. "No strange fevers or blackouts lately?"

Well, that was a strange question. Stranger because I had been having low-grade fevers all week. But as Farah had pointed out it was flu season, and the recent stress might have made me susceptible to getting sick. It would probably be better to rest and hydrate all weekend just in case I was coming down with something.

"No, none of that. But I promise to get lots of rest this weekend." That seemed to please him. He smiled that kind, fatherly smile at me, and I was momentarily warmed by it.

"You make sure to do that."

"Have a good night, Stan," I said as he opened the outer doors for me. He wished me a good night as well.

Right before I went outside, I turned back to the old security guard. "Thanks for the concern, Stan. I do appreciate you looking out for me."

He smiled. "That's my job."

What a funny way to think of his job.

The apartment was unfortunately not empty. Leta and Billy were on the couch watching a movie, snuggled up disgustingly close. Leta had made pasta and told me that there was a plate for me in the microwave. I heated it and consumed the pasta standing over the sink, listening to Leta and Billy laugh at the slapstick comedy.

As I trudged through the living room, feeling a week's worth of hard work hit me, Leta invited me to join them. I politely declined and was too tired to even avoid The Tree. It must have taken pity on me, or it chose not to act out in front of Billy because I made it to my bedroom without being whacked in the face.

After brushing my teeth and changing into pajamas, I crawled into bed and tried to read the biography of Coco Chanel that I had recently picked up. Five sentences in and my eyes became heavy. I turned the light out and called it a night, falling quickly into sleep.

The sleep was not restful though. I woke drenched in sweat, patting my skin down as the image of fire spreading all over my body stayed with me even as I opened my eyes. After assuring myself that I was not on fire, I climbed out of bed and wandered into the living room. Leta and Farah were sitting on the couch. Their conversation abruptly stopped as I entered the room.

"Good morning," I said, unsure if I should be concerned by their speculative looks.

"Good afternoon, actually," Leta said.

"Afternoon?" I rubbed the lingering bits of sleep from my eyes as I walked through the room.

"Yep, it's two in the afternoon," Farah replied.

I stopped and turned slowly to them. "Two? Wow, I must have been really tired."

"It must be all that extra time you're spending at the office. Or something else that we are not talking about." I heard the hint of disapproval in Leta's voice and answered it with a dirty look as I continued towards the kitchen.

There was some murmuring before Farah followed me into the kitchen. "You feeling alright? Having any fevers?"

What was it with people and their concern with fevers? "I'm fine."

"You've been irritable lately."

"How would you know?"

"Leta's worried." I wanted to snap at her, but there was just enough concern in Farah's voice that I couldn't bring myself to be that bitchy.

"I'm fine."

"You're looking a little flushed," she said.

I paused and realized that I felt a lot flushed. All that heat I had been feeling must have been a fever coming on. I was burning up all over. Putting a hand to my hot forehead, I closed my eyes briefly.

"I think I need to go back to bed." Maybe even take a cold shower first. "I must be coming down with something," I muttered as I exited the kitchen.

"Get some rest," Farah called out.

I nodded in response.

Leta called out, "Do you want me to make you some soup?"

Ugh! All I needed was more heat right now. "No, I'm just going to take some Tylenol and sleep it off. Thanks though."

I didn't even attempt a smile; there was suddenly not enough energy, and I needed to save what little I had on getting back to my bed.

I couldn't make out their words, but I knew Farah and Leta were talking about me as I trudged to my room. I didn't care. All I wanted now was to pass out. I felt like a nuclear explosion had gone off inside me, and I was left with nothing but the heat.

As I collapsed onto the bed, I thought briefly that this was the worst case of the flu I had ever had.

I called in on Monday. Actually, Leta called in for me on Monday, Tuesday, and Wednesday because I still hadn't regained full consciousness by then. The few times I had been awake were a blur. Bathroom, fluid, and more fluid was my mantra while I was awake. After accomplishing those three things, I fell back asleep. The fever came and went, but it did not reach the same level as it had on Saturday afternoon. Mostly, I just felt drained. As if something essential to sustaining energy had just been leeched out of me. But that was the flu for you.

Leta watched over me from a distance. The trauma of her recent illness was still with her. "I think this might all be part of the process," she would say, "but just in case it isn't."

Whatever that meant.

I found that I was able to remain conscious for longer periods by Wednesday night, but I was forced to call in again on Thursday because there was no way I would even make it through the subway ride, let alone put in a full day's worth of work. Besides, I figured that I could still be contagious, and I didn't want to infect somebody else.

Abdominal pain had added itself to my list of ailments by Thursday night, and I was still so tired. Usually with the flu, I would start to feel some improvement after the first of couple days. Though I was feeling somewhat better after four days, I began to wonder if maybe this wasn't the flu.

Unfortunately, I had enough energy to Google my symptoms, which basically told me I was dying from cancer or some other horrible disease.

Leta was amused by my insistence that I had contracted a horrible brain infection or was being eaten away by cancer, but she still expressed some concern. I think it was the highlight of her week to force feed me chicken noodle soup and shove a thermometer in my mouth every four hours. I tried not to be annoyed by it, but I was sick and the glee she took out of being my nurse was just too much for my strained patience.

She called me melodramatic for thinking that there could seriously be something wrong with me, and hinted, not too subtly I might add, that it was all related to the change she was sure I was going to make. I ignored her hints even when she became less subtle. I was sure that I had stomach cancer...or at least a horrible ulcer.

I also reminded Leta that she had not been the most ideal patient and had told me numerous times that she was dying. Of course, when I mentioned this, she stared at me blankly and said with absolute honesty that she couldn't remember any of it.

Oh, the power of self-denial.

Chapter 28

Insistent pounding filled my head. I could add headaches to the list.

Only it stopped...and started again.

Peeking an eye open, I looked up from the sofa where I had crashed. The banging was coming from the front door. Relief washed through me; I probably didn't have a brain tumor.

The banging started again.

"Go away," I called out. In good health, I would have been mortified by the rudeness. However, the banging stopped, and I settled back into the sofa with a satisfied smile.

As my eyes closed, I heard the lock turn and the door swing open.

"Well, if you can tell me bugger off, I don't think that you're dying."

I looked up again to see Farah. "What are you doing here?"

"Leta was worried about you and asked me to check on you. And you look fine to me."

She stood over me, hands on hips, and a certain look of approval.

I pushed myself up into a sitting position. Grudgingly, I admitted, "I am feeling quite better today actually." I was less convinced that I was dying from some exotic disease.

"Just a case of the flu then?"

I rubbed my sore neck. "Yeah, I think so. Though, I think something bit me. I didn't pay it much attention a few days ago because...well, I wasn't able to pay attention to really anything. But there is this bump on my neck, and it's making everything sore."

I continued to rub the spot of contention until Farah brushed my fingers aside.

"Let me take a look; I can identify most bug bites."

"A secret hobby of yours," I said dryly as I craned my neck to give her a better view.

Her expression went from curious to serious. "It can't be," she muttered to herself before grabbing my chin in hand and yanking my head further to the side. I tried to object, but her grip had my jaw locked into position.

She sniffed my neck one moment, and the next, she grabbed my face so tightly it hurt. We were face to face, and I was looking at one pissed-off werewolf. In her growling voice, she accused, "You let some one-fanged vampire bastard bite you!"

Whoa. "What!" I managed to exclaim despite the viselike grip on my face.

"This," she yanked my face to the side again. I was going to get whiplash or a torn muscle from this encounter, "is a vampire bite."

"How do you know?"

"Because it smells like a vampire. And I'd say it's about a week old."

"That was the time that I started to get sick."

"Flu, huh." She released my face and stepped away. I tried to rub the soreness from my jaw.

"I had no idea, Farah, and I definitely don't remember being bitten by anyone. I think that's the kind of the thing that a person would remember."

"Not if you blacked out." She looked pissed off and thoughtful.

"Oh, no," I muttered.

When Farah gave a small growl and a raised brow, I explained.

"The night that I got sick, I thought I had fallen asleep at my desk. Seeing as how I hadn't been sleeping that well lately, I didn't think anything of it. But when I try to think back, I can't remember falling asleep. I know that I was working on the final print, and then I was waking up. It seems kind of blurry actually."

"Sounds about right. Vampires have a way of hypnotizing their victims into not remembering. It also helps with finding willing victims."

"Don't vampires have two fangs?"

"Not your vampire it would seem."

"He's not my vampire!" I felt a flush of temper that was like the fevers I had been running all week.

Farah paused to take a step back. Even The Tree seemed to recoil from me.

"Ease there, Fiery. Listen, it would appear that there is a vampire on the loose in your office building, biting unsuspecting people. Could be male or female."

"Well, that narrows it down," I said dryly. Farah shrugged. "Are they dangerous...vampires, I mean?"

"Well, they sure aren't good for your health as you found out."

"Oh," I exclaimed with a hand to the forehead. "That explains it." To Farah's questioning look, I continued. "The women at the office have been getting sick for the past few weeks with what appeared to be the flu. Of course, no one thought anything of it. There's a vampire making everyone at work sick!"

"Yes, it would appear so."

I stood up. "You have to come to the office with me. You can sniff the bastard out."

Farah narrowed her indignant eyes though her voice held a hint of amusement. "Like a bloodhound?"

"Yeah, then we can confront him, and you'll scare him away. Problem solved. Now, where are my pants?"

"Not that easy."

I looked up from my search. "Why not?"

"Vampires are not easy to 'sniff out' as you put it."

"Why not, you could smell it on my neck."

"Yeah, there was vampire saliva on your neck. Unless this vamp goes around drooling all over the place, I won't catch a whiff of him or her. Vampires go to a lot of trouble to conceal themselves. They will prey on anyone at any time. Doesn't make them the most popular kids in school."

"So...they don't smell or stand out in any way at all?"

"Not usually."

"What about all the vampire myths? You know the ones about how they can't go out into the sunlight, or they're allergic to garlic, or how they don't have a reflection in the mirror."

"Honestly, I don't how much of that is true. Vampires are very secretive. All I know is that they are sneaky little leeches that leave you sick as hell after a feeding."

"You're telling me," I muttered. "Do they come back to the same victims?"

"Sometimes. I think it all depends on ease. They want to feed off whatever is most convenient and easiest."

"So, if this vampire works for Madame, he might just keep coming back for more as we're all so convenient and easy?"

"Can't say for sure, but I wouldn't trust anyone as far as I could throw 'em."

When I returned to work on Friday, I was still lethargic and running low-grade fevers, but I couldn't stay at home for another minute. I had dark circles under my eyes thanks to the combination of heartburn and stomach pain mixed with vampire nightmares had made my sleep anything but restful.

However, I was determined to find the vampire that had bitten me and was biting others at the firm. Of course, I had no idea of how to go about finding him. Leta was as clueless as Farah, citing again that vampires were super secretive.

Selene was a little more helpful. She was sure that the sunlight thing was a myth. The absence of a reflection in a mirror was also ruled out. So, that left me with crosses and garlic. The cross was easy. I had a beautiful one that my mother had given me years ago. I hardly ever wore it but dug it out for this mission. It was gold and simple and hung on a delicate chain.

The garlic was a little harder. It wasn't like I could wear a string of garlic around my neck without sticking out or offending someone with the smell. Leta and Selene were greatly amused by my antics. I first thought about placing cloves of garlic in my bra but when I tried that, it just felt too weird. I didn't know if I was that dedicated to the cause.

The second idea I had was to carry garlic with me and rub a bit of crushed garlic over my neck. I then proceeded to get in the personal space of every employee at Madame Advertising. I was not the most popular person at the office that week. Leta brushed it off by saying that garlic was known to help fight off infection and boost the immune system. I went with it.

No one responded to the cross and garlic combination. Neither Selene nor Leta were surprised, having worked with everyone there for several years. Nor were they really that concerned that I had been bitten by a vampire. Leta held to her conviction that it was all part of the change that was coming.

Again, I ignored her.

Selene wasn't convinced that the bump on my neck, which was little more than a tiny puncture wound, was a vampire bite. She said she had never heard of a one-fanged vampire and was fairly certain they could regenerate fangs. That was a scary concept. I tried not to think about it too much.

Neither of my friends took me seriously until we arrived at work on Thursday morning and heard about Sonia. It was a juicy piece of gossip and had everyone talking about it. Leta heard it first as she was often the center of everyone's attention. She passed it on to Selene, who passed it on to me in turn.

Glenda's assistant had been out with the "flu" just like many of us. After taking a couple of days off, she had returned to work on Wednesday looking paler than a ghost and more lethargic than a sloth. All day she had tried to reassure her co-workers that she was fine.

However, later that night when most everyone had left for the evening, she was delivering the final paperwork on an account to Glenda when she just collapsed in the hall. Glenda found her and was unable to wake her up. She called 911, and the paramedics started an IV, placed her on oxygen, and rushed her to the hospital.

Glenda informed everyone the next morning that Sonia was stable and being treated for severe dehydration, anemia, and low blood pressure. All the things that would come from a vampire drinking too much blood.

After that news, Leta and Selene stopped making jokes about my garlic.

Friday was a sad and happy day. We were closing on Nolan's account. The marketing for his perfume was complete and set to release in two months. The team held a party held in the main conference room that afternoon. Even people who hadn't been a part of the design team were celebrating. Selene, Brad, Christina, and Sarah soaked up the praises of our co-workers. The clients soaked up the fawning attentions of the female employees who were saddened that they would not get to view the attractive men anymore.

I was packing up my stuff and heading out early. Selene had given me the go-ahead to leave (it was going to be an early afternoon for everyone) after I had convinced her that my fever was higher than usual, and the antacids weren't touching my pain. I assured her that I wasn't sad about missing the celebration.

"Are you sure? You should be there. You were a big part of making this a success. Your ideas were great and so was the design. The clients loved it."

"Thanks, Selene." I truly was warmed by the praise.

"Why don't you come for just five minutes? I would hate for you to miss out on it." My aversion to joining the party confused her.

"I would but," I stopped mid-sentence when I saw Nolan talking with Christina just inside the conference room. He gave her that brilliant smile and focused his beautiful eyes completely on her. I knew how that felt. No doubt, he was flirting outrageously with her, asking HER to dinner.

Selene followed my gaze. She noted the scene taking place and turned back to me with the same confused expression. I don't know what she saw when she looked back at me, but her confusion faded. She looked back at Christina and Nolan again, and there was a knowing look on her face this time.

"I understand if you're not...feeling well enough to go. I'll let everyone know that you were sick." She rubbed my back, and I knew that she knew. I wasn't sure of the extent of what she knew. But she knew.

"Thanks," I could hear the sadness in my voice, and it disgusted me. Slinging my purse over my shoulder, I gave her a little smile. "I'll see you on Monday."

I started to walk away when she called out to me. "Elena...remember to be careful. I don't know why but I have a feeling this weekend is going to be...transformative for you."

I nodded and continued down the hall. The cubicles on either side were abandoned. Everyone was at the party. Past the reception desk, pushing through the glass door that bore the firm's name, I hit the down arrow for the elevator.

I felt him before he spoke. He was right behind me, his lips so close to my neck that I shivered. "Umm, garlic" he purred teasingly, "did you have Italian for lunch?"

I had a moment's weakness. Yes, I stood there just absorbing the lovely feeling of him behind me before I worked up the gumption to step away and face him.

I took a deep breath and set a look of disapproval on my face before turning. He smiled, looking genuinely happy to see me. The softness in his gaze almost undid me.

His fingers grazed my cheek. "I was worried about you. I left for a week to come back and find that you were very sick. Out for an entire week, right?"

I turned my head away with difficulty. "I'm surprised you noticed." I knew with the sharp stabbing pain in my entire torso and the sudden surge of emotion that I was not going to be able to keep this civil.

His eyes narrowed. "Why would I not notice?

"Oh, I think you made it very clear after our date that you were not interested. And then again when you passed me in the hall with nothing but a pleasant smile. And again, when you left for a week and didn't bother to tell me." That was more than I intended to say, but the words continued to spill from my lips. "It's not like you called me after the date to tell me what a good time you had or that you wanted to do it again."

He tried to speak, but I just kept going. "It must have been horrible to put in all that work to get me to go out to dinner only to be disappointed and uninterested at the end of it."

The elevator dinged behind me. I stepped inside without ever looking away from him.

"Good for you though for getting right back in there. I'd hate to think that you were off your game after our date."

He looked stunned as the doors closed. I saw only a sliver of him when he recovered enough to call out my name in a voice that sounded almost wounded.

I collapsed against the back of the elevator and breathed a sigh of relief that that confrontation was over. At least, I told myself it was a sigh of relief.

Chapter 29

I opened the door, definitely not expecting who was on the other side.

He leaned against the doorframe with one hand while the other held a single red rose. When he lifted his cool eyes to mine, I swore it was the most vulnerable that I had ever seen him.

"Hi." I know...great line.

"Hi," Nolan said the word with his husky voice as if it was foreign.

We stared at each other. "What are you doing here?" I asked, unable to maintain eye contact a second longer.

An almost shy smile. Almost. "Will you come somewhere with me?"

"Right now?"

He nodded as his eyes bore into me with what I can only think to describe as longing.

This was a bad idea. A really bad idea. "Where are we going?"

"It is a surprise."

Yep, bad idea. "Let me grab a coat."

He waited in the doorway as I grabbed my navy coat. I pulled it around my shoulders and pushed my arms through as he waited. My heart raced...just a bit. I reminded myself as I checked for my keys and pulled the door shut that I had been out with this guy before. And he'd easily resisted my charms.

I wasn't sure why I said yes after my meltdown earlier in the day.

That's not true. I knew exactly why I was locking up my apartment and heading out into the night with Nolan...I wanted to. I wanted to be with him, to experience the excitement that came from being with someone who just seemed to fit. It didn't matter that we hardly knew each other. Sometimes there was just a feeling of rightness with another person.

"Were you happy with the ad?" I hadn't noticed his reaction during the final presentation. I had been too busy trying not to look at him.

He motioned me to precede him down the stairs. "We were very pleased with it," he responded behind me.

It was one of those polite answers that didn't tell me anything about what he was thinking. As if reading thoughts, he added. "I loved it." I felt a little flush of warmth join the butterflies in my stomach. "You put much into it, did you not?"

I shrugged. "I was a part of the team."

"It was more than that."

With a sigh, I admitted, "The nymph was my idea. I'm glad that the team agreed, and that it worked out."

We reached the bottom floor. He held the door for me, halting me with a caress on my cheek. "I thought so. It... felt like you."

With a small smile, I walked out the door looking for the limo.

"This way."

He placed a hand on my back and led me down the sidewalk. The night was chilly, and I sincerely hoped that he didn't plan on walking to our destination. I was relieved, surprised, and slightly terrified all in that order when we stopped in front of a shiny black motorcycle. Two helmets rested on the seat, both black. I turned to Nolan with a raised brow.

He laughed, the first time all night that he seemed his normal self. "Aren't all women excited by a motorcycle?"

Excitement was not the way I would describe my feelings towards the bike. Trepidation was more like it. The bike may not have excited me, but I was excited by the man.

"Is it safe?" I asked while warily assessing it.

"Only one way to find out." I frowned at the challenge but accepted it nonetheless.

He fitted the helmet over my head and tightened the chinstrap before doing the same with his own. I watched, wondering what the hell I was doing, as he climbed on and started the purring monster of chrome and rubber.

I hesitated only a moment before climbing up behind him. He instructed me to put my feet on some thingies that stuck out. When he pulled my arms around him and told me to hold on, I felt breathless. With our bodies pressed together, I was unable to ignore the heat that flowed through my body despite the chill in the air or the resurgence of desire. As he smoothly entered traffic, I marveled at the trust he inspired.

At first, I wasn't impressed as we made our way through the city traffic. The stop-and-go seemed as about as exciting as it was from inside a car. I was disappointed to be so underwhelmed by the ultimate bad-boy experience.

Then we were out of town, and it was an experience beyond anything that I could have expected. The night was cooler as we left the congestion of the city. Even as we raced through the darkness, I felt exhilarated by the frigid air blowing past me and the heat of Nolan's body as I pressed against it. The contrast was thrilling.

He took the curves of the road with an ease that told me he was familiar with this mode of transportation. I panicked briefly with the first few we took, but as the curves stretched out into long 'S's and wide horseshoes, I relaxed into the turns. I melted into Nolan's body so that when he leaned right, I was right there with him. As one, we maneuvered the bike through each curve.

It was an incredible feeling to be so exposed, to have my feet almost floating, to have my body hovering above the road. I had never felt so free, so weightless, so wild in all my life. I was sad when he slowed down, taking a turn onto a dirt road.

The world had passed by me, and I realized as he stopped the bike. I wasn't sure how far we were from the city, but the lights and the skyscrapers were nowhere in sight. As he helped me climb off the back of the bike, I realized that there were trees all around us, and the night truly was dark this far out of the city.

Taking the helmet off, I stared up at the sky. I hadn't seen so many stars since a camping trip taken with friends just after high school graduation. I hadn't even realized that it had been that long since I had been out in the open space like this.

He stood just behind me in silence. I imagined that he was looking up at the night sky as well. "Spectacular view, isn't it?"

I turned around and looked at his beautiful face. Yes, it most definitely was. "So, we came out here to stargaze?"

Nolan looked down at me, and even in the dim light, I could see his smile.

"I thought we would have a picnic."

He took my hand and led me into the meadow. The dark shapes of trees surrounded us as we walked through the rough fall grass towards the blanket that lay spread out. An old-fashioned picnic basket rested next to it.

I sat down in the center looking out over the silent wilderness, pulling my coat more tightly around me. It was a chilly but beautiful night.

Nolan unloaded the contents of the basket. A thermos of steaming liquid, deli sandwiches, a couple of bags of chips, and the most beautiful brownie I had ever seen. Despite myself, I laughed.

"This is quite a detour from our first date."

He smiled, placing a camping lantern just to the side of the basket. It emitted a soft glow with the touch of a button. "Some women are not easily impressed. I had to make sure that our second date would be extraordinary."

How he knew that a motorcycle ride and a picnic under the stars with simple food would be more impressive than a limo, dozens of roses, and a fancy dinner was beyond me. But he was so right. Sitting under the stars munching on delicious sandwiches and sharing the hot chocolate in the thermos was the most romantic thing I had ever done.

We chatted about inconsequential things like work and the upcoming release of his company's product. Nolan seemed slightly uneasy with the topic and turned it back to my job. We talked about both being new to the city and all the crazy, unexpected things that we had seen. Like the guy at the subway terminal who only wore a cardboard skirt while singing the wrong words to famous songs. Or the woman who walked her fluffy Pomeranian with a collar with questionable rhinestones. We agreed that it was a strange and wonderful city full of unusual characters. Of course, I was sure that Nolan didn't have any idea of how unusual some of the city's residents were.

"I am impressed," I said as I brushed the bread and potato chip crumbles off my hands. He leaned in, one strong hand grabbing the back of my neck, and pulled me towards him. His lips found mine, and the kiss was more aggressive than I expected.

"I have wanted to do that since you first opened the door tonight." His lips strayed to the ridge of my cheek and my jaw. "I have wanted to do this since I came back, every single time I saw you." He whispered the words against my neck, and a shiver of pleasure went down my spine.

"Where did you go, for that week I mean?"

He stopped kissing me. His eyes looked sad for a moment as he stared at me. "I had to handle some concerns back home." He smiled and looked less sad. "I did not want to go, but sometimes we have commitments that cannot be avoided."

I nodded. How true was that?

"Did you get your business taken care of?"

His hand was massaging the tense muscles of my neck. "I did...but I have to go back."

Of course, he had to go back. He lived in Europe and had only come to the States to sell his product. I looked away, reminding myself why I was a thousand kinds of fool and telling myself this was for the best. I began to gather up the remains of the picnic.

"Yeah, of course," I could hear the disappointment in my voice.

His fingers grazed my cheek and chin, and he turned my face towards his.

"I'm working to create an office here, in the city. It might take a few months to get it set up. But I want to be here." He stared into my eyes, and I knew he meant it.

"That's great," though I said it with little enthusiasm. I pulled my chin from his grasp and returned to cleaning up.

"Today, you were angry with me. Why?"

Because I thought I had been played. Because he left without saying anything to me. Because I was hurt.

"I think I was angrier with myself. I shouldn't have gone on that first date with you, and this was a bad idea too."

His brow lowered in confusion. "This was not a bad idea. You enjoyed yourself the first time." He stilled my busy hands with his. "And you were enjoying yourself now."

"Yes, I was, I did. But you are still a client, and it was not appropriate to date you." Heartburn burned my chest and the beginnings of tears stung my eyes. "I'm sorry. It's my fault that this got out of hand."

"You're right, it is."

I was so shocked by his words that I looked at him with stunned offense. "Excuse me?" I didn't like it when he accused me of being totally in the wrong.

"If you had not been so fascinating from the first moment we met or so intriguing every meeting after. If you weren't so adorable and beautiful, I never would have pursued you relentlessly until you gave into my flirtation and eventually a date. If it were not for you,

I would not have to say that this is the most I have ever felt for a woman. I would not be so utterly enchanted if not for you and considering relocation for the mere opportunity of trying to win you over. Yes, it is all your fault."

Well, when you put it like that.

I was speechless, so overwhelmed by his speech.

He took advantage of my silence. "You thought that I snubbed you that day before I left, but I was trying to honor the position you have in your company. I was trying not to draw attention to how I feel about you. I thought that was what you wanted. And you thought that I did not want you because I had to leave for a week. This entire night was to assure you of how much I do want you. If it's not enough or you do not want me, tell me now, Elena."

Not want him? How could I not want him?

Sometimes words were the right answer, and sometimes throwing yourself into another's arms was the best answer. As I fell into him, I wrapped my arms around his neck and kissed him passionately. Though the night was cold, my body was on fire as he recovered from his surprise and kissed me back.

We stayed in each other's arms like that for a good long time. When I finally came up for air, he put his forehead to mine and smiled. "I very much like your answer."

"I thought it'd convey my feelings fairly well."

He wrapped his arms around me, and we stared up at the stars for what felt like hours.

The ride back was a bittersweet mix of elation and disappointment. Nolan was on the red eye, going home for a few days to prepare for his move to the city. So, though I was beyond excited that he would be in the city and this thing between us might have a chance, I was sad that I would not see him for a while. I reminded myself not to pout and focus on the positive.

The ride back into the city flew by faster than the first one. That was the problem with trying to hold onto something; the tighter you held the faster it slipped through your fingers.

A space right in front of my apartment building opened as he turned onto my street. He parked the motorcycle and put the purring beast to sleep. I didn't want to get off. I didn't want the night to end.

He gently took my helmet off, running his fingers through my hair before he helped me from the bike. We walked back to my apartment hand in hand. I laughed as he made a joke about the weather. It was easy with Nolan, just to walk together and hold hands. It was easy to just be with him. That was a sign of sorts, wasn't it?

A good sign, I hoped.

I told him he didn't have to walk me to the door, but he insisted, citing that the city wasn't always safe.

I laughed. "You're telling me."

"Did something happen to you?" he asked with concern as we ascended the stairs.

"No, no, not me. But a friend of mine was telling me about a few women around town that have been attacked." Most likely by a vampire, but I left that part out.

"That is unfortunate," he said, his expression thoughtful as I pulled my keys out.

I jiggled the key in the lock as he came behind me and nuzzled at my neck.

Hmm... maybe the night wouldn't have to end. Just maybe he'd want to come in tonight. My roommate didn't have to be the only one having a good time in our apartment.

I paused to enjoy the sensations flowing through my body as his lips moved from my ear and down my neck. It felt so good. I pushed the door open, eager to take this inside. He reached the base of my neck, and suddenly he hissed before quickly pulling away.

Stumbling a few feet into the apartment, I turned to him with shock and confusion. My hand rose of its own volition to the spot on my neck that he had been kissing... to the spot where I had been bitten by a vampire.

He stared back at me in anger and disgust. Someone else had had a similar reaction to the bite... Farah.

"Oh, god," I cried as I took a step back. What was I, a werewolf magnet? "Not you too!" My voice, full of betrayal and anger, pleaded.

It drew him out of his anger and disgust. His expression softened, and he stepped towards me. "Elena, I'm sorry...I...I..."

I retreated further into the apartment as he advanced, looking around for a bat, a pipe, a damn umbrella!

But he stopped abruptly in the doorway as if hitting a door. "Elena, please, just let me come in, and we can talk about this."

We stared at each other, nothing blocking the space between us. "Oh, oh, this just keeps getting better!" I cried.

"Elena, please. Invite me in." His voice was tight as he looked down the hall.

I took a step forward. "Why do you need me to invite you in? Why can't you just walk through the door?"

"Is that an invitation?"

"No!"

"Elena," his voice more resigned than strained.

"Say it. I need to hear you say it."

He snorted a soft laugh. "I am not sure that you will believe it."

"Try me. You'd be surprised what I'm willing to believe."

He started at me. Those dark blue eyes filled with sadness, yet there was a brief spark of recognition in his eyes. "I think you know."

"Say it!"

"I can't come in because I'm," he checked the hall again, his voice low, "a vampire."

My chest was on fire, and for a second, I thought I saw tiny wisps of smoke curl from my nose. I took a few deep breaths, holding my hand to my chest. Breathing was good. Breathing was good, I told myself until the painful burning ebbed.

"When did you get the bite, Elena?" his voice was angry again.

I looked up at him. "Two weeks ago. A friend of yours?"

His eyes darkened. "At one time, perhaps, but no longer."

"You know who bit me," I accused more than asked.

He didn't want to answer. I marched right up to the doorway, careful to stay inside the apartment. "I deserve to know, dammit. As do all the other women at the office who have been getting horribly sick. Was that you? Were you involved in that?"

"I did not intend for anyone to get hurt." Not an answer. "However, I will rectify the problem."

"Nolan," I yelled as he turned away.

He paused only briefly to look at me. "I will fix this and show you that you can trust me."

I called after him again, but he did not turn around a second time. I watched him go, frustrated, angry, and hurt.

Slamming the door, I stomped through the apartment. Leta was staying at her boyfriend-of-the-moment's place. Briefly, I thought about calling her and decided against it. I would have to tell her the whole story about Nolan, and with my present level of embarrassment, I wasn't sure I could admit to her what an idiot I had been. Such an idiot to date a client, to trust a stupid man, and to somehow, unknowingly get involved with a vampire. A vampire!

Had I not just been thinking that I didn't know him? The whole Miguel encounter had taught me that I didn't really know any man. He could be a wolf in sheep's clothing.

Sometimes literally.

I tried Farah, but the call went to voicemail. After leaving a message that I hoped wasn't panicked, I began to pace the apartment.

Congrats to me, I had found the vampire, only it wasn't the vampire I was looking for. Yet, I could guess who the other one was. It had to be Micah. That lousy pair of scheming bloodsuckers!

I was so mad I could feel the anger coming off me in waves of heat and little tendrils of smoke escaped my nose when I exhaled. The Tree shied away from me whenever I paced to that side of the room.

Great! This was the perfect time for Leta's prediction to come true, I thought briefly then pushed the thought aside.

No, I was so not turning into a fire elemental, not today, not any day. She was not going to be right about this. The heat I felt was just my anger. I had a lot of it.

"I'm an idiot," I said to The Tree as I stood across the room from it.

It shook its leaves in agreement.

"How could I be so stupid? You would think that I would have learned to be a little more cautious after Miguel." I ignored the puff of smoke that came out with the sigh. "This is too weird. All of it. Leta, Selene, Farah, Nolan," I looked at The Tree, "the fact that I'm venting to a tree."

The Tree seemed to shrug, as well as trees can shrug that is.

"Why didn't he tell me?" The Tree was motionless. "Okay, okay. I get it, the whole vampire thing. But still." My companion remained motionless.

"It's not unreasonable to want a little honesty in a relationship."

It started to shake its leaves in that subtle angry way. "What? I'm not holding anything back." Sudden stillness.

"I'm not. It's not like I could tell him about Leta or the others. That's their secret, and it would be wrong of me to reveal that to anyone."

The Tree nodded its uppermost branches before the lower ones resumed shaking sternly.

I knew what it was getting at. "Just because Leta thinks that I'm going to be some sort of elemental doesn't mean that she is right. I love Leta, but let's be honest; she's not the most...sane person. I would think you understand that better than anyone."

The Tree sighed. Yes, it sighed.

I collapsed on the chair. "Where does this leave me?" I watched as it raised a branch on the right and then one on the left. "I'm not sure I know what options you are talking about."

I took off my jacket as I was starting to sweat from all the heat.

"Why is it so damn hot in here?" I said irritably as I got up to turn down the thermostat. The Tree shook a single branch at me. "The thermostat was set too high."

Collapsing back in the chair, I felt the first sharp pain pierce my abdomen. "Oh, god, I'm getting an ulcer."

I let my head rest against the back of the couch as I waited for the pain to subside.

The Tree was swaying slightly. "I'm fine. Just my ulcer; I'll get some Tums and be just fine."

I got up and edged far away from The Tree as I passed by. We may have shared a moment, but I wasn't convinced The Tree could be trusted.

Looking over my shoulder at The Tree, I said, "Hey, thanks for letting me talk it out. I'm going to get some rest and maybe it will be clearer in the morning."

The Tree nodded and waved me good night.

"Yeah, you sleep," do trees sleep? "well too. Night."

I turned out the lights in the room, and after finishing my nightly routine crawled into bed. I popped a couple of Tylenol and Tums as the heartburn and random abdominal pains returned. My body was too hot to bother with the covers and the fleecy PJs I normally wore. So, in just my underwear and a tank, I settled into the mattress, hoping that sleep would claim me quickly.

By the morning, the anger had cooled, but my body hadn't. It was a rough night full of pain, fever, and disturbing dreams. As I crawled out of bed, I wondered what they were putting in the water here. I had never had such vivid dreams before here. In fact, I would give anything to not remember the nightmares of Nolan into ripping my throat, or my friends caught in a fire that I couldn't control. Fully conscious, I wondered why my dream self would think I could control fire, but dreams were symbolic, right? I just had to figure out what the fire represented in real life.

It was five am, and the first rays of the sun were just barely visible. I had tried to sleep longer, but my brain was wide awake and refused to return to REM. So, I dragged myself out of bed. Trudging to the living room, I paused to look at how peaceful The Tree was. I felt particularly warm towards it after last night, which might explain why I thought it was okay to reach out and brush my fingers over the pretty green leaves. The Tree quickly reminded me why that was a bad idea.

I was whacked in the back of the head by a leafy branch. "Ouch! Okay, okay," I surrendered as I ran from the attacking branches. "I thought we bonded," I said from the other side of the room.

The Tree just shook its leaves in that affronted way. I huffed and went to the kitchen to make a cup of tea. After grabbing a cup from the cabinet, I paused.

What a sorry mess I was.

The tears flooded my eyes and drenched my face. I knew they were coming. Temper had never really been my thing...until recently... and tears were always a sure bet when things were too overwhelming. Like they were now.

I wanted to beat myself up, again. A similar internal conversation to last night's started, only there was more self-flogging and weeping.

Eventually, I just collapsed onto the floor, my back against the cabinets. Why was I so worked up? I hadn't felt this bad over Miguel.

Of course, I hadn't liked Miguel as much as I liked Nolan. I had never reached that comfort with Miguel, but with Nolan I had. With Miguel, I hadn't thought past the next date, my biggest preoccupation with the doctor had been if lukewarm feelings were enough to continue the relationship.

With Nolan though, I had thought about more than just the next date. While we had cuddled under the stars, I imagined how things would work out after he moved to the city. I couldn't deny that as I was wrapped in his arms, I thought about how his relocation was partly, maybe more than partly, about me, and it filled me with so much...hope. Dangerous thing that.

Even now there was a glimmer of hope that we could work past this vampire thing. I mean I could almost understand why he hadn't told me. And his surprise regarding the attacks at work was so genuine that I honestly believed he had nothing to do with it. Though, he did seem to know who was responsible.

Could I date a vampire? With a sniffle, I pondered the downsides.

Well, the drinking blood thing was a little strange and potentially dangerous. I was sure that Nolan could control himself enough to not kill me... if I let him drink my blood that was. Remembering my only experience as a blood donor for a vampire, I realized I wasn't so keen on the idea of experiencing that again. It would be like getting constant bouts of the flu.

But if a vampire's girlfriend didn't give up her blood, where did he get his sustenance? Other women? Ugh!

My head hurt as I shook it. So, dating a vampire had its complications. Big complications.

The plus side... I liked Nolan. I loved how he teased me, how he listened so attentively and seemed fascinated by what I had to say. He offered up affection in a way that was so easy, and even someone as intimacy-challenged as I was could just ease into that affection. Also, I was shallow enough to admit that I just liked looking at him, and the thought of taking all that physical affection to another level was enough heat my entire body.

I groaned as I banged my head on the cabinet. Dating was hard enough. I didn't need to have it complicated by a pair of fangs and a diet of blood.

My phone beeped from the other room. I must have left it there last night. The tears dried up though I didn't feel any better. There was no quick solution to this.

Nolan was going to be gone for a few days and that gave me time to figure some of this out. Of course, that was if he was still interested. I needed to talk this out with someone other than The Tree. Glancing at the clock, I realized it was probably still too early to call Farah, and I was desperate enough to talk to Leta, but she didn't usually breeze in until noon.

My phone beeped again. With mild irritation, I rose from the floor and went to retrieve it.

There were two messages. From Nolan.

I hesitated and then unlocked the phone. Of course, I was going to read them.

The first left me surprised:

I couldn't leave without fixing this. Come to me. I must see you. My flight is at noon.

I stared at the message. He had changed flights, which meant I could go to him now. I started towards the bedroom. The Tree shook at me angrily.

"What am I doing?" I asked myself.

I would take a few days to think about this, to talk it out with sensible people who could see the situation more objectively. I couldn't just drop everything to be at his beck and call. Where was my self-respect?

Looking down at the message, I remembered that another was waiting for me. Scrolling down, I read it:

I need you.

My self-respect flew out the window. I was desperate to get rid of this aching in my chest. My emotional turmoil caused all kinds of physical pain. My joints ached, my head throbbed, and my chest filled with burning acid.

I ignored The Tree as I rushed past it, intent on getting dressed. My hair was wild, and my eyes were bloodshot from all the crying. Nothing I could do about the eyes, but I brushed my hair back into a ponytail and quickly applied make-up that would at least distract from the redness. Tumbling about the room, I rushed to dress. It was six. I calculated what time I had. Six hours minus the thirty minutes to get there minus another two hours that he would need to get to the airport to make his flight. That left me with three and a half hours. Plenty of time to talk this out.

I was almost out the door when I realized I hadn't brushed my teeth. The Tree continued to shake rather disapprovingly at me. As I moved the brush in tight circles over my teeth, I marveled at how unlike me I was acting. Never in the past would someone describe me as a tempestuous, impulsive person, but the last few weeks seemed to be a total flip of my personality. I spitted and rinsed, then frowned as I looked at myself. I wasn't sure I liked the changes. Most likely it was the result of spending too much time with my mythical friends.

That rational part of me that had been repressed as of late surfaced long enough to realize that it might be wise to leave a note. I was meeting with a vampire after all. Quickly, I scribbled out a message for Leta on a Post-It and put it on the cabinet where the cups were. She was sure to go for a cup of tea when she got home.

I also sent Farah a text telling her that I had to talk with her about Nolan. *He's not what I thought.*

A taxi was strangely easy to get this early in the morning on a Saturday. I gave the driver the name of the hotel and sat back as he drove us to our destination.

The hotel lobby was dazzling. The grand, open space glittered and glowed with the light coming from elegant glass chandeliers. The rich mahogany surfaces of the check-in desk, the floor-to-ceiling columns, and the sophisticated furniture were complimented by the color palette of reds and gold. From the perfectly kept rugs in majestic designs to the luxurious fabrics, the entire place spoke of the opulence of a king. It was tastefully arranged and combined, even if to my eye the whole effect was too much.

Figures a European vampire would pick a hotel like this. I pulled out my phone as I continued to stare at the grandeur of the lobby. I called Nolan, but no answer.

Great, I thought. Here I was, and I couldn't get a hold of him.

I glanced at the check-in desk. There was a possibility that I could get his room number from the clerk. Who was I kidding...I'd needed Leta for that kind of persuasion. Or Farah. I smiled at the thought of how they would handle this situation.

My phone beeped.

Are you here?

Okay, that was weird. He didn't pick up my call, but he could text me?

Nonetheless, I responded yes and asked where he wanted to meet. I had assumed his room, as this was the kind of conversation one would want to have in private.

I waited a few minutes for him to respond.

"Elena."

That voice made the hairs on the back of my neck stand up. I was tempted to ignore the speaker, but I knew it wouldn't work. He'd just get more irritating.

"Mr. Renier," I used his last name because it seemed to annoy him.

He tsked. "Elena, are we not on a first name basis after," he paused briefly, smiling a secret little smile, "after everything."

I'm not sure what "everything" he was talking about. We had a strictly professional relationship. "I'm waiting for someone," I said hoping that it would be enough to make him go away.

Micah gave me a sympathetic smile. "Oh, Elena. I wished he hadn't done this to you. It's just cruel."

I swallowed, suddenly more uncomfortable. "What are you talking about?"

"Nolan, of course. He's not here. He left last night to see to business at home."

"But he texted me this morning. He asked me to meet him here."

On a sigh, "I told him not to lead you on like this, but he's cruel that way."

Something was very wrong here. "I still don't know what you're talking about."

"Elena, Nolan is," he seemed to consider his next words carefully, "involved with someone else."

"What!" My voice was louder than expected and drew the attention of those in the lobby.

I avoided their gazes as Micah gently took my arm and led me down the lobby and past the grand staircase, too absorbed in my shock to object. We stopped in a corner. A single elevator dinged at the end of a short hall. It didn't look like it got a lot of use as it wasn't the main elevator. I wondered if it was designated for staff.

Micah's cold fingers caressed my cheek, pulling me out of the stupor. I pulled away from his touch.

"What do you mean he is involved with someone else? Is he married?" I shouldn't trust a word of this, but my gut kept telling me that something wasn't right.

Micah studied my face for a moment. "I suppose you could call it an engagement."

"Why should I believe you?"

He smiled sadly. "Why would I lie to you?"

Because you're a sneaky, slimy narcissist. "I don't understand why he would..."

"There's a saying...having your cake and eating it too."

Oh, that was a nice comparison. "But he texted me."

"It's all a game. He wants you to think that he needs you."

As he continued talking, I thought about how close his words were to the text I had received.

Warning bells went off. I watched his mouth as he talked, though I didn't hear a word of it. Because, as he talked and offered charming smiles, I noticed that his right canine was broken. It no doubt had happened long ago, the edge of the tooth looked worn smooth, but it was half the size of his other canine.

"Stay away from me." The words came out on a fearful breath. I took a step back from Micah, looking for an escape.

"I was not lying to you when I told you that he was spoken for, Elena. I was trying to save you from this. You are not the first he has misled."

I tried not to hear his words. They were lies, all of them. But the gnawing in my gut was not as convinced.

"I know what you are," I whispered viciously at him. Here was the bastard that had bitten me. The one who had put a coworker in the hospital.

I didn't like feeling cornered. My body was a furnace throwing off enough heat to warm the entire building and dizziness filled my head as I frantically searched for a way out. Yet, he just kept advancing.

"Ah, I see." His voice dripped with condescension. "Since that is the case, I can tell you the full truth. He is not just involved with another woman; he is the consort to our queen. A consort, you understand, is a highly revered position…in some ways. It ensures the queen's attention along with whatever favors she chooses to bestow. The quantity and quality of the favors, of course, reflect the pleasure she finds in her consort. Nolan," he smiled, "is very accomplished in earning the queen's favors."

He assessed me with his devious eyes, trying to determine if I took his meaning.

Oh, I understood quite well. Nolan was apparently very good at keeping his queen happy. It made my chest burn.

"He was gifted the perfume company by her. She gave him a little project to occupy himself when she does not have need of him." When I didn't respond to his comment, he sighed. "I feel obligated to inform you that the commitment of a consort is many years. Nolan has several left to fulfill. He was never free to pursue you."

I didn't want to believe him, and he could see it. "He was summoned back to the queen last week. That is where he was, providing her the pleasures she seeks from him."

Ow! He drove the metaphorical spike right into my chest. I could feel the pain radiating throughout the rest of my body.

"Why would I trust you? You bit me. You've been biting all the women at work, making everyone sick. And what about Sonia? She's in the hospital, right now."

He placed his hand over his chest and looked stricken with guilt. I didn't believe a bit of it.

"I couldn't deny your appeal. You called to me in a way that I have never experienced before. Your beauty, your grace, your-"

"What about the others?" I interrupted. He was an idiot if he thought I was going to buy that fake flattery.

His features hardened briefly, revealing the true depth of his irritation. I felt a surge of fear in response. A vampire had me cornered, and I already knew he could hurt people.

My heart raced and pounded against my ribs. My breaths were rapid and shallow. Somewhere in the back of my mind, I knew that this hyperventilation could lead to me passing out. But I couldn't control the functions of my body. I had never been this scared in my life.

"Elena, be reasonable," he said in that patronizing tone that was so annoying.

However, his voice seemed far away, and though he was standing right in front of me, his image blurred and swayed.

No, that was me swaying. And this wasn't fear pushing my body into overdrive.

"Oh, no," I cried as I doubled over in extreme pain that ripped from my abdomen out to the rest of my body.

"Elena?" I could barely hear his voice even as he hovered just over me. I felt only pressure as his hands gripped my arms to steady me. Heat, like hell fire itself burned from deep inside and spread out to my skin.

Just before darkness swallowed me, I felt Micah take me in his arms and watched as gray smoke rose in front of my face on a final exhale.

Chapter 31

The first thing I was aware of as I slowly came to consciousness was the warm humidity surrounding me, the heavy kind that made my skin feel constantly saturated in moisture. The heat was just right, like tanning in the sun. Maybe I had died and gone to the Bahamas. Worse things could happen.

The next thing I was aware of was the swish of hot water against my breasts, in and out. Dead and lying on a beach in the Bahamas. Even better. I just hoped that I was wearing a cute red bikini. With white polka dots. There was sure to be a pink drink with tons of alcohol and a little yellow umbrella nearby.

The third thing that reached my consciousness was the sound of grunting.

Grunting was not a part of my Bahamas heaven, not unless it was coming from an incredibly sexy man.

I pried my eyes open, struggling momentarily against the crusties that had formed. My extremely dry eyes stung as the air touched them. I blinked several times to lubricate them, and only then was I able to focus.

The good news was- that it was an incredibly sexy man grunting; the bad news was the sexy man was Nolan. I groaned and rolled my burning eyes. Apparently, I was not in paradise.

In fact, I was lying naked in a bathtub. The water bubbled at a soft boil, and the last remains of ice cubes floated around me.

"What the hell!" My voice was dry and scratchy.

I tried to clear my throat, but it didn't seem to do any good. Turning my head to gaze over the top of the old-fashioned porcelain tub, my eyes narrowed on Nolan. Had they been lasers, there would be two little holes burning through his head.

Did I mention that Nolan was tied up and gagged?

"What the hell is going on!" I cried out again. The water around me bubbled vigorously.

Nolan continued to worm his way towards me. With his hands tied behind his back and his feet bound together, it was a slow process over the carpet in the other room. He reached the open doorway and slid better on the tile of the bathroom. I noted while I waited for him to get closer that a faint burnt smell permeated the air.

An ornate gold leaf mirror hung over the tub. The intricate edges of it were blackened. The wall beneath was covered in deep rich maroon and cream striped wallpaper. Glancing at the rest of the bathroom, I saw the sink was set into a stand that looked like it might have originally belonged in Versailles. The counter was a maroon marble and the stand itself was painted cream, with gold leaf accents. The tile beneath was cream marble.

"Are you hurt?" Nolan managed to work the gag down and slide across the tile.

"I'm fine," I answered a bit too brusquely.

"When Micah brought you here, I was worried." Ah, yes, this was making more sense.

"This is his hotel room, isn't it?" The French revival extravagance was just his style.

"Yes, it is." He propped his back against the tub, breathing heavily.

"Winded by a little crawling? I thought you vampire types were tougher than that," I mocked.

"Normally, I would be." He didn't seem to take offense to my quip. "I haven't fed in almost a month; that tends to weaken us a bit." He managed a smile as he looked over his shoulder at me.

Aware of my nakedness, I covered my breasts with my hands and sank lower beneath the boiling water. "Eyes forward, mister."

He laughed. "I regret to inform you that I've seen it all already." He did turn his head away though.

"I beg your pardon!" I said in outrage.

"By the time Micah got you here, you were so hot that your clothes were starting to burn off. He tried covering you, but the sheet burned to ash. When he laid you on the bed, the counterpane went up in flames. He had no choice but to throw you in the tub. It was the only thing that would not burn."

Great! I really hoped this new body temperature of mine was temporary. Finding fire-retardant clothing could be a challenge.

"What's with the boiling water?"

"You're still burning hot apparently."

"Ah." So, I was boiling the water. "Let me guess, he put ice in here to cool me off?"

"It helped for a moment. When he first put you in there, you steamed the entire room. Water evaporated faster than it could fill the tub. Finally, Micah just surrounded you with ice." He glanced over his shoulder again. "That's what's left of the third batch."

"How long have I been here?"

"I think it's Sunday afternoon. I've been in and out myself." He turned back and rested his head on the edge of the tub. His eyes closed, and his beautiful face looked strained.

"Why did Micah bring you here?"

He opened his eyes and then looked up at the ceiling. I followed his gaze and noted the crystal chandelier. Yes, a chandelier in the bathroom. This was definitely Micah's style.

"I confronted him about the attacks, on you and the other women."

"He didn't appreciate your concern, I take it," I drooled.

He gave a small laugh. "No, apparently not."

We avoided looking at each other as silence filled the room.

"I'm sorry, Elena."

"You're going to wear those words out and then what," I threw his words back at him, and noticed from the corner of my eye that he smiled.

"It is not something that I would reveal to most people."

He turned to look at me. "Vampires are not very popular, despite what the New York Times bestseller's list says. Others look at us as parasites. Imagine the shame of having your entire existence dependent on the theft of another's blood. We avoid attracting attention by consuming donated blood, which is as appetizing as cold pizza."

Not being a fan of cold pizza, I understood his point. I rested my arms on the edge of the tub; they were heavy and stiff like I hadn't used them in weeks.

"That doesn't make it okay to drink from unsuspecting women, leaving them unable to understand why they're so sick."

"I never suspected what Micah was doing. I truly came to your firm for the promotion of my company."

"The company that your queen gave you...because you're her consort."

I stole a glance at him, my attention remaining fixed on the pain in his face. "Elena." There was so much despair in the way he said my name. So, it was true.

Tears would have fallen on my cheeks if they hadn't evaporated just as they touched my skin.

"Micah said that you are in the service of your queen and that it will be a while longer before that...service is completed."

He sighed. "He told you the truth."

I almost asked what that service included... but I didn't really want to know, even though I was sure I could guess. No, I was not going to ask.

"What kind of things do you do for the queen?" Damn, I wasn't going to ask. I felt the emotion clogging my throat as I tried to contain the tears.

He stared into my eyes, not wanting to answer any more than I wanted to hear it. "I do whatever she wishes of me." That was all-encompassing, wasn't it?

"And you aren't free to pursue other people, are you? Was Micah lying about that?"

Please let him be lying. Please, please.

Nolan laughed mirthlessly. "The queen does not share what is hers." And he was hers, that part went unsaid.

"Oh, god." I turned away as my eyes tried to water.

"I never intended...I never thought I would fall in love with someone while I was in her service, Elena."

"Oh, god." The pain filled my voice. I could feel his eyes on me.

"Elena..." His voice sounded tortured.

We were both silent.

"I can't believe you're a vampire," I said quietly.

He snorted softly, "You are a fire elemental."

"I didn't know that until very recently." With a sigh, "Are any of the stories about vampires true?"

"Such as?" He rested his head on the rim of the bathtub.

"I tried garlic, and that didn't work. You can clearly go out in the sunlight. Do you have a reflection? Are you immortal?"

He laughed weakly. "Most of the stories are not true. I do have a reflection, and I am not immortal."

"You aren't?"

"No, but vampires live for hundreds of years, aging only at the end of our lives."

Hundreds of years...with no aging...and blood drinking...

"You said that you haven't drunk in a month. How...who..."

"We have human blood donors who live with my coven. When I'm traveling, I consume frozen blood, which is not as appetizing."

"So, you don't feed on unsuspecting people?"

"No," he said firmly as he turned toward me. I didn't care anymore if he saw my naked body. "What Micah did was reprehensible."

"What would your queen say if she knew about everything that Micah has been doing? About the woman in the hospital? I guess it probably wouldn't matter to her, would it? She probably couldn't care less about what he's been up to."

Wariness filled his voice. "She most definitely will care."

I turned back to him, seeing that he was once more resting his head on the edge of the tub. "She will?"

"Micah's actions put the entire coven at risk if it were exposed. That would give others an excuse to come for us. The queen has maintained power for a very long time by encouraging those who despise us to forget that we exist. It could endanger her rule. She will not be happy.

"Micah has gone too far. Because I missed the flight, and I have not checked in with her, she came to the city."

"Your queen is in the city?"

"Yes. Micah has gone to see her. He is telling her lies about where I am and why I have not checked in."

"You could get to her. You could tell her what has been going on," I splashed bits of boiling water onto the floor as I sat up.

He turned to me with a severe look of doubt.

"You have to! Who else can stop Micah? You think that he's just going to let us go after this."

"He doesn't know how to kill a fire elemental."

"Oh, that's a comfort," my voice full of sarcasm. "When he does figure it out, do you think he's going to let me stand in his way?"

Nolan looked unsure. Maybe my words were making an impact. I started to get out of the tub. If he wasn't going to go, I would just have to find a way to see the queen myself. With my new fiery body, I could just burn my way through her guards.

My legs were shaky, and I reached for the wall to balance myself. And the wallpaper started to sizzle. I quickly pulled my hand away. A black print of my hand marred the surface of the maroon and cream stripes.

"Great," I muttered as my legs gave out, and I splashed back into the tub.

Nolan had ducked and dodged to avoid the boiling water that splattered everywhere. I let out a large sigh and watched the tendril of smoke that came with it.

"You're too hot still."

"Yes, thank you. I hadn't realized that what with the scorch mark on the wall."

He smiled. "With fire come temper and disdain."

"Are you quoting something?" He laughed. "Micah is going to come back. What will you do then?"

"He can't kill me. I'm the queen's con- I'm close to the queen."

"Yes, I know. But he's gone this far, do you think that he cares if you're the queen's lover? Besides, he's a lying, manipulative bastard who will just find a way to justify it all. Maybe kill you and pretend to know nothing about it."

He sighed as he looked at me. "I do not know if I have the strength to get to the queen. I need blood badly."

Even as I thought it, I knew it was the kind of thing I would regret. "You can take some of mine...if it will give you the strength you need."

He smiled that dazzling smile and said in the flirtatious tone I was familiar with, "Before I would have wanted nothing more; however, I fear you might run too hot for my taste."

That's right. I was so hot I was burning the wallpaper and boiling the bathwater. "I could cut my wrist and let the blood fall into your mouth." Oh, that sounded great.

He laughed. "Think of it as more a problem of spice, not heat."

Ah, so I was hot and spicy now.

"You can do this, Nolan. My life depends on you doing this." Doubt lingered in his eyes, but I decided to ignore it. "Turn around, and I'll burn the binding on your hands."

He hesitated only a moment before turning and rising to his knees. I reached out and placed one fingertip on the rope knot. I didn't want to burn him. As soon as the knot was falling apart, I pulled my finger away. He tested the bindings and was able to break through them. After pulling his hands apart, he quickly went to work on the rope tied around his feet.

When he had finished, he turned back to me. I had reclined back into the water, surrendering to the heat. I wasn't going anywhere for a while.

"I will get to the queen, and I'll return with help as soon as I can. I promise." There was a desperate vulnerability in his whole demeanor.

"I believe you." It might have been the only sincere thing I had said since waking. He took strength from that and staggered out of the room.

I pulled the plug on the water. As it drained, I turned the cold water on full blast. The sooner I could cool off the sooner I could get myself out of this awful predicament.

Hopefully, before Micah returned.

Chapter 32

It took another two hours before my body had cooled enough to even touch surfaces other than the tub. I gingerly placed my hand on the wall, waiting anxiously for the sound of burning paper. When I heard nothing but a soft sizzle, I looked under my hand. The wall was undamaged...well, it wasn't any more damaged. I snagged a towel that was burnt at the edges. It must have been a casualty when I was brought into the bathroom.

It was barely long enough to wrap around my body, the edge riding the tops of my thighs and barely covering the important parts.

I was still a bit lightheaded and dizzy, which I guess could be expected after reaching inferno temperatures. My joints popped and creaked as I slowly walked across the bathroom floor. It was no surprise that my muscles were tight in some places, and sore in others. I had been in that tub a long time. I looked around the bathroom for something else that could be used as a covering. Unfortunately, it appeared that I had burned all the other sizable towels to a crisp.

Continuing to the bedroom, I eyed the monstrosity of a bed with disgust. The gilded, over-the-top style was starting to hurt my dried-out eyes. The remains of the sheets and comforter were bundled in the center of the bed. I was impressed by the damage I had unknowingly caused.

Searching for a suitcase, I figured I could borrow some of Micah's clothes to escape the hotel, though the idea of wearing his stuff made me sick. Beggars couldn't be choosers though.

Of course, there was no obvious suitcase. When I eyed the armoire on the other side of the bed, I realized that he would have hung his expensive silk shirts and designer suits.

I stood in front of the highly polished piece of furniture sorting through his shirts, when I heard his voice outside the door.

Oh, no!

The sweater I was hoping for was not going to happen. Instead, I grabbed a navy button-up, quickly pulled my arms through the sleeves, and rushed through the buttons. I was not going to face him naked.

The door opened as I finished with the buttons and pulled my dry hair free of the shirt. That at least was convenient. Micah walked sauntered into the room, his gray pinstripe suit perfectly pressed. He studied the front room before our eyes met. With quick steps, he advanced.

I too advanced, hoping that I would be able to maneuver past him.

His eyes assessed me from head to toe, a sleazy smile parting his lips. "What an attractive look on you, and one of my favorite shirts too." His expression hardened. "Where is Nolan?"

"On his way to the queen."

He raised an eyebrow, taking off his coat as he paused by a sofa.

"Is that so? I have just returned from seeing the queen. I assured her that Nolan was not available. This will be quite inconvenient."

"Yes, I'm sure that she will figure out what a liar you are pretty quickly." We circled the furniture in the room, him in one direction and me in the other.

"A liar?" He held his hands to his chest with an affronted look. "When have I ever lied to you?"

I started to speak only to stop as I realized I couldn't think of any examples. That was what made him so sneaky; he didn't actually lie. He just twisted the truth to fit his uses.

"Damnit!" I gripped the chair in front of me in frustration.

"Careful, sweetheart, or you're going to set that on fire." He indicated the chair I was gripping in frustration.

Immediately, I looked down and saw the fabric browning under my fingers. My hands flew off and remained in the air.

"Okay, maybe you didn't lie, but what about all the women you attacked? What about me?"

"What about you?"

"You attacked me! You kidnapped me!"

"Did I?" He looked at me with the concern you would give to someone mentally unstable. "I don't remember it as an attack. Rather, I remember you quite willing. And, as for the kidnapping charge, you passed out; I merely took care of you."

I was fuming. "Taking advantage is not the same thing as willing."

He laughed.

I used his laughter as a distraction and made a mad dash for the door.

Almost...so close.

His arm wrapped around my waist from behind and pulled me away from the door. He easily lifted me off my feet as he walked back into the room. "Where do you think you are going?"

"Let me go!" I struggled, but the band around my waist was unrelenting. "What do you want with me?"

He set me on my feet though one of his hands maintained a tight grip on my arm. "First, why don't you try not to set the room on fire?" His eyes were fixed on the space behind me.

I turned, and, clear as day, was the path I had taken to the door. Little flames where footprints would have been burned into the carpet. Not sure how I did that.

He towed me with him as he stomped out the flames.

"Now, what do I want with you?" I didn't like that gleam in his eyes. "It's been far too long since I had a blood slave."

I recoiled at the thought. "I'm too hot for you."

That was my brilliant comeback to the evil mastermind.

He smiled. "No, you're not. Besides, I like a little heat. Why do you think I convinced you to come here?"

Aha! "So, you are a liar. Nolan didn't send those texts."

"True, he did not physically send them, but they were his thoughts. Not a lie."

Sneaky, slimy bastard.

"I will not be your blood slave. People will come for me. My people will come for me."

"Right, because they've come looking for you in the day and a half that you have been missing?"

Ooo, that stung. Where was my backup? Any moment now, Leta and Farah could come barging through the door.

Where were G.I. Jane and Cat Burglar Barbie?

"I left a note and messages," I informed him with satisfaction.

"Then either your messages did not contain enough information, or they don't care. Because, sweetheart, they are not here."

I was mad and scared and seriously annoyed. Maybe that was what made me so hot that Micah was forced to pull back his hand in pain. We stared at the reddened skin on his hand and arm. The sleeve of the shirt had burned away.

"One of my favorite shirts," he growled, all seductive charm gone.

I took off towards the door once more, not caring if my mad dash set the whole place to flames.

Wrenching open the door, I raced down the hall, making it past two doors before he grabbed me from behind again. The sudden jerk of my body had me falling forward. I caught myself with my hands, and the carpet beneath them burst into flame. Oh shit!

Micah's hands wrapped around me and pulled me to my feet. I turned quickly, planning to put my burning hands on him, but he was faster. He grabbed each wrist and held them out away from his body. I noticed that there were black gloves on his hands.

"Heat-resistant gloves," he said in response to my questioning glare. "You don't think I learned from my first encounter?"

He began to haul me back towards the room. I figured now was as good a time as any. I opened my mouth to scream, praying that the bystander effect was just a myth.

Except no sound came out. Instead, a steady stream of fire came out, like it would out of a flame gun. I abruptly closed my mouth. Burning hands and extreme temperatures had been quite enough. I wasn't prepared to learn that I could breathe fire like a dragon.

Micah took advantage of my shock and threw me over his shoulder. I continued to yell, and little flames shot out of my mouth. As I fought to get out of his grasp, he struggled to maintain his grip. In the process, we bumped into one wall after another, careening across the hallway. My head knocked against the doorframe as we approached his room. Momentarily stunned, I lifted my head and looked down the hall.

The wallpaper and the carpet were on fire. Not the whole thing, but there were small fires on the walls and the floor growing in size.

"Put me down! The hall is on fire." I tried hitting his back, but he simply kept walking.

"Because of you," he responded angrily.

I was about to point out that he had a part in it. I wouldn't be so hot, so to speak, and struggling if he would just let me go. However, we were back in the room, and I was dumped on the ground.

"Stay there," he said and turned back to the door.

As if!

I rolled over as soon as he turned his back and took off. I'm not sure where I thought I was going, but anything was better than staying on the floor. I circled a sofa and headed to the bedroom when I heard him growl.

"Troublesome bitch!" he shouted at me, trampling the furniture in his path as he stalked towards me.

The sofa cushion in my hand went up in flames. Realizing that I had a weapon, I picked it up and aimed it at Micah.

"Stay right there, or I'll throw it. And my aim is pretty damn good."

My aim was and had always been crap, but I figured aim didn't really count for much when the missile was flaming. Damage done either way.

He growled. "Why couldn't you be docile like the others? Difficult from the very beginning." He shoved the coffee table out of his path. It crashed into a chair and another table and the sound of the lamp hitting the floor followed.

"I tolerated you when you were nothing more than a distraction. You were even a tasty late-night snack." He flashed his one elongated fang at me with a sinister smile. "But you had to enlighten my idiot partner."

He kicked the fallen lamp, the bulb shattering. "And he had to rush to defend you."

He stood on the opposite side of the sofa, his hands gripping the frame.

"I was even going to let it go when I sent those messages to lure you here. Had you," he pushed the sofa to the side, almost removing the barrier between us, "just accepted what I was telling you, you could have walked out of here." Another push, and there was nothing between us.

I threw the flaming cushion. It flew by his head, just barely missing his shoulder, and accomplishing absolutely nothing. So much for aim not being a factor.

"But you wouldn't. I knew from the look in your eye that you were not going to let this go."

I started backing up. "You put a woman in the hospital. It was wrong to feed off all those women. It was wrong to take something that wasn't freely given."

He rolled his eyes and made a sound of disgust. "Have you always been so morally upstanding?"

However, before I could respond, he lunged towards me. He was faster than I was. His hands came around my neck before I could react. Suddenly, it was impossible to get air in.

"I did not want to do this, Elena, but I will not have you ruining everything I have worked for. I can't have you exposing any of this."

"No-lan," I managed to say.

"If he made it past the street curb, I would be amazed. The plan was to starve him, which he made so much easier since he hadn't fed in weeks. After a beating, there was little strength left. The queen will undoubtedly be upset when he's found in an alley somewhere, but he was led astray by an insignificant little elemental. By you, Elena. He renounced ever drinking again because of his affection for you. It has a bit of romance to it, don't you think?"

I tried screaming, thinking I could breathe fire on him, but I couldn't pull in air no matter how hard I tried. My chest burned in a completely new way as I struggled to breathe.

He laughed at my efforts, "Fire needs oxygen to burn, little salamander." The amusement in his laughter was pure evil.

I struggled to break his grip. He held me far from his body, and the long heat-resistant gloves protected the parts of him I could grab.

"While Nolan died of self-imposed starvation, you Elena, unfortunately, didn't survive your transition. There are always a few elementals who don't."

My vision blurred, and darkness started to creep in from the sides. I could not pass out. I knew that would be the end. With a second burst of effort, I tried to pull his gloves down, just hoping to expose vulnerable skin. It was a wasted effort though.

As my vision started to black out, I thought what a horrible way this was to go. His sinister amusement was going to be the last thing that I heard and saw. It's not how I pictured my end. And, for the first time in my life, I felt terror and despair like no other. At no other moment had I felt this deep regret and paralyzing fear. It was more than just thoughts of all the things I hadn't done. It was the uncertainty of what was next and the finality of death.

Maybe it was the summation of all that emotion that gave my body that final burst of explosive heat. Just before the curtain closed, I felt a fireball form in the pit of my stomach, building pressure until it simply exploded with heat that shot out from my entire body.

I heard Micah cry out just before the grip on my throat was released. The gasping breaths that followed the release were involuntary. My body knew what it needed, and even as I collapsed onto the ground in a circle of fire, my chest pulled deep gulps of oxygen into my system.

When my vision cleared enough, I peered through the flames and saw that Micah lay unconscious on the ground. My gaze slowly shifted to take in the rest of the space, and I realized that I had set fire to the room.

Chapter 33

"Elena! Elena, where are you?"

I heard his voice calling to me from somewhere beyond the flames.

Suddenly, water began to rain down, and I heard the shrill ringing of the fire alarm.

I was so exhausted that I collapsed onto the floor into child's pose, letting the water from the fire sprinklers sizzle as it hit my cooling skin.

"Elena?" I turned my head to see Nolan coming through the flames. It was a nice sight. He scooped me into his arms. "Are you hurt? Elena, talk to me." He sounded a bit frantic.

"I'm fine. Though I'm not so sure about the room." I smiled weakly, but his eyes continued to scan my body for injuries. My once again naked body.

"This is going to be very inconvenient," I muttered to myself.

"Wait right here," he said before rushing off. I had no plans to go anywhere.

"Here." He returned and covered me with a bathrobe that had been hiding from me earlier.

I pulled it around me and arranged the front before letting him help me stand. The water stopped as we stood up looking at each other. I glanced at the room, and it appeared that most of the flames had been extinguished. Everything that had been flammable now bore fire damage.

I also noticed the group of hauntingly beautiful men standing across the room. They parted, and a woman of smaller stature but with an imposing and powerful bearing joined us. She was exceedingly beautiful with her white-blond hair and gray eyes. They were shrewd eyes that took in everything...including how close Nolan and I stood.

I took a step back.

"Interesting," she said with a smooth voice that had just a slight accent. "Had I known what you were doing here, Nolan, I would have visited much sooner."

Her eyes held a warning as they fell on Nolan, and then swept across the room. She motioned to the men behind her with a simple hand gesture. One was instantly at her side. "Take care of security cameras and any who might have seen this."

The vampire bowed and rushed to fulfill her command.

The queen took another step into the room, her stilettos creating a squishing sound on the wet carpet. She stopped in front of a groaning Micah.

Tilting her head much like a bird would, she looked at his red and blistered body with no apparent sympathy.

"You have acted unwisely, Micah. I do not tolerate lies nor do I suffer those who disobey my edicts. You will not enjoy the punishment." She looked away, signaling again to the vampires behind her. They retrieved Micah, uncaring of his painful cries, and carried him from the room.

The queen stopped a few feet from me. Her gray eyes seemed to see right into my soul. As she stood there in observational silence, I found her to be more terrifying than Micah had been in his murderous rage. She smiled, and it was chilling.

Next, she turned to Nolan and watched him with narrowed eyes. Seconds seemed to pass as they stared at each other. Her look of anger slowly melted, though her face was still hard. She turned to leave the room with a soft word I could not understand, but one that Nolan acknowledged with a nod. Briefly, her eyes focused on me, and I felt paralyzed by fear. But there wasn't anger in her eyes.

Instead, I felt that as our eyes locked, she was analyzing me, and something she found filled her with such sadness that it leaked through the icy façade. For a tiny moment, I saw a familiar look of pain on her face, and I knew what she was feeling.

She turned quickly with the elegant knee-length dress swishing seductively with the movement of her body. The remaining vampires filed out of the room behind her without a look, without a word. Nolan and I stood in the room, both our eyes doing a dance of avoidance. That stabbing pain was there again in the middle of my chest.

I wish I could say that it was the heartburn sensation of being a newly transitioned fire elemental. However, only a broken heart caused this kind of pain. I couldn't stand there any longer with the pain and the cause of it, so I stepped towards the door. He spoke my name, and being the weakling I was, I stopped.

"It was real," was all he said in a sorrow-choked tone. Three little words, and it was suddenly hard to breathe. Two tears slipped from my eyes, leaving a watery trail on my cheeks. I pursed my lips, afraid of how pitiful my voice would sound, and gave him a nod. "Everything that you think I felt, I did. It was real."

Crack... went the sound of my breaking heart. Why couldn't he just be the bad guy? Why couldn't he just be the evil, womanizing vampire? It would hurt less.

I took a step only to stop as his chest was directly in front of me. I refused to look up. I refused to let him see me with wet cheeks and a trembling lip. I still had my pride.

His smooth hands slid down my arms, finding and intertwining with my hands. I looked up to him. His devilishly beautiful face looked so...sad.

"I never meant to hurt you." That was the best he could give me.

A meek laugh escaped. I laughed again, hearing the edge of hysteria. He looked confused, and I laughed more.

This was one of those movie moments; heartbroken girl looking up into the face of the undeniably attractive heartbreaker, our bodies only inches apart.

This was the moment where he begged for forgiveness, and I would give it to him.

This was where he would take me in his arms and kiss me passionately, and all the hurt and betrayals would cease to exist. And as cheesy romance novel as that sounded, a part of me wanted it to happen so badly.

That was when the pain exploded in my chest, stealing my breath, and causing my eyes to fill with tears because despite all the fantastical things that had happened in my life the last few months, this was reality. My being an elemental and him being a mythological creature of immense seductive power could not change the truth. A betrayal was still a betrayal. Obligations and commitments could not be ignored. He wasn't going to sweep me away.

Quite simply, magic did not fix a broken heart.

The first step was breathing. The next was to separate our hands and step back. He reached for me, but I held up a hand to stop him. I gave him my best smile.

"I know you didn't mean to, but you did, and that's something that I'll just have to get over."

"Get over?" Apparently, even vampires hope for a happy ending.

"Yeah." I gave another encouraging smile. "You made a commitment to your queen, and I hear you have a few years left on that sentence." He was not amused by my poor attempt at humor, so I went with straightforwardness instead. "Neither one of us is in a place to pursue this."

I motioned to include him and me. "I want...no, I need to be stronger than that kind of woman."

"I will not be the queen's consort forever. Like you said, it is just a few more years." Something in my face must have discouraged him. His words trailed off, and he looked as horrible as I felt.

"It wasn't all bad," I jested weakly. "I mean besides the evil partner drinking my blood and trying to kill me."

His face tightened. "You won't regret it? Humans tend to regret many things." His voice was deeper than usual.

"No, definitely not," I said with complete honesty. A sad smile was my parting gift to him. "How many girls can say they seduced a super sexy vampire? And let us not forget all the amazing kissing. Nope, no regrets there." I stepped around him and headed out the door.

"I'll never forget you, Elena."

I couldn't help but turn at those words. "Be careful, never is a long time for you."

He smiled that seductive smile I loved so much. "Never," he placed his hand over his heart.

My heart shuddered, and my eyes watered. "Take care of yourself."

I continued down the hall, my entire body hurting. My throat ached from the sobs I tightly held in, and I smiled. It wasn't real though.

I continued down the hall, self-pity welling up inside of me. But I refused to cry.

I was not going to cry.

I was bawling so hard as I let the crowd of people carry me out of the hotel like a wave in the ocean. The firemen, who I will admit I didn't glance twice at, saw me, and were sure that I was injured. They rushed me to the ambulance throwing a blanket around my shoulders and an oxygen mask around my face. It was only later that I realized how dangerous that could have been.

"Elena!" the panicked shriek got my attention. Leta rushed towards me with her arms flailing in the air.

A police officer tried to hold her back, but after whispering a few words in his ear, she was granted access. I was only slightly surprised to see Selene and Farah following behind her.

"What happened?" she yelled at me as she ran to the ambulance.

The fireman who had applied the oxygen was watching her with a wary expression. I gave him a reassuring nod to indicate that I did know the lunatic rushing at us. He stepped back to give us some room as Leta threw her arms around me.

"Are you okay? What happened? I've been so worried! Is she okay?" She turned to the paramedic, giving him a thorough once over and following it with a soft sound of approval. "Is she?"

Some things never change. The medic was momentarily stunned by Leta's presence. Shaking his head, as if that would recover his senses, he nodded. "Your friend appears to be doing just fine. Just a little shaken up, I think."

Leta nodded, and then her eyes got big. "She's not in shock, is she?"

"No, I'm not in shock," I denied.

She didn't listen to me. Instead, she was asking him if I needed emergent medical care. I replied that none of that was necessary, but they didn't appear to hear anything I said. With an exasperated sigh, I gave up. The medic could convince Leta that I was fine.

I turned away from them to find Selene and Farah watching me. Selene's eyes were alight with amusement while Farah assessed me as a dog assesses a strange animal it has never seen before; not sure if this new thing was a threat or not.

"How are you feeling?" Selene asked.

"Like I just survived the fires of hell," I replied.

Selene smirked.

"Well, it's not shock," Leta said as she joined the conversation. The medic had gone off to save other shaken-up souls.

"I'm glad we all came to that conclusion," I said dryly.

"What's with the bathrobe?" Leta asked.

"Well, at some point my body temperature got so high, my clothes burned right off. At least that was what I was told."

The three of them just stared at me. "Hmm, this could be a problem if your clothes burn off whenever you get too excited," Leta observed.

"I think it all has to do with the transition. My body temperatures shouldn't reach fabric incinerating levels again."

Selene raised an eyebrow. "You have this on good authority?"

I was about to respond but paused to realize that I didn't know a damn thing about what was normal anymore.

"Nope, it's just a hunch. I guess we'll find out, huh?"

"Might want to carry an extra set of clothes, just in case," Leta suggested practically.

"So, did you mean to burn the hotel down?" Farah asked as she stood with her hands in her jean pockets looking at the hotel.

For the first time, I took in the scene around me. Smoke billowed from the windows of the floor I had been on. People were still being evacuated from the hotel as the firemen, police, and paramedics tried to bring some order to the chaos. Cop cars formed a circular barricade around the hotel, and uniforms kept the curious crowd at a distance. A few different ambulances were parked inside the barricade with their back doors open where frightened people were being evaluated and treated.

"That was not the plan, no." I looked at Farah who seemed highly amused by it all. "New uncontrolled powers, a showdown with a vampire, and a few drapes went up in the process." I shrugged my shoulders and looked at the smoke billowing out of the hotel windows. "Maybe the linens went up too."

"Did you take him down?" she asked with sudden seriousness.

I played offended. "Of course, I took him down! And, then I let his coven cart him back to wherever it is he came from to endure the wrath of his queen."

"Coven? There was a whole coven here?" Farah asked.

"It's a really long story."

"When you say vampire...Nolan is a vampire?" Leta asked with genuine shock.

I jumped off the back of the ambulance. "That is an even longer story."

Selene put her arm around my shoulders. "How about I buy you a drink, and you tell us all about it?"

"Hell, I'll buy you dinner just for roasting a vampire," Farah said from the other side of me.

"First, some clothes. And then, a drink...or two while I tell you the whole story."

Leta wanted me to take Monday to recover. Honestly, I think she was afraid I was going to burn all my clothes off again, which is probably why she was packing a bag of my clothes to take to the office. "Can't be too prepared," she said to me.

I nodded and let her do whatever made her happy. I wasn't too worried about my clothes going up in flames.

After taking a long cold shower and telling the story to my friends over a few glasses of wine, my body had settled back down to a somewhat normal temperature. I now ran at what would be a low-grade fever for most.

Despite the transition, the fight with Micah, and the heartbreaking goodbye to Nolan, I felt better than I had in weeks when Monday morning came around. It was like all that heat I had been fighting just settled into the pit of my stomach, making me feel warm and balanced.

I wasn't ready to face the ramifications of what I had become, but I wasn't denying it anymore either.

"Look at you," Stan said as I approached the building that housed Madame Advertising. "There's a glow about you, Ms. McNeal. You look good and healthy. There's something more too." He stared at me with a smile, trying to pinpoint what was different.

"I feel more...fiery than before." I smiled at my inside joke.

Stan smiled and gave me a wink. "I always pegged you for a firecracker."

If only you knew, Stan. I returned the smile. "Yep, I guess I didn't realize it until recently though."

"You've got plenty of time to figure it out, Ms. McNeal." He tipped his hat to me with a knowing smile and turned away. "Plenty of time," I heard him say to himself as he got lost in the crowd of pedestrians.

I shook my head and wondered how it was that Stan always seemed to know what to say.

Because as usual, he was right. There was plenty of time to figure it out. To figure it all out.

I took a deep breath.

This was just the beginning, I reminded myself as I pulled open the glass door and headed to work.